AN
ENCHANTMENT
OF
RAVENS

MARGARET ROGERSON

MARGARET K. McELDERRY BOOKS

New York   London   Toronto   Sydney   New Delhi

MARGARET K. McELDERRY BOOKS
An imprint of Simon & Schuster Children's Publishing Division
1230 Avenue of the Americas, New York, New York 10020
This book is a work of fiction. Any references to historical events, real people, or
real places are used fictitiously. Other names, characters, places, and events are
products of the author's imagination, and any resemblance to actual events or places
or persons, living or dead, is entirely coincidental.
Text copyright © 2017 by Margaret Rogerson
Jacket illustration copyright © 2017 by Charlie Bowater
All rights reserved, including the right of reproduction in whole or in part in any
form.
MARGARET K. McELDERRY BOOKS is a trademark of Simon & Schuster, Inc.
For information about special discounts for bulk purchases, please contact Simon &
Schuster Special Sales at 1-866-506-1949 or business@simonandschuster.com.
The Simon & Schuster Speakers Bureau can bring authors to your live event. For
more information or to book an event, contact the Simon & Schuster Speakers
Bureau at 1-866-248-3049 or visit our website at www.simonspeakers.com.
Interior design by Sonia Chaghatzbanian and Irene Metaxatos
Jacket design by Sonia Chaghatzbanian
The text for this book was set in Sabon LT Std.
Manufactured in the United States of America

10 9 8 7 6 5 4 3
CIP data for this book is available from the Library of Congress.
ISBN 978-1-4814-9758-9 (hardcover)
ISBN 978-1-4814-9760-2 (eBook)

To my mom and dad, with love.

One

MY PARLOR smelled of linseed oil and spike lavender, and a dab of lead tin yellow glistened on my canvas. I had nearly perfected the color of Gadfly's silk jacket.

The trick with Gadfly was persuading him to wear the same clothes for every session. Oil paint needs days to dry between layers, and he had trouble understanding I couldn't just swap his entire outfit for another he liked better. He was astonishingly vain even by fair folk standards, which is like saying a pond is unusually wet, or a bear surprisingly hairy. All in all, it was a disarming quality for a creature who could murder me without rescheduling his tea.

"I might have some silver embroidery done about the wrists," he said. "What do you think? You could add that, couldn't you?"

"Of course."

"And if I chose a different cravat . . ."

Inwardly, I rolled my eyes. Outwardly, my face ached with the polite smile I'd maintained for the past two and a half hours. Rudeness was not an affordable mistake. "I could alter your cravat, as long as it's more or less the same size, but I'd need another session to finish it."

"You truly are a wonder. Much better than the previous portrait artist—that fellow we had the other day. What was his name? Sebastian Manywarts? Oh, I didn't like him, he always smelled a bit strange."

It took me a moment to realize Gadfly was referring to Silas Merryweather, a master of the Craft who died over three hundred years ago. "Thank you," I said. "What a thoughtful compliment."

"How engaging it is to see the Craft change over time." Barely listening, he selected one of the cakes from the tray beside the settee. He didn't eat it immediately, but rather sat staring at it, as an entomologist might having discovered a beetle with its head on backward. "One thinks one has seen the best humans have to offer, and suddenly there's a new method of glazing china, or these fantastic little cakes with lemon curd inside."

By now I was used to fair folk mannerisms. I didn't look away from his left sleeve, and kept dabbing on the silk's glossy yellow shine. However, I remembered a time in which the fair folk's behavior had unsettled me. They moved differently than humans: smoothly, precisely, with a peculiar stiffness to their posture, and never put so much as a finger out of place. They could remain still for hours without blinking, or they could move with such fearsome swiftness as to be upon you before you could even gasp in surprise.

I sat back, brush in hand, and took in the portrait in its entirety. It was nearly finished. There lay Gadfly's petrified likeness, as unchanging as he was. Why the fair folk so desired portraits was beyond me. I supposed it had something to do with vanity, and their insatiable thirst to surround themselves with human Craft. They would never reflect on their youth, because they knew nothing else, and by the time they died, if they even did, their portraits would be long rotted away to nothing.

Gadfly appeared to be a man in his middle thirties. Like every example of his kind he was tall, slim, and beautiful. His eyes were the clear crystal blue of the sky after rain has washed away the summer heat, his complexion as pale and flawless as porcelain, and his hair the radiant silver-gold of dew illuminated by a sunrise. I know it sounds ridiculous, but fair folk require such comparisons. There's simply no other way to describe them. Once, a Whimsical poet died of despair after finding himself unequal to the task of capturing a fair one's beauty in simile. I think it more likely he died of arsenic poisoning, but so the story goes.

You must keep in mind, of course, that all of this is only a glamour, not what they really look like underneath.

Fair folk are talented dissemblers, but they can't lie outright. Their glamour always has a flaw. Gadfly's flaw was his fingers; they were far too long to be human and sometimes appeared oddly jointed. If someone looked at his hands too long he would lace them together or scurry them under a napkin like a pair of spiders to put them out of sight. He was the most personable fair one I knew, far more relaxed about manners than the rest of them, but staring was never a good idea—unless, like me, you had a good reason to.

Finally, Gadfly ate the cake. I didn't see him chew before he swallowed.

"We're just about finished for the day," I told him. I wiped my brush on a rag, then dropped it into the jar of linseed oil beside my easel. "Would you like to take a look?"

"Need you even ask? Isobel, you know I'd never pass up the opportunity to admire your Craft."

Before I knew it Gadfly stood leaning over my shoulder. He kept a courteous space between us, but his inhuman scent enveloped me: a ferny green fragrance of spring leaves, the sweet perfume of wildflowers. Beneath that, something wild—something that had roamed the forest for millennia, and had long spidery fingers that could crush a human's throat while its owner wore a cordial smile.

My heart skipped a beat. *I am safe in this house,* I reminded myself.

"I believe I do like this cravat best after all," he said. "Exquisite work, as always. Now, what am I paying you, again?"

I stole a glance at his elegant profile. A strand of hair had slipped from the blue ribbon at the nape of his neck as if by accident. I wondered why he'd arranged it that way. "We agreed on an enchantment for our hens," I reminded him. "Each of them will lay six good eggs per week for the rest of their lives, and they must not die early for any reason."

"So practical." He sighed at the tragedy. "You are the most admired Crafter of this age. Imagine all the things I could give you! I could make pearls drop from your eyes in place of tears. I could lend you a smile that enslaves men's hearts, or a dress that once beheld is never forgotten. And yet you request eggs."

"I quite like eggs," I replied firmly, well aware that the

enchantments he described would all turn strange and sour, even deadly, in the end. Besides, what on earth would I do with men's hearts? I couldn't make an omelette out of them.

"Oh, very well, if you insist. You'll find the enchantment in effect beginning tomorrow. With that I'm afraid I must be off—I've the embroidery to ask after."

I stood with a creak of my chair and dropped him a curtsy as he paused at the door. He gave an elegant bow in response. Like most fair folk he was adept at pretending he returned the courtesy by choice, not a strict compulsion that was, to him, as necessary as breathing.

"Aha," he added, straightening, "I'd nearly forgotten. We've had gossip in the spring court that the autumn prince is going to pay you a visit. Imagine that! I look forward to hearing whether he manages to sit through an entire session, or hares off after the Wild Hunt as soon as he's arrived."

I wasn't able to school my expression at the news. I stood gaping at Gadfly until a puzzled smile crossed his lips and he extended his pale hand in my direction, perhaps trying to determine whether I'd died standing up, not an unreasonable concern, as to him humans no doubt seemed to expire at the slightest provocation.

"The autumn—" My voice came out rough. I closed my mouth and cleared my throat. "Are you quite certain? I was under the impression the autumn prince did not visit Whimsy. No one has seen him in hundreds . . ." Words failed me.

"I assure you, he is alive and well. Why, I saw him at a ball just yesterday. Or was it last month? In any event, he shall be here tomorrow. Do pass on my regards."

"It—it will be an honor," I stammered, mentally cringing

at my uncharacteristic loss of composure. Suddenly in need of fresh air, I crossed the room to open the door. I showed Gadfly out and stood gazing across the field of summer wheat as his figure receded up the path.

A cloud passed beneath the sun, and a shadow fell across my house. The season never changed in Whimsy, but as first one leaf dropped from the tree in the lane, and then another, I couldn't help but feel some transformation was afoot. Whether or not I approved of it remained to be seen.

Two

TOMORROW! GADFLY said tomorrow. You know how they are about mortal time. What if he shows up at half past midnight, demanding I work in my nightgown? And my best dress has a tear, I can't get it mended by then—the blue one will have to do." While I spoke, I massaged linseed oil into my hands and set at them with a washing cloth, scrubbing my fingers raw. Usually I didn't bother cleaning the paint off myself, but usually I didn't work for fair folk royalty, either, and I had little idea what trivial nonsense might offend him. "I'm low on lead tin yellow, too, so I'll have to go into town this evening—shit. Shit! Sorry, Emma."

I lifted my skirts away from the water spreading across the floor and dove for the fallen bucket's handle.

"Heavens, Isobel, it'll be all right. March"—my aunt lowered her spectacles and squinted—"no, May, would you clean that up for your sister, please? She's having a hard day."

"What does *shit* mean?" May asked slyly, flouncing down at my feet with a rag.

"It's the word for when you spill a bucket of water by accident," I said, aware she would find the truth perilously inspiring. "Where's March?"

May gave me a gap-toothed grin. "On top of the cabinets."

"March! Get off the cabinets!"

"She's having *fun* up there, *Isobel*," May said, slopping water over my shoes.

"She won't be having fun when she's dead," I replied.

With a bleat of delight March hopped down from the cabinets, kicked a chair over, and went bounding across the room. She came toward us, and I lifted my hands to ward her off. But she was heading not for me but for May, who stood up in time to crack heads with her, which gave me a momentary respite while they tottered about in a concussed daze. I sighed. Emma and I were trying to break the habit.

My twin sisters weren't precisely human. They'd begun life as a pair of goat kids before a fair one had had too much wine and enchanted them on a lark. It was slow going, but I reminded myself that at least it *was* going. This time last year they hadn't been house-trained. And it worked in their favor that their transformative enchantment had rendered them more or less indestructible: I'd seen March survive eating a broken pot, poison oak, deadly nightshade, and several unfortunate salamanders without any ill effects. For all my concern, March jumping off cabinets posed more danger to the kitchen furniture.

"Isobel, come here a moment." My aunt's voice interrupted my thoughts. She watched me over her spectacles until

I obeyed, and took my hand to scrub off a smudge I hadn't noticed.

"You're going to do well tomorrow," she said firmly. "I'm sure the autumn prince is the same as any other fair one, and even if he isn't, remember you're safe inside this house." She wrapped both her hands around mine and squeezed. "Remember what you earned for us."

I squeezed her hands back. Perhaps at that moment I deserved being spoken to like a little girl. I tried to keep the whine out of my voice as I replied, "I just don't like not knowing what to expect."

"That may be so, but you're more prepared for something like this than anyone else in Whimsy. We know it, and the fair folk do too. At market yesterday I heard people saying that at this rate you might be headed for the Green Well—"

I snatched my hand back in shock.

"Of course you aren't. I know you wouldn't make that choice. The point I'm trying to make is that if the fair folk see any human as indispensable, it's you, and that's worth a great deal. Tomorrow will be *fine*."

I released a long breath and smoothed out my skirts. "I suppose you're right," I said, privately unconvinced. "I should go now if I want to get back before dark. March, May, don't drive Emma mad while I'm gone. I expect this kitchen to look perfect when I come home."

I gave the overturned chair a significant look as I left the room.

"At least we didn't shit all over the floor!" May shouted after me.

When I was a little girl, a trip into town had been nothing short of an adventure. Now I couldn't leave fast enough. My stomach wound a notch tighter every time someone passed by the window outside.

"Just lead tin yellow?" asked the boy behind the counter, neatly wrapping the chalk stick in a twist of butcher's paper. Phineas had only been working here for a few weeks, but he already possessed a shrewd understanding of my habits.

"On second thought, a stick of green earth and two more of vermilion. Oh! And all your charcoal, please." Watching him retrieve my order, I despaired at how much work awaited me tonight. I needed to grind and mix the pigments, select my palette, and stretch my new canvas. In all likelihood tomorrow's session would only involve completing the prince's sketch, but I couldn't stand not being prepared for every possibility.

I glanced out the window while Phineas ducked out of sight. A patina of dust coated the glass, and the shop's location in a corner between two larger buildings gave it a dark, shabby, out-of-the-way air. Not even a single, simple enchantment brightened its lamps, sang out when the door opened, or kept the corners free of dust. Anyone could see that the fair folk never gave this place a second glance. They had no use for the materials used to make Craft, only the finished product itself.

The establishments across the street were a different story entirely. A woman's skirts vanished into Firth & Maester's, and I knew from that brief sighting alone that she was a fair one. No mortal could afford the lace gowns sold there. And no humans shopped at the Confectionary next door, whose sign advertised marzipan flowers, sweets made from almonds imported at great cost and danger from the World Beyond. Enchantments, and enchantments alone, were worthy payment for Craft of such caliber.

When Phineas straightened, his eyes shone in a way I recognized all too well. No—"recognized" wasn't the right word. I dreaded it. He shyly brushed a lock of hair away from his forehead as my heart sank, and sank, and sank. *Please,* I thought, *not again.*

"Miss Isobel, would you mind taking a look at my Craft? I know I'm not like you," he added in a rush, scrambling to keep his nerve, "but Master Hartford's been encouraging me—it's why he took me on—and I've practiced all these years." He held a painting to his chest, self-consciously concealing the front side as though it weren't a canvas but his very soul he feared exposing. I knew the feeling intimately, which didn't make what came next any easier.

"I'd be more than happy to," I replied. At least I had a great deal of experience in faking a smile.

He handed it to me, and I turned the frame over, exposing a landscape to the shop's dim light. Relief flooded me. Thank god, it wasn't a portrait. I must sound horribly arrogant saying so, but my Craft was held in such high esteem that the fair folk wouldn't commission anyone else until I was dead and gone— and until they actually realized I was dead and gone, which might take several additional decades. I despaired for every new portrait artist cropping up in the wake of my fame. Perhaps Phineas stood a chance.

"This is very good," I told him honestly, passing his painting back. "You have an excellent grasp of color and composition. Keep practicing, but even in the meantime"—I hesitated—"you might be able to sell your Craft."

His cheeks flushed, and he grew an inch taller right in front of me. My relief went cold. Often, the part that followed was worse. I braced myself as he asked the exact question I feared. "Could you . . . do you think you could refer one of your patrons to me, miss?"

My gaze wandered back to the window, where Mrs. Firth herself was arranging a new dress for Firth & Maester's shop-front display. When I was young, I had thought her a fair one for certain. She possessed flawless skin, a voice sweeter than a songbird's call, and a tumble of chestnut curls too lustrous to be natural. She had to be verging on fifty but barely looked a day over twenty. Only later, when I learned to read glamours, did I realize my mistake. And as the years passed I grew disenchanted with enchantments, which were just as much a lie. No matter how cleverly they were worded, all but the most mundane, practical spells soured with age. Those that weren't cleverly worded ruined lives. In exchange for her twenty-two-inch waist, Mrs. Firth couldn't speak any word beginning with a vowel. Last October the Confectionary's head baker had accidentally bargained away three decades of his life for bluer eyes, and left his wife a widow. Yet still the allure of wealth and beauty swept Whimsy along, with a vision of the Green Well hovering at the very end like the promise of heaven itself.

Sensing my reluctance, Phineas hastened to add, "Not anyone important, mind. That Swallowtail looks like he might be the right sort of fair one. I see him in town sometimes, buying Craft on the street. And they always say fair folk of the spring court are kinder in their dealings."

The truth of the matter was that no fair one was kind, whatever house they came from. They only pretended to be.

The thought of Swallowtail coming within ten yards of Phineas made me taste bile. He wasn't the worst fair one I'd met by any stretch of the imagination, but he'd twist words until he convinced the poor boy to bargain away his firstborn child for fewer pimples.

"Phineas . . . you're probably aware my Craft means I spent more time with fair folk than anyone else in Whimsy." I met his eyes across the counter. His face fell; he was doubtless thinking I was about to turn him down, but I forged onward through his unhappiness. "So believe me when I say that if you want to deal with them, you must be careful. Not being able to lie doesn't make them honest. They'll try to deceive you at every turn. If something they offer sounds too good to be true, it is. The enchantment's wording must leave *no* room for mischief. None."

He brightened so much I feared all my efforts were in vain. "Does that mean you're going to recommend me?"

"Maybe, but not Swallowtail. Don't trade with him until you've learned their habits." Chewing on the inside of my cheek, I glimpsed out of the corner of my eye a man emerging from Firth & Maester's. Gadfly. Of course that was where he would have gone for his embroidery. Though I must have been nearly invisible standing inside the dark shop across the way, he looked unerringly toward me, beamed, and raised a hand in greeting. Everyone on the street—including the gaggle of young women who'd been waiting for him outside—eagerly craned their necks to find out who was important enough to merit his attention.

"He will do," I declared. I placed my coins on the counter and shouldered my satchel, avoiding the new heights of elation dawning on Phineas's face. "Gadfly is my most esteemed patron, and he enjoys being the first to discover new Craft. Your odds are best with him."

I meant that in more ways than one. Phineas would be safest with Gadfly. Had I not dealt with him first at the tender age of twelve, even with Emma's help, I likely wouldn't have lived to see my seventeenth birthday. Even then, I still couldn't shake the feeling I was doing Phineas a double-edged favor, granting him a dearest wish that was bound to either destroy or disappoint him in the end. Guilt chased me toward the door without a word of good-bye. But with my hand on the knob, I froze.

A painting hung on the wall beside the entry. Faded with age, it depicted a man standing on a knoll surrounded by oddly colored trees. His face was obscured, but he held a sword that glinted brightly even in the gray light. Pale hounds swarmed up the knoll toward him, suspended in midleap. The hair stood up on my arms. I knew this figure. He was a popular subject of paintings done over three hundred years ago, when he stopped visiting Whimsy without explanation. In every remaining work he was always standing in the distance, always battling the Wild Hunt.

Tomorrow, he'd be sitting in my parlor.

I shoved the door open, curtsied to Gadfly, and hurried through the throng of curious bystanders with my head down. Exclamations followed in my wake. Someone called my name, perhaps hoping for the same favor as Phineas. Now that Emma had said it, I saw the truth written all over everyone. They were watching, waiting for me to accept an invitation I would rather die than spend half a second considering. I could never explain to any of them that to me, the Green Well's reward wasn't heaven. It was hell.

The sun hung low in the sky as I made my way home. My shoes tapped along the path through a wheat field to the rhythmic buzzing of grasshoppers, and the light's steep angle intensified the summer heat until the back of my neck grew sticky with sweat, cool every time the breeze blew my hair aside. The town's crooked, brightly painted rooftops descended out of sight behind me, concealed by rolling hills my narrow path split like the part in a woman's hair. If I walked quickly, I could make it back in precisely thirty-two minutes.

It was always summer in Whimsy. Here the seasons didn't change according to the passage of time as they did in the World Beyond, an idea I could barely fathom. While I walked my walk that never changed, the painting's oddly colored trees haunted me like a recent dream. Autumn was to all accounts a dreary time, a withering of the world when birds vanished and the leaves discolored and fell from their branches as though dying. Surely what we had was better. Safer. Endlessly blue skies and eternally golden wheat might be boring, but I told myself, not for the first time, that it was foolish to long for anything else. A person could suffer worse things than being bored—and in the World Beyond, they did.

A whiff of decay jogged me from my frustrated thoughts. This part of the path wove near the forest's edge, and I cast a wary glance into its shadows. Dense honeysuckles and briars flourished like a barrier beneath the branches. In days long past, during the less friendly time before iron was outlawed, farmers had risked their lives driving iron nails into the outermost trees to ward off fairy wickedness. The sight of the old, bent nails, rusted and twisted almost beyond recognition, always gave me a prickle of unease.

Sweeping my gaze across the undergrowth again, I saw nothing amiss. No doubt I was being paranoid about a dead squirrel rotting somewhere nearby. Reluctantly reassured, I checked my satchel for the fourth or fifth time just to make sure I hadn't left anything behind at the store—an odd habit of mine, as I never made such mistakes. When I looked up, something was wrong. A creature stood on the rise of the next hill, beside the lone oak that marked the halfway point home.

My first thought was that it was a stag. A tremendously big one, but it was the right shape, more or less: four legs, two antlers. Then it turned to look in my direction, and right away I understood it wasn't.

Just like that the wrongness spread. The breeze dropped away, and the air grew still and oppressively hot. The birds stopped singing, the grasshoppers stopped buzzing, and even the wheat drooped in the stagnant air. The stench of decay grew overwhelming. I dropped down to my hands and knees, but it was too late.

The not-a-stag stood watching me.

Despite the heat, a fever chill shivered over my skin and crystallized in my stomach. I knew what it was, this not-a-stag. I also knew I was dead. No one could run or hide from a fairy beast. This creature had risen from a barrow mound, a grotesque union of fairy magic and ancient human remains. Some acted as servants and guards to their masters. Others crept from the earth unbidden. One such monster killed my mother and father when I was a little girl, so terribly Emma hadn't let me see their bodies, and I was going to die the same way. I don't think my mind could quite process this, because my next thought was that I shouldn't have wasted money buying pigments; I was never going to use them now.

The fairy beast lowered its head and bellowed across the field, a deep, rousing, and putrid sound, as though someone had blown into an ancient, once-exquisite hunting horn stuffed full of rotting moss. It swung its heavy body around, antlers first, and sprang down the hill.

I lunged from my crouch and ran. Not toward the safety of my house half a mile in the distance, but away from it, into the field. If I was going to do anything of value in my last moments alive, I might as well try to lead the thing as far away from my family as I could manage.

The wheat parted around my hiked-up skirts. Stems crunched beneath my boots, and prickly seed heads scratched welts across my bare arms as they whipped past. My satchel bounced against the backs of my thighs, cumbersome, slowing me down. Grasshoppers shot out of the way as if flicked from the field by an invisible hand. At first I heard nothing but the rasping of my own breath. None of it felt real. I might as well have been running through a field for the fun of it, on a lovely day beneath a flawless blue sky.

Then a shadow's coolness touched my sweaty back, and darkness enveloped me. The wheat thrashed like waves in a storm-tossed ocean. A hoof slammed down beside me, burying itself deep in the soil. I threw myself backward, stumbled, and fell, floundering among the shafts. The fairy beast loomed over me.

A proud stag's guise rippled over it like the reflection of sun on water. In the dark spaces between the illusion lay a skeletal form of decomposing bark held together by vines that shifted like tendons, a hollowed skull-like face, antlers that were not truly antlers but instead a pair of crooked branches wound tight with thorny briars, each one as long as a man was tall. A sickness lay over it; as it snorted and raised a quivering leg, bark sloughed away and tumbled across the ground. Shiny beetles swarmed out of the pieces, skittering over my stockings as they fled in every direction. I retched at the taste of rot coating the inside of my mouth.

The fairy beast reared up, blocking out the sun. I thought my last sight on earth was going to be the constellation of maggots weaving in and out of its belly. Therefore I wasn't certain how to react when the monster simply collapsed in front of me into a soft, tumbling heap of worm-eaten wood. Centipedes longer than my hand spooled out into the grass. Two huge, spotted moths took wing. The grasshoppers began buzzing again right away as though nothing had happened, but still I lay clammy and trembling on the ground, blood pounding in my ears. With a repulsed cry, I kicked at the pile. Bone fragments scattered along with the bark. The human corpse that gave it life had been destroyed.

"I've been tracking that beast for two days, and I might not have caught up to it if you hadn't drawn its attention," said a warm, lively voice. "It's called a thane, in case you're interested."

My gaze snapped up from the fairy beast's remains. A man stood before me, so eclipsed by the sun I couldn't make out his features, only that he was tall and slender and in the process of sheathing a sword.

"Drawn its—" I stopped, baffled and more than a little offended. He spoke as if this were sport, as though my life mattered not at all; which of course told me everything I needed to know. This figure might look like a man, but he wasn't one.

"Thank you," I backtracked, choking down my protests. "You've saved my life."

"Have I? From the thane? I suppose I have. In that case, you're most welcome—oh. I don't know your name."

A frisson of unease rattled me like a thunderclap in the dead of night. He didn't recognize me, which meant he didn't visit Whimsy often, if at all. Whoever he was, he was bound to be more dangerous than the fair folk I normally dealt with. And like all of his species he couldn't resist seeking my true name. I paused, evaluating my mind and senses, and came to the relieved conclusion that he hadn't put me under a malicious charm, one that might make me speak more freely or reveal secrets I ought not. Because no one used their birth name in Whimsy. To do so would be to expose oneself to ensorcellment, by which a fair one could control a mortal in body and soul, forever, without their ever knowing—merely through the power of that single, secret word. It was the most wicked form of fairy magic, and the most feared.

"Isobel," I supplied, scrambling to my feet. I dropped him a curtsy.

If he realized I'd given him my false name, he showed no sign. He stepped right over the pile in one long-legged stride, bowed deeply, and took my hand in his. He raised it, and kissed it. I hid a frown. Supposing he had to touch me, I rather wished he'd helped me up instead.

"You're most welcome, Isobel," he said.

His lips were cool against my knuckles. With his head ducked before me I only saw his hair, which was unruly—wavy, not quite curly, and dark, with just the slightest red tint in the sun. Its fierce unkemptness reminded me of a hawk's or raven's feathers blown the wrong way in a strong wind. And like Gadfly, I could smell him: the spice of crisp dry leaves, of cool nights under a clear moon, a wildness, a longing. My heart hammered from terror of the fairy beast and the equal danger of meeting a fair one alone in a field. Therefore I beg you to excuse my foolishness when I say that suddenly, I wanted that smell more than anything I had ever wanted before. I wanted it with a terrifying thirst. Not him, exactly, but rather whatever great, mysterious change it represented—a promise that somewhere, the world was *different*.

Well, that simply wouldn't do. I hoisted my annoyance back up like a flag on a mast. "I've never known a kiss on the hand to last so long, sir."

He straightened. "Nothing seems long to a fair one," he replied with a half-smile.

By my reckoning he looked a year or two my elder, though of course his real age might have been more than a hundred times that count. He had fine, aristocratic features at odds with his unruly hair, and an expressive mouth I instantly wanted to paint. The shadows at the corners of his lips, the faint crease on one side, where his smile became crooked—

"I said," he remarked, "nothing seems long to a fair one."

I looked up to find him staring at me in perplexed fascination with the smile still frozen on his face. There was his flaw: the color of his eyes, a peculiar shade of amethyst, striking against his golden-brown complexion, which put me in mind of late-afternoon sunlight dappling fallen leaves. His eyes instantly bothered me for a reason other than their unusual hue, but try as I might I couldn't put my finger on why.

"Forgive me. I'm a portrait artist, and I have a habit of looking at people and forgetting about everything else while I'm doing it. I did hear what you said. I just don't have an answer."

The fair one's gaze flicked down to my satchel. When he returned his attention to me his smile had faded. "Of course. I imagine our lives are beyond human comprehension, for the most part."

"Do you know why the thane came out of the forest into Whimsy, sir?" I asked, because I got the sense he was waiting for some sort of validation regarding his mysteriousness, and I wanted to keep the conversation both short and practical. Fairy beasts were rarely glimpsed here, and its presence was beyond troubling.

"This I cannot say. Perhaps the Wild Hunt flushed it out, perhaps it merely felt like wandering. There have been more of them about lately, and they're causing an awful mess."

"Lately" could mean anything to a fair one, my parents' deaths included. "Yes, dead humans do tend to be messy."

His eyebrows shifted minutely, creating a furrow in the middle, and his gaze sharpened to scrutiny. He knew he'd upset me somehow, but in typical fair folk fashion wasn't able to divine why. He was no more able to understand the sorrow of a human's death than a fox might mourn the killing of a mouse.

One thing I knew for certain: I didn't want to linger long enough for him to decide that his confusion offended him and the cause of it deserved revenge in the form of a nasty enchantment.

I ducked my head and curtsied again. "Whimsy's people are grateful for your protection. I'll never forget what you've done for me today. Good day, sir."

I waited until he'd bowed again before I turned back toward the path.

"Wait," he said.

I froze.

Behind me, the sound of wheat shifting. "I said something wrong. I apologize."

Slowly I looked over my shoulder to find him watching me, looking oddly uncertain. I had no idea what to make of it. Fair folk were known to extend apologies on occasion—they valued good manners highly—but most of the time they followed a double standard according to which they expected humans to be the polite ones, while doing everything in their power to avoid acknowledging their own misbehavior. I was flabbergasted.

So I said the only thing that came to mind: "I accept your apology."

"Oh, good." His half-smile reappeared, and in an instant he went from looking uncertain to looking quite pleased with himself. "I'll see you tomorrow, then, Isobel."

I'd already started walking by the time his words sank in and I realized what they meant. I whirled around again, but the fair one, who could be none other than the autumn prince, was gone: wheat swayed around the empty path, and the only sign of life in the entire field was a single raven winging away toward the forest, with a red sheen on its feathers where they caught the fading light.

Three

I STILL had no idea when the prince might arrive, and with my aunt in town making a house call, the responsibility of emptying our kitchen of goat children fell to me. Easier said than done.

"He called our names weird!" May shrieked, while March sobbed silently next to the stove. Never had I loathed the baker's boy more, though truth be told he was quite nice, and he did have a point.

I squatted down and took them both by the shoulders. "Well, when Aunt Emma and I named you," I said reasonably, "you were goats. You were already familiar with March and May by then, and we weren't certain whether the enchantment would last, so we decided not to make changes."

March gave a strangled sob. I needed a different tactic. "Listen, I have an important question. What are your favorite things?"

"Scaring people," said May, after a moment of thought.

March opened her mouth and pointed into it.

Oh, god. "Those things are weird, aren't they?"

May eyed me warily. "Maybe . . ."

"Yes, they're definitely weird," I said in a firm voice. "So weird isn't really bad, is it? It's good, like scaring people or eating salamanders. Harold was paying you a compliment."

"Hmmm," May said. She didn't look convinced. But at least March had stopped crying, so for my sanity's sake I declared this round a partial victory.

"Now, come on. The two of you need to play outside until our guest leaves. Remember, don't go past the edge of the wheat field." As I pushed them toward the door a slimy coil of unease stirred in my stomach. If another fairy beast emerged from the forest . . .

Such events were extraordinarily rare, and I couldn't forget how easily the prince had dispatched the monster yesterday. Surely we were safe with him visiting. But the uneasiness wouldn't pass, and I added: "If you hear the grasshoppers go quiet, come back to the house right away."

May peered up at me with her eyebrows bunched in suspicion. "Why?"

"Because I said so."

"Why can't we just play in the house?"

I propelled them down the stoop while our rickety kitchen door banged shut behind us. I noted with relief that it looked perfectly normal outside. The chickens muttered to themselves as they stalked across the yard, the trees rippled in a lively breeze, and shadows raced over the rolling hills. Yet May kept staring at me. I realized my stomach was still clenched tight as a fist and it must show on my face.

"You already know the reason," I said briskly, stomping down my guilt.

Honestly, there were multiple reasons. May had knocked over my easels on more than one occasion. March exhibited an insatiable appetite for Prussian blue. But most of all, fair folk didn't like having them around. My theory was that the twins embarrassed them, being visible proof of one of their mistakes, and unintentionally powerful proof to boot. I knew for a fact they couldn't be ensorcelled: March and May were their true names. If the fair folk could use that knowledge against them, they would have done so by now.

March gave a delighted bleat and went capering over to the woodpile, but May didn't look away. "Don't worry, we won't get hurt," she said finally, soberly, and patted my knee. Then she tore off after her sister.

My eyes stung. Busily, I straightened my skirts and shoved a few stray hairs behind my ears. I didn't want them to see I was affected, and I didn't want to admit it to myself, either. When I focused on keeping everything in order, I didn't have to think about what had happened to my parents, or why the event still gripped me with panic twelve years later when I hadn't even been there, seen or heard a single part of it. Yet obviously, I didn't hide my fear well enough. Even May could see it.

A raven's hoarse croak sounded from the tree shading the yard.

"Shoo!" I said, hardly looking up. Ravens scared away the songbirds that nested in our bushes, and Emma and I made every effort to return the favor.

My unease faded in the warm sun and the sight of March and May scrambling on top of the logs. From a distance, the only way to tell them apart was the pattern of white splotches on their otherwise pink skin; May had one that went over her left cheek and half her nose. Their curly black hair was identical, as was the gap between their front teeth, and their startlingly fiendish eyebrows. They looked like a pair of cupids who had decided they liked shooting people with real arrows better. They were horrible. I loved them so much.

But I couldn't forget that the prince was coming, and apprehension lapped restlessly at the dark shores of my subconscious.

The raven croaked again.

This time I did look up. The raven turned its head to and fro, eyeing my frown. It ruffled its feathers and hopped smartly along the branch. When it emerged into the light, my breath caught in my throat. Its back had a red sheen, and it seemed to me its eyes were an unusual color.

I lunged into a swift curtsy and then dove inside, torn between hoping the raven wasn't the prince after all and the knowledge that if that was the case, I'd just curtsied at and promptly fled from a bird. The loose kitchen door went thud, thud, thud behind me.

A fourth thud sounded, but it wasn't the door banging. It was a knock.

"Come in!" I called back. I looked around, and wished I hadn't.

At random, I seized a pot and shoved it into the washbasin. I'm not sure whether it was even dirty. But that was all I had time to do before the door swung open again and the autumn prince stepped inside. The doorframe was made for average-sized humans, and he had to duck to avoid hitting his head on the lintel.

"Good afternoon, Isobel," he said, and gave me a courtly bow.

I'd never had a fair one in my kitchen before. It was a small room with rough stone walls, floorboards so worn with age they sagged in the middle, and one high window that let in a bit of light, just enough to draw special attention to the stack of unwashed dishes beside the cupboard and the sad-looking lump of peat still smoldering in our little chest-height hearth.

Meanwhile the prince looked as though he'd just stepped from a gilded carriage drawn by half a dozen white stallions. I didn't well remember what he'd been wearing the day before, but if it had looked like this, I would have. His close-fitting dark silk coat nearly brushed the ground behind his boots, cloaklike, lined with copper-colored velvet. He wore a matching copper circlet on his brow, and though his wild hair seemed to have developed a life of its own and swallowed much of the circlet, I made out that it was shaped like intertwined leaves and speckled green with verdigris. He had a raven-shaped cloak pin attached to his collar, no doubt a relic from a previous era. The sword from the day before still hung at his waist.

Yes, there he was, standing mere inches from a moldy onion skin I hadn't swept up that morning.

I had already violated the standards of etiquette. What I said next needed to be thoughtful and poised. I blurted out instead, "What happens if you can't bow back?"

Occupying himself while I mustered myself, the prince had turned to stare intently at a ladle. Now, he stared at me instead.

What are you? his mystified amethyst eyes seemed to say. "I don't believe I understand."

The saggy floorboards were bound to give way eventually. Maybe they'd do me a favor and make it happen now.

"If someone bows or curtsies at you, and you aren't able to return it right away," I heard myself explain.

Understanding lit his expression, and his familiar half-smile reappeared. He leaned toward me and met my eyes as though confiding a great secret. Perhaps he was. "It's terribly uncomfortable," he said quietly. "We have to look for whoever did it until we find them, and can't think about anything else in the meantime."

Oh. "I suppose I just did that. I'm sorry."

He straightened, seeming to forget about me in an instant. "Finding you was my pleasure," he said warmly, though rather distantly, and picked up a meat skewer. "Is this a weapon?"

I carefully took the skewer from him and set it back down. "Not by design, no."

"I see," he said, and before I could stop him he crossed the kitchen in three great strides to inspect a skillet hanging from a nail in the wall. "This is almost certainly a weapon."

"It isn't . . ." This was the most tongue-tied I'd ever been in the presence of a fair one. "Well—it can be utilized as one, certainly, but it's for cooking." He looked around at me. "Craft to make food," I clarified, because his eyebrows were drawn together in polite consternation verging on alarm.

"Yes, I know what cooking is," he said. "I was merely astonished that so many tools of your Craft can double as armaments. Is there anything you humans don't use to kill one another?"

"Probably not," I admitted.

"How peculiar." He paused to look around at the ceiling. Disquieted by what he might choose to comment on next, I cleared my throat and curtsied.

With a slight frown, he turned around and bowed back.

"Ordinarily I take clients in the parlor, which is this way. Should we get started? I wouldn't like to take too much of your time."

"Yes, certainly," he replied, but as we walked through the hall he continued glancing upward, and soon halted altogether to place his hand against the white plaster wall. I stopped too and waited for him to finish with a tight smile on my face, which was really more of a means of keeping myself from screaming in exasperation.

"There's a very strong enchantment on this house, and an odd one at that," he remarked finally.

"Yes." I started walking again, relieved to hear the swish of his coat follow. "It was the first thing I worked toward when I began painting these portraits—it took me an entire year to earn. No fair one—"

"May harm an inhabitant within this house's walls so long as you live," he finished at a murmur. "Impressive work. Gadfly's?"

I nodded, resisting the urge to look over my shoulder. As the parlor's distinct smell rolled over me I adopted a more formal tone out of habit. "I've enjoyed his patronage for years. May I ask why you think it's odd?"

"I've never seen an enchantment like it before. Nor would I have expected something like this of Gadfly."

Now it was my turn to almost come to a dead halt. I kept myself moving with a physical effort, entered the parlor, and

went about mechanically arranging the charcoal I'd need for the day's sketch. Had the enchantment gone bad? Had I said something wrong to Gadfly all those years ago, left an accidental loophole in the terms of our arrangement? The possibility was so sickening my hands and feet started going numb.

"As a prince, I could destroy most enchantments if I wished," he went on, still looking around at something I couldn't see. "But when I said this one was strong, I meant it. It's far beyond even my power. Gadfly must have spent a great deal of energy to achieve such a working, which is out of the ordinary, since I've never seen him so much as get up out of a chair unless he had to. He must enjoy your Craft immensely. I'm beginning to understand why he was so persistent in recommending I have a portrait done."

I blew out a steadying breath.

One thing the prince had said sounded off—Gadfly had given me the impression he'd had nothing to do with this appointment—but I was so relieved the thought fled my mind almost instantly.

"I had no idea," I said. "You're the first to tell me—no one else has ever mentioned it."

The prince brushed past, his sleeve caressing my arm. The parlor appeared to interest him greatly. It was the largest room in my house, and the most cluttered, though we took pains to keep it neat. At present the only unoccupied piece of furniture was the settee beside the window. In the corner to my left there was a varnished side table on which sat a crystal vase containing two peacock feathers, a set of imported china, a stack of leather-bound books, and an empty birdcage. The brocade chairs next to it were piled high with mismatched drapes, rugs,

and curtains in every color and pattern imaginable. The rest of the room went on similarly, in each nook and cranny a different collection of curiosities, as though the parlor were a miniature, eclectic museum of human Craft. My chair and easel sat unassumingly in the very center.

The prince seemed too distracted to reply, so I continued: "When working with human patrons, portrait artists usually travel to their homes and paint them there. Because I can't do that with fair folk, of course, we choose furniture and decorations and arrange them to your liking here in this room."

"It restricts us," the prince murmured, touching his fingertips gently to the birdcage. He ran them down the thin metal bars. I remembered the raven sitting outside and wished I'd had the presence of mind to put the cage in another room, even as I wondered what on earth he was talking about. Never once had a fair one acted anything but pleased to surround themselves with the parlor's gaudy props.

He snatched his fingers away and turned around. His pensiveness vanished into a smile like morning mist dissolved by the sun. "Gadfly's enchantment, that is. Why none of us have mentioned it to you before. It feels like having a pair of shackles around our wrists, as light as spider-silk but strong as iron. No fair one enjoys commenting on their own weakness."

"But you're an exception, sir?"

"Oh, not at all. I don't enjoy it either." His smile deepened, and the crooked dimple reappeared on his cheek. "I just have little regard for discretion, as you might have noticed."

Indeed, I had. He was unlike any other fair one I'd ever met.

"Is there a proper way to address you as prince?" I deferred, crossing the room to start sorting through the fabrics for a backdrop that would complement his wardrobe.

"We don't observe such formalities," he said, and glanced at me. "I would have thought you already knew that." *How?* I wondered. It wasn't as though I had fairy royalty over for dinner. "In any case, my name is Rook."

I couldn't help but smile. "That's fitting, sir."

His eyes moved, searching my face, and it seemed to me his own smile grew even more familiar, confidential in a way I hadn't known a fair one could manage. Standing next to him, I became aware that the top of my head only reached to his chest. My cheeks warmed.

Good lord! I had a job to do.

"I think this brocade would suit you," I said, lifting a heavy rust-colored silk with copper embroidery.

He paused to look at it, almost impatiently. I always found this part interesting. One could learn precious little about fair folk, but occasionally their aesthetic choices opened windows into their souls (if they had them, that is—always a controversial matter at church). Gadfly enjoyed stuffing his frames full of as many expensive-looking trifles as possible. Another patron, Swallowtail, preferred only functional objects that had been used before: half-burnt candles, books with cracked spines and feathered corners.

Rook shook his head at the brocade and bent to inspect a row of blown-glass vases. He examined statuettes and mirrors, baskets full of wax fruit, chemistry bottles, quill pens, strangely arresting in his silence and grave concentration. I couldn't begin to imagine what he was thinking. Finally he came back to the birdcage and looked up to find me watching him. His mercurial smile returned.

"I've decided I don't want anything in my portrait," he declared, and went over to the settee. He sat down with one arm stretched across the back and a knowing regard that told me he'd figured out exactly why I'd been watching him. "If you must stare at something for hours on end, I'd prefer it to be me alone."

I struggled to keep my expression serious. "How gracious of you, sir. It will take me far less time to finish your portrait with you as the sole subject."

He sat a little straighter and frowned, a trace of petulance darkening his aristocratic features.

What was I doing? It was easy—so easy—for a fair one's pique to turn to dangerous ire. This wasn't like me. So many years of being cautious, and in a matter of minutes I'd started slipping up. Swallowing my words, I went over to my chair, arranged my skirts, and selected a stick of charcoal. I pushed every other thought aside.

It's difficult to explain what happens when I pick up a charcoal stick or a paintbrush. I can tell you the world changes. I see things one way when I'm not working, and an entirely different way when I am. Faces become not-faces, structures composed of light and shadow, shapes and angles and texture. The deep luminous glow of an iris where the light hits it from the window becomes exquisitely compelling. I hunger for the shadow that falls diagonally across my subject's collar, the fine lighter filaments in his hair ablaze like thread-of-gold. My mind and hand become possessed. I paint not because I want to, not because I'm good at it, but because it is what I must do, what I live and breathe, what I was made for.

My concerns fell away along with the scrape of charcoal

across paper. I didn't notice the soft black flakes sifting down, dusting my lap. First a circle, loose, energetic, capturing the shape of Rook's face. Then vigorous wider lines sketching in the ensnaring tousle of his hair, his crown.

No.

I tore the paper off my easel, let it fall to the ground, and started in on a new one. Face, hair, crown. Eyebrows, dark and arching. A crooked half-smile. The blocky frame of his shoulders. Good. Better. There were two Rooks in the room now, both watching me. Neither was more real than the other.

Beyond my easel, the living Rook tilted his head. He shifted where he sat. I felt him observing me and didn't care, lost in the fever of my Craft. But with the small portion of my mind reserved for other thoughts I noted he was getting restless, and remembered what Gadfly had said to me the day before—something about Rook having trouble sitting still.

"Wait," he said, and my charcoal scraped to a halt. I looked at him, looked at him, my eyes adjusting back to the living world as though I'd just stared too hard at an optical illusion. Something about him seemed troubled. Briefly, I worried he was about to cancel his session.

"Is it"—he frowned, grasping for words—"fixed? The portrait? Can you make a change to it?"

I let go of the breath I'd been holding. So that was all. "I can make any change you'd like at this stage. Once I begin painting it will become more difficult, but I'll still be able to make alterations up until the end."

For a moment Rook didn't say anything. He looked at me, looked away, and then unfastened the raven pin and put it in his pocket. "Excellent," he said. "That's all."

I would be lying if I claimed I wasn't curious. The pin was, of course, an item of human Craft, like everything else he wore. Long ago, Rook had been well known in Whimsy. And one day, to all accounts, he'd simply stopped visiting. Fair folk coveted Craft above all other things. What calamity might shake one of the habit, and did it have anything to do with the article he'd just removed?

Or perhaps—more likely, almost certainly—the pin was simply out of fashion, or he was tired of wearing it, or he'd just decided it clashed with the color of his buttons and wanted it remade. He was a fair one, not a mortal boy. I couldn't fall into the trap of sympathizing with him. It was his kind's oldest, favorite, and most dangerous trick.

I fell back into my work. His likeness was filling in well, yet a flaw began bothering me as I refined the sketch. Somehow, his eyes were wrong. I dabbed charcoal from the paper with the lump of moistened bread I kept on my side table and started over, but each time I redid them they grew no closer to perfection. From the folds of his eyelids to the curve of his eyelashes, every detail was exactly true to his image—but the sum of them failed to capture his . . . well, his soul. I'd never encountered this problem with a fair one before. What on earth was wrong with me today?

My charcoal stick broke. One half rolled across the floor-boards and vanished under the settee. I started to get up, but Rook bent and retrieved it for me. Before he returned to his seat he paused and looked at my work. I thought I heard a barely audible intake of breath.

He leaned forward to look at it more closely. "Is that how you see me?" he asked, in a quiet and marveling tone.

I wasn't certain how to answer. To me the unnameable flaw overwhelmed the drawing, made it unsightly. "It's how you look, sir," I settled on. "But it still needs a great deal of improvement. I'd like to work on it more before we're done today."

Rook touched his crown, almost self-consciously, as he sat back down. He hesitated, then put his arm back where it had been before. After a pause he adjusted its placement to make it exact.

The remainder of the session passed in silence. Not the rigid silence I usually felt in the presence of Rook's kind, but a warmer and more tentative stillness. It reminded me of the time I'd gone to sit under my favorite tree in town to read in the shade, and found another girl already there doing the same thing. We'd passed hours together after saying only a brief hello. By the time we went home I felt we were friends even though we'd only exchanged a single shy word. Later, I found out she'd left with her parents for the World Beyond.

I realized how late it was when two curly-haired heads rose up behind the window. Rook remained oblivious to the twins peering inside until May stuck her face to the glass like a suction cup and puffed out her cheeks. Then he turned, but not in time to see them duck down, leaving only a shrinking fog on the windowpane. The sun had nearly set. I still hadn't figured out what was wrong with Rook's eyes.

A trace of disappointment moved his brow when I told him we were finished.

"Can I come back again tomorrow?" he asked.

I looked up from untying my apron. "Gadfly has a session scheduled. The next day?"

"Very well," he said, annoyed—but not at me, I sensed.

I'm not sure what came over me next. When he opened the door he didn't walk out straightaway, but rather lingered as if he wanted to say something else, just wasn't certain what. The exact same feeling gripped me. Our eyes met, forging a connection across the room. I drew a breath and then said boldly, chastising myself all the while, "Are you going to return as a raven?"

"More likely than not, I think."

"Before you leave, may I see you change?"

He hadn't expected that question. Several emotions crossed his face at once: hope, caution, pleasure. None of them exactly human, but I still couldn't help but feel they had more substance than the aloof facsimiles of sentiment other fair folk tried on like hats, pale imitations no more real than their glamour.

"It will not frighten you?" he asked.

I shook my head. Neither one of us looked away from the other. "I am not easily frightened."

A spark flared in Rook's eyes. Rustling filled the house, the sound of a faraway wind rushing through dry leaves. It rose and rose in volume until I felt the cool wind surrounding me, tugging at my clothes, wild with the intoxicating spice of nighttime forest, shocking me again with that unnameable thirst for change. The cast-off charcoal drawings fluttered where they lay, then blew across the room. As the sun tipped below the horizon, the birdcage flashed blinding gold for an instant before my parlor plunged into shadow.

Rook seemed to grow taller, and darker, and fiercer. His purple eyes blazed impetuously, untouched by his subtle half-smile. A whirlwind of black feathers rose from the floor to engulf him.

I must have blinked, because the next thing I knew the papers lay still against the wall and a raven watched me with half-spread wings from atop the birdcage. The last of the dying light shone on its glossy feathers and glittered in its eyes.

The wind had stolen the breath from my lungs. I knew no words to describe what I had just seen. "That was marvelous," I whispered finally, and gave the raven a curtsy.

With a trace of humor, the bird dipped its head before it flew out the door.

Four

SEPTEMBER PASSED so quickly I felt I'd dreamed it. I finished Gadfly's portrait and soon afterward gained another patroness, Vervain of the house of summer. But it seemed to me my days were spent with Rook and Rook alone.

Halfway through the month, I'd delayed bringing up the matter of payment as long as I could. Usually my clients made the first move, eager to ensnare me in their thorniest temptations, but I suspected the prince hadn't dealt with mortals in so long he'd fallen out of practice. Having to broach the subject myself left me unaccountably nervous. I pretended it was due to the anxiety of facing a deviation from my normal routine. But the real reason was that I didn't want to listen to Rook offering me roses whose perfume would make me forget all my childhood memories, or diamonds that would make me care for nothing but gems ever after, or goose down that would steal away my dreams. I knew that part of him existed, but I didn't want to see it. And that sentiment was more dangerous than all the enchantments he could offer me combined.

Three times I set down my brush and opened my mouth before finally, on the fourth try, I found the courage to speak. He looked up from the cup of tea he'd been analyzing—rather suspiciously, I thought—and listened.

"Yes, of course," he said when I was done. Then he astonished me by asking, "What type of enchantment would you like?"

I paused to reevaluate. Perhaps he preferred watching mortals orchestrate their own undoings. In that case, I'd have to be extra careful. I weighed each word on my tongue. "Something to warn me if I or a member of my family is in danger." I took a moment to review the request's weaknesses and went on, "For the purpose of this enchantment my family includes my aunt Emma and my adopted sisters, March and May. The sign must be subtle, so as not to draw unwanted attention, but also clear, so I won't miss it when it happens."

He deposited the teacup on the side table, folded his arms, and gave me a crooked smile. I steeled myself. "Ravens," he suggested, disarming me yet again.

Ravens? I couldn't decide whether the idea owed itself to vanity, a depressing lack of creativity, or both.

"Pardon my directness," I replied, "but ravens can be quite noisy. If I were running from a"—I wavered and changed course—"a highwayman, for example, I don't believe a flock of birds squabbling over my hiding place would be to my advantage."

"Ah, I see. In that case, well-behaved ravens. They will mind their manners."

"You are strangely persistent, sir. Is there anything about these ravens I might come to regret?" Frustration hardened my voice. I couldn't figure him out. There had to be *some* catch. God help me, I *needed* there to be one, to remind me what he was. "They won't torment me with foreknowledge of my own death, or keep me sleepless at night, or descend in droves whenever I'm about to stub a toe?"

"No!" Rook exclaimed, rising halfway from his seat. He caught himself, shoved his sword out of the way, and sank back down looking unsettled. I stared. "I am not up to any mischief," he went on, sounding equally frustrated. "You do not seem as though you would allow it, in any case, if I tried."

My stranded words formed a lump in my throat. A fair one never lied. I tore my gaze away from him, away from that look in his eyes I couldn't put to name—or canvas.

"No, I wouldn't. Given your assurances, ravens would be— acceptable." Mortified by how stiff I sounded, I clenched my fists until my fingernails dug into my palms. "We can discuss the remaining terms tomorrow."

He brightened at the mention of "tomorrow" and bowed his head in assent. "I look forward to it," he replied eagerly, and just like that, all was forgiven. Stifling a smile, I picked up a palette knife by accident before I found my brush.

After he left, I couldn't shake the notion that he'd insisted on ravens for a reason. I was almost finished cleaning up by the time the explanation occurred to me. My cheeks warmed, and a wistful pang plucked a sweet, sad chord in my stomach. It was simple, really. He didn't want me to forget him once he'd gone.

The remaining weeks blurred together. The season didn't turn. Yet there in my parlor, while the fields outside simmered beneath a summer sun, a vital change swept through me. When Rook wasn't there, I thought about him. During our sessions, my heart pounded as though I'd just run a mile. I tossed and turned half the night, tortured by the cipher of his unpaintable eyes, driven restless and half-wild by the moonlight spilling through my window, which I swore was brighter than any moon preceding it. This must be what the awakening of spring was like, I thought. I was alive in a way I never had been before, in a world that no longer felt stale but instead crackled with breathless promise.

Oh, I knew that how I felt toward Rook was dangerous. Incredibly, the danger made it *better*. Perhaps all those lonely years of keeping a polite smile frozen on my face had driven me a bit off-balance, and the madness just didn't kick in until I'd had a taste of something new. Walking on a blade's edge every time we exchanged a curtsy and a bow, knowing one misstep could topple me into mortal peril, made the blood sing in my veins. I exulted in my own cleverness. Of all the Crafters in Whimsy, I knew fair folk best. As the days trickled through my fingers like water, slipping past no matter how fiercely I held on to them, hurtling me toward the inevitable end of a moment I wanted to last forever, my assurance that I could handle Rook strengthened to iron.

And I might have continued believing that if I hadn't figured out what was wrong with his eyes during our very last session.

"Gadfly told me the first time you painted him, your feet didn't reach the floor," Rook said, which was how it started. "He spoke as though it was merely . . . Isobel, how old are you? I've never thought to ask."

"Seventeen," I replied, breaking free from the painting to watch his reaction.

During our first few sessions he'd sat stiff as a board, apparently under the impression he'd interfere with my work if he moved so much as a hair. Now that I'd assured him I was far enough along that his posture didn't matter, he sprawled sideways on the settee so he could glance out the window constantly, as though it pained him to miss even one cloud or passing bird. But even so he spent most of his time looking back at me. The rapport between us had grown perilously casual.

His reaction wasn't quite what I anticipated. For a long moment he only stared, his expression close to shock or even loss. "Seventeen?" he repeated. "Surely that's too young to be a master of the Craft. And you're already fully grown, aren't you?"

I nodded. I would have smiled if it hadn't been for the look on his face. "It is young. Most people my age don't perform at this level. I started painting as soon as I could hold a brush."

He shook his head. His gaze drifted to the floor. Preoccupied, he touched his pocket.

"How old are you?" I inquired, perplexed by the air of melancholy that had fallen over him.

"I don't know. I can't—" He looked out the window. A muscle moved in his jaw. "Fair folk hardly pay years any mind, they pass so quickly. I don't believe I can tell you in a way you'd understand."

What must it be like? To meet someone, to forge a connection, all in the span of one golden afternoon—only to find out that for her, each passing minute was a year. Each second, an hour. She would be dead before the sun rose the next day. A keen, quiet pain twisted my heart.

That was when I saw the secret hidden deep within his eyes. Impossibly, it was sorrow. Not a fair one's ephemeral mourning, but *human* sorrow, bleak and endless, a yawning chasm in his soul. No wonder I hadn't been able to identify the flaw. That emotion didn't belong to his kind. Couldn't belong.

Time stopped. Even the dust motes glowing in the air seemed to go still.

I had to be sure of what I'd seen. I crossed the room in a trance and brought my hand to his cheek so lightly I barely touched him. He hadn't been paying attention, and he made the smallest movement—almost a flinch—before he looked at me. Yes, the sorrow was truly there. Along with it, hurt and confusion, to a degree that I wondered whether he even understood what he felt, or whether it was as alien to him as so many aspects of the fair folk were to us.

"Have I offended you?" he asked. "I'm sorry. I didn't mean to imply . . ."

"No, you haven't." Somehow my voice sounded normal. "I've just noticed something I need to work on before your portrait's finished. Could you hold your head like this for a few minutes?"

Aware that I was taking an immense liberty, I raised my other hand, cupped his face, and gently turned it toward my easel at just the right angle for the light to strike his eyes. He allowed me to handle him in silence, his breath warming my wrists, watching me all the while.

This was our last day together. The first and final time I'd ever touch him. The knowing of it pulsed between us like a heartbeat. With our gazes locked, another truth became unmistakable. I felt a connection between us as tangibly as a handshake or a grip on my shoulder. I knew he felt it too.

Dizzy, I stepped back and slammed the door on it before it could take form. Dark spots swam around the edges of my vision and cold panic squeezed the air from my lungs. Whatever this was, it had to end. Now.

Walking along a blade's edge was only fun until the blade stopped being a metaphor.

Mortals cared little for the Good Law's cryptic edicts, but one of its rulings applied to us all the same: fair folk and humans weren't permitted to fall in love. Almost a joke, honestly. The sort of thing Crafters wrote songs about and wove into tapestries. It never happened, never could happen, because despite their flirtatiousness and their fondness for attention, fair folk couldn't feel anything as real as love. Or so I'd thought. Now I doubted everything I'd been told about Rook's kind, everything I'd observed, the neat, sensible rules I'd taken for granted my entire life. Laws didn't exist without reason—or precedent.

And its penalty? Oh, you know how these stories go. Of course it's death, with one exception. To save her life—to save both their lives—the mortal must drink from the Green Well. But only if the fair folk don't catch them first.

"If you would remain still for me, please," I said. My request came out coolly, and my chair's creak sounded miles away. As I lifted my paintbrush, I dared not look at Rook and witness his reaction to my changed demeanor.

When the world failed me, I could always lose myself in my work. I withdrew into this sanctuary, where all my other concerns faded beside the demanding compulsion of my Craft. I narrowed my focus to Rook's eyes, the full, mellow aroma of oil paint, the sensual gleaming trail my brush spread across the textured canvas, and nothing more. This was my Craft, my purpose. We were here for Craft alone. His veiled expression was something only a master could achieve, and I was determined to do it justice. The technique lay in the shadows of his irises—deep, mysterious, and clouded, like the darkness a boat cast onto the bottom of a clear lake. Not the thing itself, but the shape of the ghost it left behind.

And while I worked the fever filled me, the thrill of my talent, an awareness that I was about to complete a portrait unlike any painted before. I forgot who I was, swept up in this force that seemed to surge through me from both within and without.

The light faded, but I didn't notice until the room grew dim enough to leach the color from my canvas. Emma was home; she made quiet sounds moving about in the kitchen, trying to keep her presence unobtrusive as she smuggled the twins upstairs. My wrist ached. Stray hairs clung to my sweaty temples. Without warning, I paused to shape my brush and realized I was finished. Rook looked back at me, his soul captured in two dimensions.

A horn blast sounded in the distance.

Rook leapt up across the shadowy room, tension in every line of his body. His hand went to his sword. My first muddled thought was that it was another fairy beast, but the sound wasn't right: high and nasal, pure of tone. I became sure of this when the horn sounded a second time, shivered, and dropped away.

A chill rippled across my back. Though one rarely hears it in Whimsy, one never forgets the Wild Hunt's call.

"Isobel, I must go," Rook said, belting on his sword. "The Hunt has intruded on the autumnlands."

I stood up so fast I knocked my chair over. It cracked like a musket shot against the floorboards, but I didn't flinch. "Wait. Your portrait's finished."

He stopped with his hand on the half-open door. Awfully, he wouldn't look at me. No—couldn't. I knew then, without a speck of doubt, that he planned on vanishing from the human world once more, utterly and, as far as my own mortal life was concerned, permanently. Neither of us could afford to tempt fate. Once he left, we'd never see each other again.

"Have it prepared to be sent to the autumn court," he said in a hollow voice. "A fair one named Fern will pick it up in two weeks' time." He hesitated. But then the horn sounded again, and he only added, "One raven for uncertain peril. Six for danger sure to arrive. A dozen for death, if not avoided. The enchantment is sealed."

He ducked below the lintel and dashed out the door. Just like that, he was gone forever.

Now I have to tell you how foolish I am. Before that gray and lifeless time following Rook's departure, I'd always scoffed at stories in which maidens pine for their absent suitors, boys they've hardly known a week and have no business falling for. Didn't they realize their lives were worth more than the dubious affection of one silly young man? That there were things to do in a world that didn't revolve solely around their heartbreak?

Then it happens to you, and you understand you aren't any different from those girls after all. Oh, they still seem just as absurd—you've simply joined them, in quite a humbling way. But isn't absurdity part of being human? We aren't ageless creatures who watch centuries pass from afar. Our worlds are small, our lives are short, and we can only bleed a little before we fall.

Two days later, I made a mental inventory of Rook's unfavorable qualities, prepared to indulge in some vicious criticism. He was arrogant, self-centered, and obtuse—unworthy of me in every way. Yet as I fumed over our first meeting, I couldn't help but remember how swiftly he'd apologized to me, no matter that he hadn't had the slightest idea what he was apologizing for. I recalled the look on his face exactly. By the end of the exercise, I only felt more miserable.

Three days later, I pressed the half dozen preparatory charcoal sketches I'd done of him between sheets of wax paper, bundled them up, and hid them at the back of my closet, resolving not to look at them again until I no longer craved seeing his face like prodding a fresh bruise. The golden afternoon was over. By the time Rook remembered me, if he ever did, I'd be long dead.

I ate. I slept. I got out of bed in the morning. I painted, I did dishes, I looked after the twins. Every day dawned bright and blue. During the hot afternoons, the buzzing of the grasshoppers blurred into a monotonous throb. It was for the better, I told myself, swallowing the mantra like a lump of bitter bread.

It was for the better.

Two weeks later, Fern arrived as promised and took the portrait away in a crate packed with cloth and straw. After the third week I'd started feeling a little like my old self, but there was something missing from my life now, and I suspected I'd never be exactly the same again. Maybe that was just part of growing up.

One night I went into the kitchen after dark to find Emma asleep at the table, her hand curled around a tincture bottle in danger of tipping over, with pungent half-ground herbs sitting in her mortar and pestle. It wasn't an unusual discovery.

"Emma," I whispered, touching her shoulder.

She mumbled indistinctly in reply.

"It's late. You should go to bed."

"All right, I'm going," she said into her arms, muffled, but didn't move. I took the tincture from her hand and sniffed it, then found its stopper and set it aside. I knew what I would find if I smelled Emma's breath.

"Come on." I draped her limp arm over my shoulders and pulled her upright. Her ankles turned before she found her footing. Going up the stairs proved as interesting as I expected.

People mistook Emma for my mother all the time. Children, mostly, and out-of-towners—people who didn't know what had happened to my parents, or that as Whimsy's physician Emma had been the one who'd tried to save my father's life and failed. Unlike my mother, he hadn't died instantly. To all accounts, it would have been better if he had.

So I suppose I couldn't stay angry at Emma for her vices, even when they occasionally made me her keeper rather than the other way around. A patient must have died today, though I'd long ago stopped asking once I'd made the connection. Most of all, I could never forget I was the reason she was still in Whimsy. If it hadn't been for me, the responsibility of raising her sister's daughter, the child of the man who died in her arms, she would have left for the World Beyond as soon as she could. In a place where enchantments reigned supreme and the creatures who traded them had no use for human medicine . . . well, her ideal life lay elsewhere.

Emma was missing something too, and I'd do well to remember that.

"Can you take your shoes off?" I asked, lowering her to the edge of her bed.

"'M all right," she replied with her eyes closed, so I did it anyway, and tucked them under the bed skirt so she wouldn't trip on them if she got up during the night. Afterward, I leaned down and kissed her forehead.

Her eyes squinted open. They were dark brown, almost black, like mine—large and intense. She had the same freckles spattered across her fair skin and the same thick, wheat-colored hair. Before everything happened, I remember her and my mother joking that the women in our family reigned supreme: they passed their looks down without any input from the men whatsoever.

"I'm sorry about Rook," she said, reaching up to give a strand of my identical hair an affectionate tug.

I froze. My mind reeled, teetering at the edge of a precipice. "I don't know what—"

"Isobel, I'm not blind. I knew what was going on."

Acid soured my stomach. My voice came out thin and tight, prepared to rise stridently in defense. "Why didn't you say anything?"

Her hand flopped down to the coverlet. "Because I couldn't tell you anything you didn't already know. I trusted you to make the right choice." Lanced with guilt in the face of Emma's understanding, my hostility deflated. Somehow the emptiness it left behind felt far, far worse. "Also, I worry about you. Your Craft keeps you so busy and isolated you haven't had a chance to experience . . . well, so many things. We'd have a hard time getting by without the enchantments. But I wish—"

A thump shook the ceiling, followed by a maniacal cackle. I

welcomed the interruption. The more Emma spoke, the harder I wrestled with the tears prickling the backs of my eyes.

"Oh, hell. The twins." Her voice scraped like sandpaper. She gave the rafters a resigned look.

I rose swiftly. "Don't worry. I'll check on them."

The old stairway to the attic creaked beneath my weight. When I entered the twins' bedroom, a tiny slope-ceilinged nook barely large enough for two beds and a dresser, they'd already initiated a pretend sleep routine, which wouldn't have fooled me even without the stifled giggling.

"I know you're plotting something. Out with it." I went over to May and tickled her. Rarely did she confess without torture.

"March!" she shrieked, thrashing beneath the covers. "March wants to show you something!"

I relented, and regarded March with my hands on my hips, trying to look stoic. Judging by the way her cheeks were ballooned out, she was about to squirt water all over my face or possibly something even less pleasant. I couldn't show weakness. I tapped my foot and raised an impatient eyebrow.

"Bleeeghhh," she said, and ejected a live toad onto her quilt.

I shook my head at May's hysterical laughter. "Well, at least you didn't swallow it," I reasoned, lunging after the moist and traumatized creature. I snatched it before it made a bid for freedom down the stairwell. "Now settle down, all right? Emma's having one of her nights." They didn't know what this meant, only that it was serious, and I'd think of some way to bribe them for being on their best behavior.

"Fine," May sighed, flopping over in bed. She watched me with one eye. "What are you going to do with it?"

"Put it somewhere far away from March's mouth." *And*

hope it recovers from the nightmares, I thought, shutting the door behind me.

I drifted through the house, moonlight making foreign shapes of the parlor's clutter. A half-finished Vervain smiled at me coldly from the easel, wearing an expression that might as well have been carved onto a wigmaker's mannequin. Working with her came as a shock after Rook, even though I knew she was only a return to normality, whatever that meant in my case.

I crept through the kitchen and outside onto the damp grass, where I set the toad free. It sprang away into the weeds, toward the forest. From here, across the moon-silvered field, the tops of the trees poked above the horizon like a cloud bank.

A breeze stirred the wheat and sighed through the grass, chilling the dew on my toes. The wind blew from the forest's direction and for a moment I imagined I caught a whisper of that crisp, wild, wistful smell, Rook's smell, the one that seized my heart and wouldn't let go. I knew what it was. Autumn.

All at once my chest swelled with unnameable longing, an ache lodged at the base of my throat like an unvoiced cry. Lives to be lived awaited me out there, far from the safety of my familiar home and confining routine. The whole world waited for me. I felt pierced through with longing. Oh, if only I were the type to scream.

I wiped my toady hands off on the grass and stepped back.

A fluttering of wingbeats came from the old oak.

I turned, the breeze lifting my hair, and saw a raven in the tree. But which was it—a raven for peril, or a raven I loved?

Before I could move, Rook stood over me. I only had time to think, *Both.* For this wasn't the Rook I knew. As the feathers shed from his form and gathered into a sweeping coat, they revealed a face livid with fury. No half-smile softened this hard, frozen mask, those amethyst eyes burning like conflagrations.

"*What did you do?*" he snarled.

Five

ROOK'S BEWILDERING question chilled me to the core. Mutely, I shook my head. I needed to get inside.

Anticipating my move, he crowded me against the side of the house and pinned me there. He didn't touch me, but a clear threat radiated from the arms bracketing my shoulders, the strong hands gripping the wood beside my face. With escape eliminated as an option I found I couldn't look away from him. His normally expressive mouth was compressed into a thin, bloodless line as he waited for me to answer. I would have welcomed any change in his icy expression, even for the worse, to give me some indication of what was going through his head.

"Rook, I don't know what you're talking about," I said, sounding as daunted as I felt. "I haven't done anything."

He drew up to his full height. I'd forgotten how tall he

was—I could barely tip my head back far enough to see him. "Stop playing the fool. I know you sabotaged the portrait. Why? Are you working for another fair one? What did they give you to betray me?"

"Give—what are you *talking* about?"

In his eyes, a flicker. But if I'd gotten through to him, he steeled himself quickly against his doubts. "You did something to it, between the last session and when it was sent to me. There's a wrongness to it now. Anyone who looks at it can tell."

"I painted you. That's all. That's all my Craft involves, how could it be . . ." *Oh.* Oh, no.

"You did do something," he hissed, his fingers curling against the wall.

"No! I mean, I did, but it wasn't some sort of—scheme, or—or sabotage. I swear. I painted you exactly as you are. I saw it, Rook. I saw everything, though you might try to keep it hidden away."

Well. I may be an artistic prodigy, but I've never claimed to be a genius. Only at that moment did it occur to me that Rook's secret sorrow might be secret for a reason. It could be a secret even to him.

"You saw everything?" His voice grew menacingly quiet. He leaned over me, caging me in with his body from all angles. "What do you think you saw, Isobel, with your mortal eyes? Have you ever seen the splendors of the summer court, or witnessed fair folk as old as the earth itself slain in the glass mountains of the winterlands? Have you watched entire generations of living things grow, flourish, and die in less time than it takes you to draw a single breath? Do you recall what I am?"

I shrank against the boards digging into my spine. "I could

change it for you," I said, wondering if I'd just lied to him. Even though my life might very well depend on it, I found the prospect of destroying my perfect work unimaginable. It was the only example of its kind in the entire world.

Rook barked a bitter laugh. "The portrait was unveiled publicly before the autumn court. All my house has seen it."

My mind went blank. "Shit," I agreed eloquently, after a pause.

"There is only one way to repair my reputation. You're coming with me to stand trial in the autumnlands for your crime. Tonight."

"Wait—"

Rook withdrew. Dazzled by the moon shining directly into my eyes, I found myself marching after him across the yard toward the shoulder-high wheat. My legs moved in fits and jerks, like a marionette's legs controlled by a puppeteer. Senseless panic seized me. No matter how fiercely I railed against my body's betrayal, I couldn't stop walking.

"Rook, you can't do this. You don't know my true name."

He didn't bother turning around as he spoke. The sweep of his coat was all I had to go on. "If you were ensorcelled, you wouldn't know it—you would follow me willingly, believing you'd made the decision on your own. This is nothing more than a trifling charm. You seem to have forgotten what I am after all. There is only a single fair one in all the world stronger than I, and two others my equal."

"The Alder King," I murmured. In the distance, the trees swayed.

Rook stopped in his tracks. He turned his face to the side, presenting me with a view of his profile, though he didn't quite look at me, as if unwilling to take his eyes off something else. "Once we're in the forest," he said, "do not speak those words. Do not even think them."

A chill gripped me. The only thing I knew about the Alder King was that he was the lord of the summer court and he had ruled fairykind forever. His influence spread far, locking Whimsy in its eternal summer. In that moment it seemed the trees were leaning together, whispering. Waiting for me to walk past those rusty, crooked nails and walk beneath their boughs, so they could watch and listen. I'd almost reached the edge of my yard, and felt as though I were about to step beyond a pool of lantern light into an endless darkness crawling with horrors. No, I didn't just feel like it—I was.

I couldn't scream. If Emma ran outside I had no idea what might happen to her, and the idea of the twins seeing this sickened me. But I couldn't just march after him like an unresisting puppet, either, straight into the shadowy forest ahead.

Swallowing hard, I bunched my skirts in my hands and gave his back an awkward top-only curtsy.

He spun on his heel and bowed, glaring as though he might kill me on the spot. As soon as he'd turned around and taken another step, I curtsied again. We repeated this odd ritual four times, his expression growing increasingly furious, before I felt the charm controlling my legs creep farther up my body, petrifying my waist to the rigidity of a porcelain doll's. So much for that plan.

We plunged into the field. Wheat swished all around me, tickling and scratching, catching on the rough fabric of my clothes. When I looked over my shoulder I saw no lights on in the house. Was this the last time I'd ever see my home? My family? The silver-lined shingles and eaves, the big old oak by the kitchen door were suddenly so dear to me that tears sprang unbidden to my eyes. Rook didn't notice my distress. Would he care at all if he saw me weeping? Perhaps. Perhaps not. Either way, it couldn't hurt to find out.

I flexed my fingers. Good—my arms were still free. I found the pocket hidden among my skirts' loose folds and started picking at a seam with my fingernails.

"Rook, wait," I said. Another hot tear skated down my cheek and dripped inside my collar. "If you care anything for me at all, or ever did, stop for a moment and let me compose myself."

His pace slowed, dwindled to a halt. My own marching didn't wear off until I stood close behind him, which was exactly what I'd hoped for.

"I—" he began, but I didn't get a chance to hear what he'd been about to say.

I seized his hand and squeezed it tight, making sure the ring I'd picked out of my pocket seam pressed against his bare skin. It wasn't just any ring. It was forged from cold, pure iron.

He swayed where he stood, as though the ground had dropped out beneath him. Then he tore his hand from mine and started back, rounding on me with his teeth bared in a feral snarl. My stomach lurched. Over the years, observing the individual imperfections in each fair one's glamour, I'd put together a picture of what they looked like underneath. As it turned out, I still wasn't prepared for the sight.

In his true form Rook resembled some hellish creature spawned from the forest's heart—not hideous, precisely, but terrifyingly inhuman. The life had leached from his golden skin, leaving him a sickly tallow gray, with hollow cheeks and hair that tangled about his face like the shadows cast by a briar thicket. His luminous eyes reminded me of a hawk's, soul-piercing and devoid of mercy or feeling. His fingers were uncanny in their length and jointedness, and I could tell by the way his clothes hung from him that he had grown gaunt as a skeleton beneath them. Worst of all were his teeth, each one needle-sharp behind his peeled-back upper lip.

Almost instantly his returning glamour filled in his cheeks, tamed his hair, and brought color to his ashen face, but the frightful image had been seared into my memory forever.

"How dare you use iron against me," he rasped, agony strangling each syllable. "You know as well as I that it's outlawed in Whimsy. I should kill you where you stand."

I struggled to keep my voice steady while my heart flung itself against my ribs. "I know your kind is bound by your word. You value fairness highly. If you were to slay me for carrying iron, would it not be fair and necessary to carry out the same punishment toward anyone else guilty of an identical offense?"

He hesitated. Staring at me, he nodded.

"Then if I'm to be killed, so must everyone in Whimsy down to the last child. We all secretly carry iron from the day we're born until the day we die."

"You dreadful—" Under other circumstances his consternation would have been comical. "First you betray me, and now—now you tell me—" He groped for words. Clearly he wasn't accustomed to being beaten at his own game. Because of course the fair folk couldn't go about killing everyone in Whimsy; they coveted Craft too much to even consider it.

I drew a fortifying breath. "I know I can't escape you.

Charming me to walk makes no difference, aside from using energy you could spend on something else." This, I admit, was a complete gamble, but the way Rook pressed his lips together told me I'd struck close to the mark. "So let me walk freely, let me keep my iron, and I'll go with you willingly—in body if not in spirit."

He stepped back from me once, twice, three times through the wheat, then pivoted and stalked off toward the trees. I stumbled after him, the charm's evaporation his only answer.

My mind clamored for escape. But I knew I'd harm my chances, perhaps destroy them for good if I tried running now. I had no choice but to follow him through the field, through the weeds, and into the forest waiting beyond, where only a handful of humans had set foot before—and not one among them returned.

Every muscle in my body clenched with the expectation of more fairy devilry, but my initial obstacles proved surprisingly, unpleasantly mundane. My breath blew harshly in my ears and my skirts clung to the sweat on my legs as I trudged through the undergrowth. Burs burrowed their way into my stockings, and I tripped over roots and stones every other step. Meanwhile Rook might as well have not existed, he slipped through the vegetation so smoothly. Every once in a while a branch did catch on his shoulder, only to pull back, release, and smack me in the face, but I think he was doing that on purpose.

"Rook."

He said nothing.

"It's getting too dark—the moonlight's gone. I can't see."

A fairy light bloomed above his upraised hand. It was purple, the same color as his eyes, and about the size of a fist, vaporous and shimmering. It floated down to skim along the ground, edging the leaves with a spectral glow. My mother telling me to never follow such lights numbered among my earliest memories.

On and on we trudged.

"Um." I'd gone for as long as I could without bringing this up. "I, um, need to relieve myself." When he didn't show any indication of hearing I added, "Right now."

His head turned a fraction, his profile lined with fairy light. "Do it quickly."

I certainly wasn't going to linger with my underthings down in a dark forest next to a fairy prince. He seemed to expect me to squat down and pee where I stood, which I suppose made little difference; we weren't on any sort of path. But I still wanted to maintain some semblance of dignity, so I crashed a few steps through a stand of honeysuckles and settled down on the other side. The light bobbed obediently at my heels.

I almost screamed when I glanced over my shoulder to find Rook looming behind me.

"Turn *around*!" I exclaimed.

Again that mystified look he'd first given me in the kitchen, but it vanished so swiftly I couldn't be sure I'd truly glimpsed it. "Why must I?" he asked, in a cold and princely tone.

"Because this is private! You've spent the entire walk with your back turned, surely you can manage it again for a few seconds. And I won't be able to do anything with you watching."

That, at least, got through to him. But as I wallowed there in the underbrush like a nesting hen with my skirts piled up around me, Rook's fine coat fabric brushing my hair whenever he shifted, my bladder simply wouldn't cooperate. Even more so when I glanced around the woods for a distraction and saw a mushroom circle nearby. Each toadstool cap was as wide as a dinner plate, the moss between them peppered with tiny white flowers. Legend had it that fair folk used portals like these to travel the fairy paths. The thought of a second fair one appearing suddenly out of thin air made my insides clench tighter.

A horn sounded. All the hair stood up on my body at the high, quavering melody, and I'm not proud to say I ended up watering the honeysuckles right then and there.

Rook seized my arm, pulling me to my feet as I wrestled my clothes to rights.

"The Wild Hunt," he said. He drew his sword in front of me and dragged me back through the bushes with the other arm across my chest as though he were holding me at ransom. "It shouldn't have found us here, especially not so quickly. Something's wrong."

Complaining wasn't in order at a moment like this, so I kept my mouth shut, but I couldn't help clawing at his arm in protest. He was wearing his raven pin again, and it was at just the right height to stab me in the back of the head.

"Stop that. As soon as the hounds lay eyes on us they'll go straight for you. Slaying them alone is child's play, but protecting a mortal at the same time . . . you must do whatever I tell you, without hesitation."

Throat dry, I nodded.

A spectral shape bounded toward us through the undergrowth, emitting a faint light of its own. This was no living hound, but a fairy beast. It took the guise of a white hunting dog with long legs and flowing fur, but I knew to look beyond the surface, and soon enough its glamour flickered, so quickly I was left with only the impression of something old beneath the illusion, something dead, dark and clotted with vines and dead leaves. Silently it launched itself over the honeysuckle, its soft liquid eyes fixed upon me. I caught a stench of dry rot before Rook's sword darted out and reduced it to a clattering rain of twigs entangled with human bones. A quiet, musical sound rose from it when it died, almost like a woman's sigh.

A chorus of howls swelled through the forest. I shuddered in Rook's arms. The wintry lament was so lonely, so hauntingly sad I found it difficult to believe those voices belonged to beasts that wanted to kill me.

Listening to this, Rook made a contemptuous noise; I felt the vibration of it in his chest. He sheathed his sword and turned me around.

"There are over a dozen of the creatures, and they'll all be upon us at once. We cannot fight. We have to run." It was obvious the idea of fleeing rankled him.

"I can't—"

"Yes, I know," he said, casting me an unreadable glance. "Stand back."

Wind crashed through the trees, sweeping a dizzying flurry of leaves through the forest that broke against Rook like a wave. Then he was gone, and a massive horse stamped and snorted in his place, watching me with unnervingly pale eyes. It was unmistakably him in the same way the raven had been. The fairy light now hovering above my shoulder revealed a hint of auburn in its otherwise black coat. Its mane and tail were wild, thick and tangled. It lowered itself to its knees beside me with an impatient toss of its head.

I was about to break yet another rule of life in Whimsy.

If an unfamiliar dog follows you at night, don't stop to look at it. If you wake up to find a cat you don't recognize sitting in your yard, watching your house, don't open the door. And most of all, if you see a beautiful horse near a lake or the edge of the forest, never, ever try to ride it.

As Emma would say, *Oh, hell.*

I yanked my ring off and returned it to my pocket. As eager as I was to revenge myself upon Rook, forcing him back into his normal form just in time for the hounds to devour me seemed rather counterproductive. I paused just long enough for a fortifying breath, then climbed astride his broad back with my skirts bunched around my thighs and buried my fingers in his mane.

He lurched upright, powerful muscles bunching beneath his coat, and took off at a ground-swallowing canter. Even clinging to him as if my life depended on it—well, my life did depend on it—I barely stayed on: I lifted clean off his back every time his hooves struck the ground, then slammed down afterward with such painful, tailbone-jolting force I already felt my rear going numb. Whenever he dove sideways to avoid a tree, I slid precariously. He breathed between my legs like a forge's bellows, and with each shift of his ropey muscles I was reminded that I sat atop a creature ten times or more my own size. The ground was very far away.

I didn't like riding horses, I decided.

The howling followed us, growing ever closer. Soon I made out elegant white shapes darting through the forest on either side. The two nearest hounds sped up and angled inward to cut us off. A gap in the canopy admitted a shaft of moonlight, and when they bounded across it, their spectral fur gave way to the emaciated bark-skinned frames beneath. Thorny jaws gaped and empty pits stared where their eyes should have been.

Rook gave a brash snort and lunged forward, eating up the distance between us and the hounds. They turned, teeth flashing, far too late—he trampled them to kindling beneath his hooves.

I sensed a trace of smugness in his loping stride and the way he eyed the other hounds, now falling behind us, with his ears flattened to his skull, daring them to come closer. As they say, pride goeth before a fall. We entered a clearing and Rook lurched to a halt before he collided with the figure standing at the center of it, directly in our path.

I had never seen a fair one of the winter court. They didn't visit Whimsy. Sometimes I wondered what they looked like without any use of human Craft, not even clothes. Now I had my answer.

The being was extraordinarily tall, taller than Rook, and wore no glamour. Its bone-white skin was stretched tight across a thin, angular face surrounded by a weightless corona of equally white hair. I formed only this vague impression of its features, for its eyes drew my attention and kept it. They were jade green in color, like polished stones, and at once inscrutable and magnetic, animated with the cruel, luminous interest of a house cat watching an injured mouse die. I knew at once that I looked upon a creature so distanced from anything human it wouldn't be able to imitate our ways even if it wanted to.

From toe to collar it was clad in black bark armor that appeared to have simply grown over its body, whorled and ridged with age, leaving its head alone exposed. It made a stilted, courtly gesture, drawing attention to its yellowed, inches-long claws as it swept a hand before its chest. Rook jerked his nose down in what I supposed passed for a bad-tempered bow.

"Oh, Rook!" it exclaimed in a high voice not unlike the hounds' unearthly howling. "I didn't know you had company! This is interesting, isn't it? What do you suppose we should do?"

Those terrible eyes fixed on me and the fair one smiled, but though its mouth moved, the rest of its face remained exactly the same.

Rook pawed at the ground, then reared up halfway, taking me by surprise. His head snapped back and I managed to keep my seat by wrapping my arms around his neck. His pulse pounded against my arms and sweat dampened his silky fur.

"Don't worry, I shan't do anything now." My paralyzed brain noted belatedly that it—she—was female, or at least sounded that way. "The game's changed, after all. We simply must come up with a new set of rules. It wouldn't be sporting to fight to the death here in this clearing, not after you've been held up by a mortal. Hello there," she added, leaning to the side for a better look at me. The gracious smile still hung in place unchanged, as forgotten as a hat tossed onto a coatrack.

"Good evening," I returned, aware that aside from Rook, fine manners were my only protection.

"I am Hemlock, of the house of winter." Quieter than an owl's flight, hounds rushed inward from every corner of the clearing. They milled around her legs and pressed their narrow heads against her hands. "Since before the oldest tree in the forest put forth its first root, I have been master of the Wild Hunt."

Was it just my imagination? Or did I really hear the hounds whispering among themselves—a gentle murmur that sounded like women speaking in hushed, anxious tones behind a closed door?

I swallowed, trying not to think about what was inside

them. "It's a pleasure to meet you. My name is Isobel. I'm, um, a portrait artist."

"I haven't the slightest idea what that means," Hemlock replied, smiling. "Now, Rook—"

Rook danced sideways and gave her a bloodcurdling equine scream.

"Oh, don't be rude! We mustn't carry on just because we're at war with each other. As I was going to say, before you interrupted me, I think we should even out the odds by giving you a head start. If my hounds catch up with you again, then I can have a proper go at ripping you to shreds. How does that sound?"

He snaked his head forward and snapped at the air between them. I realized with dread that he wanted to stand his ground. I turned my face into his mane so Hemlock wouldn't see me speaking to him.

"Please go," I breathed. "You might be able to survive this, but I wouldn't make it through, and without me you'll never mend your reputation."

The skin twitched on his shoulders as though dislodging a fly.

"Are your court feuds truly worth it?"

His head turned. One of his eyes fixed on me, and it was awful seeing the intelligence in it, an intelligence that didn't belong anywhere near the animal's shape he wore.

"Please," I whispered.

Rook jerked as if I'd taken a crop to him, and veered around Hemlock and her hounds to gallop into the waiting darkness.

"Do hurry, Rook!" Hemlock cried behind us, a shrill, almost desperate call. "I'll be after you soon! Run as fast as you can!"

I wrapped Rook's long mane around my wrists and risked

a glance over my shoulder. Hemlock's armor blended so well with the forest I saw only her ghastly pale face receding until the branches and leaves obscured even that. The Wild Hunt's horn sounded again. It occurred to me I'd gotten quite a good look at Hemlock, and she hadn't been carrying one.

Rook ran like the devil chased at his heels. I focused only on not falling off, blind to the scenery whipping past. For a time all I knew was the pounding rhythm of his hooves and the furnace heat rising from his back, the hard, stinging chunks of dislodged earth that pelted my legs. Then a bright shape tore past my face and lodged in my collar. At first, I didn't recognize the fluttering yellow scrap as a leaf. When I did, everything changed.

I raised my head. My breath caught. Wonder poured through me, brighter than a sunrise spilling over the horizon, headier than a glass of sparkling champagne.

We were in the autumnlands.

Dim as it was, the forest glowed. The golden leaves flashing by blazed like sparks caught in the updraft of a fire. A scarlet carpet unrolled before us, rich and flawless as velvet. Rising from the forest floor, the black, tangled roots breathed a bluish mist that reduced the farthest trees' trunks to ghostly silhouettes, yet left their foliage's luminous hues untouched. Vivid moss speckled the branches like tarnished copper. The crisp spice of pine sap infused the cool air over a musty perfume of dry leaves. A knot swelled in my throat. I couldn't look away. There was too much of it, too fast. I'd never be able to drink it all in—I needed to absorb every leaf, every chip of bark, every flake of moss. I clenched my fingers in Rook's mane, ravenous for my paintbrush, my easel. Sitting up straighter, I let the wind rush over me and fill my lungs to bursting. It still wasn't enough.

After seventeen years of living in a world that never changed, I felt as though I'd just flung off a stifling wool sweater and felt the breeze on my skin for the very first time. Nothing would ever be enough again.

When his pace slowed, the absence of the wind tearing at my clothes and the sound and motion of his pounding gallop left me strangely bereft. My thoughts whirled, and the blood buzzed in my veins. Every sound seemed muffled after the wild ride—his hooves barely disturbed the cushioned forest floor; steam gusted from his nostrils in perfect silence. Finally, he lowered himself to his knees in the middle of a glade. I slid off on legs weakened to the point of trembling and turned in a slow, unsteady circle.

No horn sounded in the distance, no baying of hounds disturbed the misty air. No droning grasshoppers here—only the music of crickets, the liquid peeping of frogs, the quiet plop of acorns falling from trees. Not a single raven roosted above me. The danger had passed.

Therefore, when I completed my revolution, I froze at the sight of Rook back in his normal form, standing with his sword drawn.

And I forgot to think altogether when he turned the blade upon himself.

Six

I DIDN'T protest. I didn't scream. Whatever he was doing, I was neither willing nor able to stop him.

He didn't look at all weary or disheveled as he knelt with his right sleeve rolled up to the elbow, the sword laid across his hand. A curl of damp hair clinging to his forehead was the only sign that remained from our reckless flight, the sweat that had previously soaked his neck and shoulders. Calmly he looked aside, and then he drew the blade across his palm in one vicious stroke. Blood spattered the moss below. It was a paler color than human blood, and thicker, as though mixed with tree sap.

Once the shock wore off I understood Rook was working some fairy magic. Whatever it was, I hoped it hurt. Perhaps it would even weaken him in a way I might use to my advantage.

"You said there were only two other fair ones as powerful as you," I said, curtsying for his attention. "I thought you meant the regents of the spring and winter courts. But is Hemlock one of them?"

He wiped his hand off on the moss, bent over his knee in a seamless bow, and stood. The cut had vanished—though I had no way of knowing whether it was truly healed or merely disguised by his glamour. The latter struck me as something he would do out of pride.

"All of us have different gifts, some more than others. I can change my shape and as prince I command the power of my season. Hemlock is known for her prowess in battle, but she is no winter lord. Perhaps—if all my magic were exhausted, or if I chose not to use it—I might meet her in physical combat as an equal." His lip curled. I wondered how often he wished he could lie.

"Her fairy beasts must be a danger to you, then," I ventured, sensing an opportunity to learn more about his weaknesses. "If not one or two at a time, the entire pack fighting at her side."

He sheathed his sword in a violent motion and strode over to me, stopping only when we almost touched, staring down. I felt his breath on my upturned face. My heart skipped a beat. He was a little winded, after all.

"They are a danger to *you*, mortal, not I. You saw how I fared against the thane. How many times do I have to remind you? I am a *prince*."

"Yes, I know!" I didn't budge an inch. "It's not as though you've given me a chance to forget it."

He squared his shoulders and bared his teeth as if I'd just slapped him.

I schooled myself, resisting the urge to reach for my ring. "I just don't understand any of this. Fairy beasts, the conflict between your houses, why on earth the Wild Hunt's been after you for centuries if Hemlock knows she can't win. I suppose it's too much for my foolish mortal brain to take in."

Rook relaxed. Annoyingly, he didn't register the sarcasm.

"Hemlock is the Huntsman," he replied. "She obeys the call of the winter court, which ever seeks to spread its frost across the autumnlands."

"The horn," I murmured. "It commands her. She doesn't have a choice."

He nodded. "For her, the Hunt is everything. It is her only purpose. She will hunt until she dies and at last must hunt no more."

Wind rustled through the canopy, and leaves pattered like rain across the clearing. I thought of Hemlock's ghastly face receding into the dark, the way she'd screamed at us to run. A shiver coursed through my body. The chill bite of the autumn air was finally catching up with me.

Or was it? For then I wondered if I had shivered at all, because the trembling went on and on, heaving the ground beneath my feet. I staggered back, but there was no escape from the peculiar quickening that followed. Beginning at the point where Rook had spilled his blood, a tide of moss starred with tiny, pale blue flowers no bigger than the tip of my little finger surged forward, unfurling across the glade, foaming partway up the tree trunks— and my own legs. I yelped and pulled my boots free, sending clumps of moss flying as I gave my skirts a vigorous shake.

"Turn around," Rook said aloofly, watching me sidelong. For a moment he'd adopted his old tone, as though we were friends in my parlor again, and it seemed a correction was in order.

But turn I did, unable to help myself. The glade's trees were growing, stretching higher and higher, their branches spreading toward one another overhead. Where they met in the center, they laced together under the glittering night sky. Smaller saplings struggled up from the moss between the larger trees to seal the gaps, putting forth trembling new leaves already resplendent in autumn colors. All of this happened nearly noiselessly, with only a quiet creaking, groaning, and snapping of expanding wood to mark the change.

It was as though I had watched the glade age a century in a matter of seconds. But no glade would age like this naturally: I stood in an open space in which the trees spread around and above me like a cathedral. Their branches were so tightly interwoven they resembled flying buttresses; no amount of craftsmanship could capture the majesty or wonder of this living antechamber. Looking straight up left me dizzy. Scarlet leaves drifted from the silent heights, passing through shafts of moonlight on their way down.

I whirled around. "Your blood did this."

Rook stood watching me, a conflicting clamor of emotions in his eyes: fascination observing my human response. Hope that I would find what he had created beautiful. And beneath that, sorrow, as raw as an open wound.

Desperation flashed across his features. He struggled to compose himself, but couldn't. Finally he turned on his heel and put his back to me with a dramatic billow of his coattails, drew his sword a few inches, and pretended to inspect the blade.

"You'll be safe here tonight," he said imperiously. "The Hunt won't be able to sniff us out in a rowan glade, and even if Hemlock did chance upon this place by accident, no fairy beast, no fair one alive could breach the magic I have just wrought."

The knowledge that he was only telling the bare, unembellished truth made the breath catch in my throat. He was arrogant verging on insufferable, but god—the power he possessed. And here he was, as confused as a child by his own emotions, dragging me to trial over a painting. I couldn't believe that just that morning I thought I'd been in love with him. I shook my head. Incredible.

"Ten thousand verging on five years old," I muttered to myself, testing the ground with my shoe.

"What did you say?" Rook inquired frostily.

Of course fair folk had impeccable hearing. "Nothing."

"You did say something, but whatever it was, I'm certain it's beneath me." He slid his sword back in with a snap. "Now lie down and get some rest. We begin again at sunrise."

Loath as I was to follow orders, I wouldn't do myself any good staying awake out of sheer stubbornness. I wandered around the glade until I found a lump in the moss I could put my back against—an engulfed tree stump, I thought—and curled up on my side facing Rook, who remained standing, facing away. I worked my ring back onto my finger, grateful to have at least some measure of protection, however small. But now I faced a different problem. I couldn't imagine how I was going to sleep.

Emma and the twins probably hadn't noticed I was gone. They would in the morning, when they found my bed empty. What would Emma do? She'd given everything up to raise me. She'd promised on my father's deathbed to take care of me. And now I'd vanished in the night without a word. Unless I was very lucky, and very clever (I had to remain honest about my odds), she'd never know what had happened to me. She'd wait for me forever. It seemed too cruel to bear.

She had enchanted chickens guaranteed to each lay six eggs a week, I reminded myself. A cord of firewood magically appeared outside the house every other month. Another fair one delivered a fat goose once per fortnight; and oddly, due to an awkwardly worded agreement, a pile of exactly fifty-seven walnuts materialized on the doorstep whenever a thrush sang in our oak tree. The twins would give her trouble, but she'd be all right. Wouldn't she?

Several paces away, Rook had finally sat down. He sat elegantly with one arm propped up on his knee. Perhaps he knew I was watching and arranged himself in his handsomest pose accordingly. No—he thought I was asleep. Somehow I knew this to be the case, because he'd taken off his raven pin and was turning it over in his hands. Beyond him the scarlet leaves continued sifting down through the moonlight, like rose petals illuminated by silvered stained glass.

Heartsick, I wondered if Emma would think I'd run off with him on purpose. Just hours ago she had proven how well she knew me. If that was the case, she had to realize that no matter how wary I was of fair folk, I'd wanted to see Rook again more than anything else in the world. Maybe she'd be tortured forever by the possibility that her regretful words had encouraged me to run away. That I'd decided taking care of my family was a burden after all, and I'd abandoned her and the twins without bothering to say good-bye.

It occurred to me then that my imagination was conjuring up increasingly unrealistic, maudlin scenarios, but wallowing neck-deep in misery, I was powerless to stop it from happening.

I thought of Emma taking too much of her tincture and collaps-
ing. I thought of the twins going through my room, searching
for any sign of where I'd gone, and finding Rook's drawings in
my closet. A hot tear spilled over. I breathed through my mouth
so Rook wouldn't hear me snuffling through my clogged nose.
Eventually, I cried myself to exhaustion. My eyelashes drooped
and my vision blurred. I didn't remember falling asleep.

When I woke up, everything was golden. The light caressing my
face was golden, and the warmth was golden too. I felt like I was
suspended in honey or amber. An autumn fragrance surrounded
me, engulfed me, underlain with a wild, masculine but not-quite-
human smell that at once comforted me and settled like molten
gold deep in my body, melted and poured into a crucible.

Also, someone was combing my hair with his fingers.

"Stop that!" I cried, bolting upright in alarm. Rook's coat
fell from my shoulders and I cast around until I found him
behind me, wearing a self-satisfied smile. "What do you think
you're doing?"

"You have a few twigs left in your hair," he said, and reached
toward me again.

I intercepted his hand with my own ring-wearing one, or at
least tried to, because he was up like a shot before I managed it,
glaring down at me.

"Rook," I said, trying to keep my voice steady, "before I get
up, you have to promise to never touch me again without my
permission."

"I can touch whomever I please."

"Have you ever stopped to think that just because you *can*
do something doesn't mean you should?"

His eyes narrowed. "No," he said.

"Well, this is one of those things." I saw he didn't understand. "Among humans it's considered polite," I added firmly.

A muscle jumped in his cheek, and his smile had faded. "Well, that doesn't sound in the least reasonable. What if you were being attacked, and I had to touch you to save your life, but I couldn't because I needed to request your permission first? Letting you die wouldn't be polite."

"Fine. You can touch me in that case, but every other time you need to ask."

"And why do you suppose I shall agree to your absurd mortal demands?" Peevishly, he snatched his coat from me and flung it back on himself without bothering to put his arms through the sleeves.

"Because I can make your life miserable all the way to the autumn court, and you know it," I replied.

He stalked off across the glade. I got the feeling he needed to throw a tantrum before giving in. Sure enough, he soon returned with a stormy expression as the land changed all around him. The moss wilted brown while thorny brambles erupted forth at his heels, grasping like fingers until they grew into an eldritch-looking tangle as high as my waist. I hadn't expected something quite so dramatic: each thorn was as long as my finger, so sharp it glistened in the morning light. All my instincts shrieked at me to get up and run before they reached me. But that was the reaction Rook wanted, so I remained where I sat.

The brambles writhed up all around my body, stretching crooked, twitching tendrils toward my clothes. Their thorns rattled together threateningly. I gave them a stern look. I knew a bluff when I saw one. Eventually the brambles subsided, rather sulkily, and froze in place. Rook stood over me encased within his bramble sea in a white-lipped state of high dudgeon, the final proof that I had won.

"Well?" I asked.

"I give my word that I will never touch you without your permission, except if I need to spare you from harm," he declared. To his credit he said it in a regal tone, with none of the petulance I expected.

I sighed in relief. "Thank you, Rook."

"You're welcome," he said automatically, and frowned. This was like bowing; he had to respond to common courtesies whether he liked it or not. He recovered from the indignity by flinging his arm out theatrically. Two of the trees hiked up their roots and shuffled aside, in a rather hasty, anxious way, as though they were a pair of bewildered matrons at whom he'd just hurled a billiard ball. Their bent trunks formed a new archway to the forest beyond.

"Hurry along, then." He swept toward the archway. A leftover root whisked solicitously out of his path. "Not only do I expect your little mortal legs will cover a disappointing amount of ground, we're already an hour delayed."

And whose fault is that? I thought.

However, as I crunched after him through the brambles, which disintegrated at a touch, my eyes fell on the neat pile of twigs and leaves he had taken from my hair—and despite myself I smiled.

We passed slender, white-barked birches, their yellow leaves shimmering and clattering like gold coins in the breeze. We passed stony brooks that wended between hillocks of moss, their water the color of milk with snowmelt. We passed ash trees that had shed half their foliage at once, pooled about their roots as a maiden might drop a shift. A stag and doe paused to watch us go by before they leapt away through the light-filled mist, casting their shadows against the air like a paper screen.

The first unpleasant landmark we came to was a riven oak. It had been struck by lightning sometime long ago, and sections of its trunk were charred black, the bark raised and glittering with beads of hardened sap. A few brown leaves still clung to its lower branches. Rook stopped to examine it. It looked out of place among the birches, watchful, malevolent. A prickle of unease warned me to keep my distance.

"Is that an entrance to a fairy path?" I asked, crunching along parallel to it.

He spared me a glance and resumed walking. "Yes. But we won't travel that way."

"You can't bring humans on them?"

"Oh, we certainly can. I merely find it inadvisable."

By that he could mean anything. Perhaps the effort would be a drain on his power, or it would alert the wrong fair folk to our presence. He didn't seem open to further questions, and I didn't see how learning more might help my cause, so I didn't bother asking.

Midday came and went. The sun shimmered through the leaves, freckling the ground in dappled patterns I would have found captivating if I'd been less preoccupied by my growing discomfort. My thighs and buttocks ached from last night's ride. I was dirty; I had mud all over my legs, and my skirts were stiff with burs and dried horse sweat. I knew for a fact I smelled abominable. And god, I was starving.

Meanwhile Rook looked exactly as he had when he'd come to fetch me the night before. His boots shone and not a single wrinkle marred his coat. The only thing disheveled was his hair, but that didn't count, since it always looked that way.

We arrived at a long embankment descending into a ravine. Rook descended gracefully as I shuffled and skidded through the leaf litter until I finally considered the possibility of giving up and sliding down on my rear. While I frowned at the ground, Rook's hand extended into my field of vision. I didn't want his help, but it was better than making a fool of myself, so I placed my fingers in his. We seemed able to touch each other without a word as long as I was the one who initiated it.

His skin was cool and his grip deceptively light. He helped me down the embankment and back up the hill on the other side as though I weighed no more than a feather. My stomach rumbled when we crested the top. To my dismay it wasn't an ordinary rumble, either: my innards summoned forth a booming growl, followed by a series of long, drawn-out squeals.

Rook started back in alarm. Then, catching on to my condition, he gave me a knowing smile. Which was interesting—most fair folk didn't understand the concept of human hunger, not truly. And earlier, he'd spoken as if he'd already tried taking a human on the fairy paths himself. Had he traveled with a human before?

Honestly, I should have suspected even earlier. He had human sorrow in his eyes, after all, and there was only one way he could have learned it.

"I haven't eaten since supper yesterday," I said when my stomach finally, mercifully went quiet. "I don't think I can go on much longer without food."

"Only yesterday?"

"I assure you, most humans aren't accustomed to going a full day without a meal." He continued looking deeply skeptical, so I added in a steadfast tone, "I'm feeling quite poorly. In fact, I can't take another step. If I don't eat soon, I may die."

His hair practically stood on end. I almost felt bad for him. "Stay here," he said urgently, and vanished. The leaves he'd been standing on eddied as though stirred by a draft.

I looked around. My stomach somersaulted, and my mouth went dry. The sparse, mossy undergrowth afforded a clear view into the far distance. I saw no tall figure, no raven winging through the forest. Rook truly did appear to be gone.

Run, I thought. But trying to urge my feet to move was like being four years old again, shifting at the foot of my mother's bed after a nightmare, unable to speak a word to wake her. The forest slumbered too. How easily would I draw its attention, and was I really prepared for *that* nightmare?

As it turned out I needn't have even bothered thinking about it. Something thumped into the leaves behind me, and I turned to find Rook standing over a dead hare.

"Go on," he said when I didn't move, glancing between me and the animal.

I shuffled forward and picked it up by the scruff of its neck. It was still warm, and watched me with its shiny black eyes. "Um," I said.

"Is there something wrong with it?" His expression became guarded.

I was ravenous. I was sore. I was terrified. And yet looking at Rook I imagined a cat proudly bringing its master dead chipmunks, only to watch the two-legged oaf lift these priceless gifts by the tail and fling them unceremoniously into the bushes. Before I knew it I'd dissolved into laughter.

Rook shifted, torn between uneasiness and anger. "What?" he demanded.

I sank to my knees, the hare on my lap, gulping in air.

"Stop that." Rook looked around, as if concerned some-one might witness him mismanaging his human. I howled even louder. "Isobel, you simply must control yourself."

He might have traveled with humans, but he most assuredly hadn't dined with us.

"Rook!" I half-wailed his name. "I can't just eat a rabbit!"

"I don't see why not."

"It's—it needs to be cooked!"

For an instant, before he slammed the door shut on his expression, horror and confusion gripped him. "You mean to say you can't eat anything at all without using Craft on it first?"

I took a shuddering breath, calming down, but knew I'd go off again at the slightest provocation. "We can eat fruit as it is, and most nuts and vegetables. But everything else, yes."

"How can this be," he said to himself quietly. That was all it took; I gave a strangled sob. He crouched and scrutinized my face, which I'm sure at that moment looked anything but attrac-tive. "What do you require?"

"A fire, to start with. Some . . . some branches to make a spit out of, I suppose. Or maybe we could cut it up and skewer it? I've never cooked a rabbit outdoors before." I might as well have started reciting an incantation. "Wood," I revised for him. "Some kindling about this size"—I spread my hands—"and a long, thin, sturdy stick with a pointy end."

"Very well." He rose. "I will bring you your sticks."

"Wait," I said, before he could vanish again. I held up the hare. He tensed. "Can you skin this for me? You know, remove the fur? And it needs to be in pieces, too. I can't do any of that without a knife."

"How very mortal you are," he said disdainfully, and seized the hare from my hand.

"Oh, and take the insides out first, please," I added, undeterred.

He halted just as he was about to disappear, shoulders stiff. "Will that be all?"

A devilish part of me wondered how far I could push him. If I pretended it was necessary for my Craft, could I command him to stand on his head or turn in a circle three times while he prepared the hare? Only my empty stomach's increasingly urgent demands prevented me from having some fun at his expense. "For now," I replied.

Less than twenty minutes later we sat in front of a badly smoking fire, which had seemed hopeless until Rook tired of watching me rub two twigs together and set the kindling ablaze with a flick of his long fingers. He cast impatient glances at the sun while I turned a haunch (at least I think that's what it was—fair folk weren't scrupulous butchers, as it turned out) over the flames. Grease dripped from the meat, hissing when it struck the smoldering wood. My mouth watered, and I tried not to dwell on the likelihood that under better circumstances, I would find the odor rank rather than appetizing. I'd never known rabbit to smell quite like this. But as long as I kept charring it by accident, at least it probably wouldn't make me sick.

Waiting for me to finish, Rook gave his seventh dramatic sigh. I'd started counting.

"You give it a try, if you're so bored," I said, handing over the skewer. He took it between his thumb and forefinger. After examining the meat, turning it to and fro, he flippantly lowered it toward the fire.

Instantly, a change came over him. At first I thought he had spied something awful in the forest behind me, and I jerked around with my skin crawling. There was nothing there. Yet he still wore the same expression: his eyes wide and stricken, his features utterly still, as if he'd just received news of someone's death, or was dying himself. It was terrible in a way I cannot describe. I've painted a thousand faces and never seen such a look.

What was happening? I scrabbled for an answer until I realized—Craft. We could transmute substances as easily as we breathed, but for fair folk, such creation did not exist. It was so contrary to their nature it had the power to destroy them. Astonishingly, even something as simple as roasting a hare over an open flame seemed to count as Craft according to whatever force governed his kind.

No more than a second or two had elapsed before Rook's glamour began flaking away like old paint, revealing his true form, but not the way I remembered it. His skin was desiccated and gray, his eyes fading to lifelessness. It was as though I watched lights go out within him one by one, dimming with every heartbeat.

And I knew that if I did nothing, in another moment he'd be gone.

I would be free. I could escape—or at least try. But I thought of the forest cathedral, the scarlet leaves sifting down in silence. The look on his face when he'd transformed into a raven in my parlor. The smell of change on the wild wind, and the way he had let me turn his head, his eyes on mine full of sorrow. All those wonders crumbling to dust, without a trace of them left in the world.

So I lunged across the fire and tore the stick from his hands.

Seven

HE CRIED out when the stick left his grasp, a sharp, haunting sound of anguish—pain, but also loss. Color flooded back into him, his glamour following behind, though he still slumped to the side and had to catch himself with a hand against the ground before he fell.

"Isobel," he croaked uncertainly, looking up at me.

My voice came from far away, swept downstream by the blood rushing in my ears. "It was Craft. Cooking. When I offered it to you, I didn't know. I had no idea."

His attention fell to the stick I held, a piece of wood with a lump of rabbit flesh smoldering on the end. I shared his disbelief. Almost impossible, that something so ordinary could harm him.

"We should—we should go." He was so out of sorts he nearly sounded human. He staggered to his feet and turned first one way and then another, unable to get his bearings. "We haven't covered nearly enough . . . have you eaten? Are you still hungry?"

"I can eat as we walk," I said quietly, stunned to see him reduced to this. From Emma's instruction, I recognized the symptoms of shock.

"You aren't going to die?" he asked.

I shook my head. Toying with him didn't seem nearly as amusing now.

"Good." His hand went to his sword, perhaps seeking out its reassuring solidity. He next patted his pockets with a disquieted air until he found the raven pin on his breast and squeezed it. "In that case—"

He cut himself off and whipped around, every muscle in his body tensed. At first I thought he'd gone mad. Then I heard it too: a high, unearthly sound in the distance. Howling.

"I suppose it was only a matter of time before the Wild Hunt caught up with us," I said reasonably, suddenly feeling strongly that someone ought to behave in a reasonable and reassuring way, even if that person, unfortunately, had to be me. "It sounds like we have a good head start, at least."

"No, it was not only a matter of time. We are deep in my domain, *my* realm. Hemlock should not have been able to track us this far so easily."

"Perhaps the difference is that I'm with you now. As you might have noticed, I do have a bit of a, um. Smell."

He barely spared me a glance, passing up the ripe opportunity to criticize my mortality. The longer he remained rattled, the more apprehensive I became. He didn't see the Wild Hunt as a serious threat. So was it just his recent near-death experience making him act like this, or something more—something I didn't know about?

Coming back to himself, he released his raven pin as though it had scalded him. "We need to be out of the autumnlands before dusk." And with that, he fixed on a direction and set off.

I snatched up as much of the cooked meat as I could carry, sloshing after him through the ankle-deep leaves. "Wait, out of the autumnlands? What do you mean? I thought we were traveling to the autumn court."

"We are. Just not the same way we were before."

"May I ask where we're going, then?"

"To the place where Hemlock's power wanes, farthest from the winter court. It will be harder, perhaps impossible for her to track us in the summerlands."

The landscape changed gradually. The sun sank behind the hills, casting long, straight shadows behind the trees and saturating everything in russet light. Thicker-trunked oaks, elms, and alders crowded out the slender birches and ashes. A melancholy air hung over this part of the forest: the leaves were brown or a dull rust red, and fungus mottled the roots and marched up the trunks, yellow and fleshy in character. Out of curiosity I placed my hand on the bark next to one of these mushroom colonies, only for the bark to peel away in my hand. The exposed wood beneath was pale and spongy, and wood lice scampered away into its crevices.

I dropped the bark, which burst rotten on the ground, and hurried to catch up with Rook several paces ahead.

"We should be reaching the summerlands soon, shouldn't we?" I asked, just for conversation's sake. The quiet here bore down like a physical weight. I couldn't help but feel as though something might be listening, an impression that intensified the longer we remained silent.

"We are in the summerlands. We have been for some time."

"But the trees—"

"Are not of autumn," Rook replied. "No, these trees are dying." Tension narrowed his eyes and set his jaw. "I have heard . . . whispers, that in some places, the summerlands have gone—amiss. I've never had occasion to see the blight with my own eyes. I confess it's worse than I expected."

"Surely the forest can be healed. I watched you raise an entire glade with a few drops of your blood."

"Here, only one person holds such power." His gaze flicked to me, the warning in their amethyst depths clear as a length of exposed steel. "And he uses his lifeblood as he sees fit."

The trees grew larger and farther apart. The knotted roots bulging across our path reminded me of diseased veins. Immense stones thrust up from the ground at intervals, standing higher than I was tall, draped in thick mantles of moss and bloodred ivy. The late sunlight produced one last burst of gold that sparkled through the failing leaves, and in this light I saw a face staring out at me from the next stone we passed.

I halted. My blood froze.

It wasn't an actual face. It was carved into the rock. But such was its realism that my mind registered the being as a living thing before logic caught up with me. Speckled with moss and bearded with vines, his grave visage was both ancient and pensive, his closed eyes sunken into webs of wrinkles. A crown of interwoven antler tines rested upon his unforgiving brow. At that moment I seemed to look upon an ailing king laid out on his deathbed, a sovereign whose cruel, mirthless conscience ruminated on all the wrongdoings of his long life without remorse. But no, I knew instantly my impression was wrong. This king did not know death. He slept, perhaps, but did not die. He never would.

I looked around, and found the same face on every stone. Without a shadow of a doubt, these engravings were Craft. Humans hadn't been permitted in the forest for thousands of years. I couldn't imagine the age of them, and what might drive the people of that forgotten era to carve, over and over again, the terrible countenance of the Alder King.

The Alder King.

Drooping motionlessly since we'd arrived, the leaves rattled in a hot, stale breeze.

The Alder King, my traitorous thoughts whispered again, naming the nameless fear clutching at me from all sides. *The Alder King.* Now that I'd started it was impossible to stop.

"Isobel." Rook strode out of a thicket, pushing aside the branches of a buckthorn shrub. I hadn't noticed he'd gone anywhere. He went to grab my shoulder, but his hand froze a hairsbreadth above my dress. "We need to leave. Quickly."

"I didn't mean to—" The thicket drew my gaze and what I saw there silenced me. Beyond the wild buckthorn hedge lay a clearing with more of the carven stones arranged in a circle. At the center of the circle, a hill bulged from the ground. It was perhaps fifteen feet long and half that wide, and its rounded back stood taller than the tops of the stones. A barrow mound. Rook had been talking about a different danger entirely.

A flap and flutter of wings sounded in the stillness. A croak, and then another. I looked up. An entire flock of shiny-eyed ravens roosted in the trees above us, watching, waiting.

A dozen ravens for death. What about a score—a hundred—more?

"You thought his name," Rook said, after a pause. "You're thinking it even now."

I dragged my attention back to him; I knew dread gripped every inch of my expression.

He didn't seem angry with me. His expression was neutral, a layer of ice under which fearsome currents raced unseen. I wished he'd looked angry. This was worse. It meant that whatever was about to happen was so awful he couldn't afford to waste time feeling anything at all.

"Prepare to ride," he said, stepping back.

Just as it had when he'd transformed the night before, a wind gusted through the trees carrying forth a whirlwind of leaves. I braced myself for his shape to shift as soon as it struck. But this time the wind died as it approached, and the leaves wafted uselessly the last few feet, scattering around his boots. Rook scowled. He stood straighter, and soon another, stronger wind roared up from the depths of the forest. But it too petered out before it reached him.

The barrow mound drew my gaze again and again. All those ancient stones, all of them facing inward, like wardens standing guard over a prisoner. For millennia they had watched it, unable to look away.

By now the heat felt oppressive. A faint smell of putrefaction hung in the air. One of the ravens gave a single, grating call, harsh as a saw rasping against metal.

"Why can't you change?" I asked, without ever taking my eyes from the mound.

Rook dismissed his latest attempt at transformation with a flick of his hand, though a defiant glint shone in his eyes and he looked none the worse for wear.

"This place won't allow me to. It appears we have stumbled upon the resting place of a Barrow Lord."

Well, that was that. I wasn't waiting around to introduce myself to something called a Barrow Lord, capitalized. I gathered up my skirts, preparing to run. Then something about the way he'd said "appears" caught up with me. "Oh, god. This is the first time you've come across one, isn't it."

"They are seldom encountered," he said grudgingly. Noticing my stance, he added, "No, do not flee. It is already awake beneath the earth—it knows we are here. It cannot be outrun, and would only overtake us with our backs turned. This time, we stand and fight." His gaze flicked to me again. "Or rather, I do, while you do your best to stay out of the way."

He'd dispatched a thane with a single sword thrust. He'd called destroying the Wild Hunt's hounds child's play. But that knowledge was cold comfort with an entire flock of ravens roosting over my head, and the fact that this time, Rook had been willing to retreat without a word of complaint.

"What is a Barrow Lord, exactly?" I asked.

"In this matter, you might prefer ignorance."

"Believe me, I never do."

"If you insist," he said, reluctant. "Most fairy beasts rise with a single mortal's bones lending them life." I nodded; I had known as much already. "Barrow Lords are aberrations—each one a mass of remains, entangled with one another in death. They are tormented creatures, enraged, at odds with themselves. We do not nurture their growth. They quicken on their own, in places where the mortals of ages past buried victims of war or plague."

As if hearing itself spoken about, the mound quivered. Soil shifted and tumbled to the ground. A grotesque sound emanated from within: the damp sucking of something moist coming apart deep below the earth. Whatever this thing was, it was bigger than a thane. Bigger than all the hounds combined.

Rook unsheathed his sword and strode toward the mound, projecting a casual ease and confidence that struck me as being as fake as his glamour. Whether he was wearing it for my benefit or his own, I couldn't guess.

As soon as he reached the stone circle's outer edge, the mound heaved in earnest. It bulged first in one place and then another like a larva attempting to split its cocoon. Carrion beetles poured from the earth in rivulets, along with some sort of dribbling fluid. The stench of wet decay struck me like a punch to the gut. Helplessly, I doubled over and retched.

One last straining swell, and the mound disgorged its contents. A lopsided form burst forth, slumping over Rook at twice his height, lumps of dirt cascading off its sides. No illusion softened this monstrosity. It had the correct number of appendages in more or less the expected places, but that was all I could say in its favor. Its flesh was the skin of a decomposing log, riddled with disease and fungus. Its head, a hollow bark cave with two empty sockets from which a pair of mushroom clusters grew, wiggling about on long stalks with a life of their own. Right away the stalks twisted simultaneously, pointing the mushrooms' caps down at Rook. Eyes. Those were its eyes.

Pressure built at the back of my skull. In the distance, or behind a closed door, voices argued. A little girl sobbed.

Impatiently, someone scolded her. A man bellowed in wordless agony. The Barrow Lord gave a convulsive ripple, almost over-balancing itself. Its frame was bearlike, but its front legs—its arms, I found myself thinking—were overlong, and it struggled to maintain its drooping upright stance. It was trying to make itself human again, I realized, in the only way it could.

Rook's sword flashed, opening a slice along the beast's underbelly. Its putrid skin split without effort. He stepped back just in time to avoid the slippery cascade of fungus that spilled from the wound, halting one neat inch from the tips of his boots.

The voices stopped. Then they all screamed in unison. The Barrow Lord's arm lashed out, scoring the statue in front of which Rook had stood a split second earlier, spraying chips of stone and moss. It slashed at him again and again, senseless and unpredictable in its maddened violence, forcing him to retreat beyond its reach. His back touched the hedge, and he began circling it, his steps easy, a cat circling a hound unafraid.

It shambled after him, lunging clumsily over the standing stones. Rook was trying to draw it away from me. But as soon as I had that thought the little girl's voice called out, strident, and the Barrow Lord paused. In a sudden, wet contraction, the mushrooms rolled backward to look at me instead. I stumbled back blindly. I heard the groan and crash of trees toppling, my gaze fixed only on the horror hurtling in my direction—it was so rotten pieces of its body peeled away as it ran, dislodged by the concussive force of its stride.

Rook appeared between us. His sword flashed once, twice. The arm the Barrow Lord had raised to cut me down exploded porously on the forest floor. Beetles swarmed in the cavity left behind. Missing a limb, its unbalanced weight dragged it backward, and it collapsed against a pair of the carven stones, skin rupturing, pushing the monuments aslant.

For a moment I thought Rook had won. The fall had left the beast in ruins. Mucus glistened, seeped from the wreckage of its hide. But already it struggled back upright, wet fungus-slimed roots slopping out of its stump to form a new arm. Its head weaved from side to side, dripping. The voices consulted one another in an agitated murmur.

Rook adjusted his grip on his sword as he stalked back into the fray, crushing debris beneath his heels. Out flashed the blade. Chunks of wood flew. He could go on like this for days, chipping away at the monster without rest. If it hadn't been for the need to keep me alive, I suspected, the Barrow Lord wouldn't have posed much of a threat to him at all.

Something grabbed my ankle.

I looked down.

A human skeleton, held together with vegetable sinew, had clawed free from the Barrow Lord's severed limb. Shuddering nightmarishly, it flung its other hand up to seize my skirt in its bony fingers. Tumorous mushrooms bulged between its ribs, forced its jaw ajar. It clutched at me, dragging itself higher grip by hard-won grip. Closer than all the other voices, a woman sobbed and pleaded.

"I can't help you," I whispered, turned inside out and shaken empty by horror. "I can't . . ."

Rook was there. He seized the corpse by its skull and wrenched it off me, crushing the brown, age-brittled bone like an eggshell. Then he looked over his shoulder. Without hesitation, he seized me by the shoulders and pushed me aside. I landed in the bushes, the breath dashed from my lungs, just in time to see the Barrow Lord swat him. Rook slammed against a tree trunk several yards away and slumped to the ground, his sword skittering across the clearing.

Oh, god.

The Barrow Lord only had eyes for me now. It lumbered forward until I lay in the fetid darkness of its shadow. Ravens launched themselves shrieking from the trees to claw and peck at its back, flap wings in its face, but their calls soon turned to shrill squawks of desperation as their feathers stuck to the Barrow Lord's hide. Skeletal hands surfaced, clutching at them greedily, pulling them inside. The birds struggled and thrashed, but soon all that remained was a beak here, a wing there, pro-truding at random from the monster's rancid flesh. Some of them kept twitching.

The Barrow Lord lowered its head to my level.

Its head alone was the size of a log, the round mouth-hollow broad enough for a person to crawl into. The mushrooms twisted and turned. A hot gust blew out, and then another.

Surely I was too small, too weak to pose this creature any danger. The voices whispered among themselves. The little girl giggled.

A ragged wail tore from my chest, and I sank my fingers into its spongy face. This gave me enough purchase to haul myself up and seize one of its eye clusters with my other hand, the one wearing the iron ring. Instantly the mushrooms wilted. They turned gray and brittle, shriveling in my grasp.

All the voices groaned in unison, from that faraway room I'd begun to think of as hell, and the Barrow Lord took a step back, dragging my legs across the ground. I gave the eye stalks one last squeeze, feeling them crumble away. I only needed to buy myself another second. Because out of the corner of my eye, I saw Rook getting up.

He had one hand inside his coat, holding his chest, and the look on his face was terrifying to behold, contorted with pain and fury. His steps weaved; I wondered if he'd make it.

He did.

I let go and tumbled to the ground as he staggered up to the Barrow Lord's face, pulled the bloody hand from his coat, and thrust it straight into the monster's mouth. First there came a cracking sound, wood splintering and snapping. The Barrow Lord's body convulsed and canted stiffly to one side. Then thorny branches as thick around as my torso burst from every inch of its flesh, skewering it a hundred times over, pinning it in place like a grisly statue. I wasn't sure if it was dead. I'm not sure that it even mattered.

One last branch pushed slowly out of its remaining eye, and yellow leaves unfolded inches from my nose.

"Rook," I breathed. "You did it. You—"

But a thump interrupted me. I pushed the leaves aside to find Rook collapsed, unconscious, with his glamour bleeding away.

Eight

THE FIRST thing I noticed upon dropping to my knees next to him was that his clothes were torn and dirty from the battle, and wrinkled by travel. I hadn't gotten a good look at them when he'd lost his glamour earlier that afternoon, and the change was shocking: in an instant he'd gone from prince to vagabond. Somehow it hadn't occurred to me that he might use his glamour to alter his clothing's appearance, too. Most astonishingly of all, until now the enormous tear across his coat front where the Barrow Lord had struck him had been completely invisible to my eyes.

"How much magic do you waste on vanity? For heaven's sake, you could barely stand." My hands shook as I slipped off my ring, put it away, and undid the buttons down his front. "It wasn't as though the Barrow Lord and I cared how you looked, you know."

I spread his coat open, and his head lolled to the side. His mouth was slightly parted. I had decided not to look too closely at the sharp teeth showing behind his lips, but as it turned out I needn't have even bothered thinking about it, because the wound on his chest demanded all my attention and then some.

I didn't have a basis for comparison, but I could make an educated guess that with his glamour on, his chest wouldn't look so gaunt, each of his ribs showing clearly through his skin. I just wished I couldn't see *that* much of his ribs. Not all of the white showing amid the blood belonged to his torn-up shirt.

The wound was long and gruesome, running from his collarbone on the left side all the way down over his ribs to the right. A human with that injury would have been dying of blood loss. Thankfully he didn't seem to be bleeding out, but I'd have felt a great deal more optimistic about the situation if he had been conscious, smugly informing me that the bone-deep gash in his chest was only a flesh wound.

"Rook," I said, patting his cheek and trying not to cringe. His jutting bones and hollow face conjured an echo of the skeleton crawling up my legs. "You're a prince, remember? Wake up and infuriate me, please."

He turned his face toward my hand and moaned.

"You'll have to try a little harder than that." I balled up some of his coat and pressed it against his chest. Then, remembering the night before, I took his right wrist and turned his hand palm up. So he'd used his glamour to hide the cut after all. Yet his hand was healing quickly—if I hadn't known otherwise I would have believed the wound a week old or more.

I started when I realized his eyes were slitted open. He was watching me. "You're still here," he murmured, half-delirious.

Quickly, I set his hand back down. "Where else would I be?"

"Running."

"If you hadn't noticed, this forest is full of things that want to kill me. Even their dismembered limbs want to kill me. As loath as I am to admit it, I'm better off taking my chances with you."

"Perhaps," he said. He tried to move, and his eyes rolled back in his head.

"Don't be cryptic. What do I need to do to get us out of here? Rook?" I patted his cheek again.

"Help me stand. No—fetch my sword first, and then . . ."

I got up and cast about for his sword. The clearing had transformed in just the short time I'd been kneeling. The Barrow Lord's petrified remains were almost unrecognizable now, engulfed by a giant tree still unfurling new branchlets. Golden leaves rained down steadily, depositing a bright accumulation of foliage through which I shuffled on my quest to find Rook's weapon. Finally I found it, only because its hilt poked out of the leaves.

When I came back, the falling leaves had nearly covered him. I ran the last few steps, stumbling once over a concealed root on the way, and brushed him off while he watched me in silence—too weak, I supposed, to remark upon the strangeness of my behavior. Even I couldn't say for certain why the sight of him vanishing into the forest floor alarmed me so. Only that there was something funereal about it. Something final, as if the earth were swallowing him up.

When I was done he tried to take the sword from my hands, but there was no strength in his grip. I had to help him guide it back into its sheath.

A question ached on the back of my tongue, embedded like a fishhook, tugging forth the awful words. "Are you dying?" I blurted out in an odd tone of voice, almost an accusation.

He frowned. "Is that what you want?"

"No!" My vehemence seemed to surprise him, so much so that I felt I had to defend my answer. "If I wanted you dead, why would I have taken the stick from you this afternoon?"

"You gave it to me first."

"Not knowing what would happen—nor did you." I struggled for words. "What you're doing to me, it isn't right. Of course I don't want to be your captive. But there's a difference between that and wanting you dead." Did he understand that? His wandering gaze suggested otherwise. Did human feelings matter to him at all? "Perhaps you ought to know," I added harshly, "because it's over and done with now, that two days ago I thought I was in love with you."

His eyes sharpened, striving through the haze of pain to focus on my face. Then he looked aside and let his arm flop out on the ground, a futile movement, as though he were reaching for something just beyond his grasp. He looked so inhuman. It didn't satisfy me to have gotten a reaction out of him at last—I just felt cold.

"Help me to my feet." It was an effort for him to speak. The air wheezed in and out of his lungs, a quiet gasp with every inhale. I wondered if one of his ribs had broken and punctured a lung, a danger Emma had explained to me one night with a tincture in her hand, and if so, whether anything could be done about it.

But Rook spoke first, saying, "We must return to the autumnlands. I cannot heal myself here. There is something wrong with this place—a corruption I cannot explain." He paused for breath. "With luck some good will have come of it all the same, and the Hunt will have been thrown off our trail."

I gathered his slung-out arm over my shoulder and did my best to lift him. He managed to rise, but only by leaning on me heavily, and when his weight shifted he made an anguished sound, almost a sob, that sent a keen dart of sympathy lancing through my own chest.

"Shouldn't you call for other fair folk?"

He sucked in a breath and replied in a rasping, gusty voice, "No."

"This isn't the time to be stubborn. Surely your own court would be equipped to help you." I didn't say "better equipped," because I had nothing at all to offer him. It didn't escape me that he still hadn't answered my earlier question. He hadn't told me he wasn't dying.

"No," he said again.

I set my jaw and began walking us back the way we'd come. Rook pointed out a different direction, and I adjusted our path. Though I suspected he was lighter than a human man, he leaned more weight on me than I could comfortably bear, and the vast difference in our heights made lugging him along an awkward trial. I kept my eyes averted from his gaunt face, and after a time, his blood started soaking into my dress. It didn't smell at all like human blood—it had a crisp, resiny scent like a tree bitten by an axe.

It was almost full dark now. It wasn't as easy to see here as it was in the autumnlands, where the trees brought color to the night. Rook's hand did something in the air, a twisting motion that made his glamourless fingers look even more insectile, and after a moment I realized he was trying, and failing, to summon a fairy light.

Dread trickled down my back, pooling at the base of my spine. What if we were attacked again? He had no power left.

"I cannot seek help from my own kind." His breathy, gasping words startled me after so long a silence. "We retain our sovereignty not through the love or respect of our courts, but through power alone. To see me weakened so, by a mere Barrow Lord, my court would wonder whether I might be replaced, and whether any one among them might be the right person to do it. Already there has been doubt cast on my suitability as prince. Not once, but twice. I hoped to undo the second." He paused, regaining his strength. I realized he was talking about the portrait and my trial. But what was the first? "A third show of weakness would mean my end, without question."

I shook my head. "That's cruel." All of it was. Him to me, and them to him.

"Such is our nature. It may be cruel, but it is also fair." He looked down.

My vision was fading, but in the hard lines of his profile I saw that he doubted himself. I recognized the rage when he had stolen me away for what it truly was—fear. Fear that his power was slipping. Fear that there was something wrong with him, that he wasn't worthy of his crown, and that others could see it now too.

Because I had painted it in his eyes, as plain as day.

"I don't think it's fair at all," I said, anger pitching my voice low.

"Only because you are a human, the strangest of all

creatures." He spoke in little more than a whisper. "What if I told you I could send you back to Whimsy? There is power in a fair one's death, enough to show the way."

"Don't toy with me." Tears started in my eyes.

"I'm not," he whispered. "I'm not."

Hoped to undo the second, he had said. *Not hope.*

I didn't say a word after that, because I didn't have any that would make sense to him. All I had were human emotions, no doubt as clamoring and riotous to a fair one as a flock of squabbling parrots, and no way to quiet them down. When I finally did speak, it was only to let him know I could walk no farther. At that point he barely clung to consciousness. He went to free himself, and slid from my shoulder like a sack of grain, his tall form crumpling down.

My heart leapt sideways before I saw that he had caught himself on his hands. With a groan, he turned over and sprawled onto his back. One hand was at his wound again, and I resisted the urge to tell him to stop touching it, as if he were a child.

I realized what he was doing when he pulled the hand away and held it over the ground. He waited, and I felt his regard.

"If I don't leave you tonight?" I asked.

"The chance will have passed. The Hunt will pick up your scent too quickly."

I swallowed once, twice. Surely I was mad. I glanced at his bloody hand. "We're still in the summerlands."

"I am a prince yet," he said, and looking at that inhuman, sharp-boned face, lying in repose in a tangled nest of curls, those eyes feverish with resolve, I thought, *Yes, you are, aren't you.*

I lifted the folds of my skirt and sat down on a rock.

It was all the answer Rook needed.

He plunged his hand into the soil, long fingers grasping down. This was no offering to the earth, but a command to it, and the forest surged around us. Bramble roots as wide around as kitchen tables heaved up from the ground, bristling with thorns longer and more wicked than any sword. When they reached their full height they branched, heaving higher, knotting together, until they gathered us up in a fortress like something out of an old tale, a place where a cursed princess slept imprisoned. I was gladdened by the sight of those vicious thorns more than I could say, and wondered whether the stories would have gone any differently if the princesses had been the ones telling them.

When the last tendrils snarled into formation beneath the moon, shattering it like a broken mirror, Rook sighed and went still.

Waking up that morning was worlds different than the morning previous. The jagged scraps of sky showing through the brambles were so overcast I couldn't tell whether it was before dawn or after. Dew had settled on me overnight, leaving my clothes sodden and my skin so clammy my fingers and toes had gone numb. I was immediately conscious of how sore I felt, and how disgusting a state I was in. Of my entire body only my shoulder felt warm, but in a moist, disagreeable way that set my skin crawling. I found it covered in moss where Rook's blood had soaked through my dress, and hastily peeled the growth off in clumps.

Then I rolled over, and found Rook dead beside me.

He lay sprawled a few feet away in exactly the same position I'd last seen him. His hand was still buried in the dirt, and his face was sepulchral. I wouldn't have thought it possible for him to grow any paler overnight, but he seemed to have done so.

I went to him, my damp, grimy skirt flapping against my legs as I moved. I stood over his body and for a moment just looked. I'd gambled everything on his survival—more than was wise, I admitted to myself, as a gray bleakness engulfed me, chased by a weak flutter of hope.

Because I was wrong. He had to be alive. His spilled blood had turned to moss overnight, but his body remained whole. If he were dead, I wouldn't be looking at him now, not intact, not like this.

I dropped to my knees and splayed my hand across his chest. When I felt it rise and fall shallowly beneath the rags of his coat, I breathed out an uneven laugh, shaken by relief. I reached for the coat's edge to peel it back from his wound. My sleeve caught on his raven pin, and cold metal sprang against my wrist. I pulled away. I'd tripped a catch. The bird had a hidden compartment inside.

I would be lying if I claimed the secret it revealed surprised me. There were precious few explanations for Rook's behavior, and this was proof of the most likely one: a curl of blond human hair nested inside the compartment, carefully tied together with blue thread.

I remembered how he'd insisted on removing the pin for his portrait. Even then he had fumbled to protect himself, his reputation, from his damningly mortal grief. He wore it still, though the pin's tarnish and antique craftsmanship gave it away as two or three hundred years old.

Gently, I closed the pin, but I had to press down on his chest to secure the latch, and I think it hurt, because his eyes flew open. Their unearthliness in the light of day gave me an unpleasant jolt. They were glassy, burning with fever. He tried to move and started panting.

"I feel strange," he announced, struggling to focus on the empty air beside me.

"You look strange." I steeled myself and touched his forehead, which proved hot as an oven against my chilled fingers. "I was under the impression fair folk didn't get fevers," I said, concerned.

"What's a fever?" he demanded with a scowl, which didn't improve my fears.

"It happens when a wound goes bad. I'm going to touch this." I indicated his clothes and he tensed, but nodded. While he waited for me to do my work he took his hand out of the dirt, inspected it, then cast about for something to wipe it off on. I had the annoyed suspicion he considered my dress before he victimized a patch of moss instead.

I peeled his coat open, and my stomach flopped over. The flesh around the wound had turned black. Black veins spiderwebbed out of it, vanishing beneath the edges of his clothes. How extensively had the poison spread? I dragged his coat and the shirt underneath open farther, undoing buttons toward his waist without a care for preserving his modesty. Or my own, for that matter, as while I'd educated myself thoroughly on the subject, I'd never seen a man undressed.

Rook propped himself up on an elbow. Despite his weakness, he suddenly looked very interested in whatever I might be doing. Then his eyes alit on his chest. He cried out in disgust and seized his clothes from my hands, fastened the buttons back up, and stood with more alacrity than I would have thought possible. I evaluated him warily. In some ways he had greatly improved. But as fevers went, this could be the final blaze before his body burned itself to ashes.

"You can't just pretend it isn't there," I told him, climbing to my feet.

"But it's hideous," he replied, as though this were a reasonable objection.

"Festering wounds are always hideous." I ignored the affronted look he gave me at the word "festering," perhaps under the impression that I'd just insulted him. "Do you have any idea why this is happening?"

He turned his back to me, lifted his collar rather squeamishly, and peered under it. "That land wasn't . . . right. The Barrow Lord shared its affliction, and appears to have passed it on to me. Temporarily, of course."

That didn't sound good at all. "Rook, I think you need medical treatment."

"And you know how to treat me? No. So I thought. We resume our course toward the autumnlands, which should not take long now that I can walk unaided." He avoided my eyes as he said this. Last night clearly wasn't one of his proudest moments. "Whatever turn my wound has taken, it won't matter once I can properly heal. Therefore we're better off leaving without delay."

I grudgingly admitted that in this matter, he knew better than I. He strode to the edge of the brambles, weaving only a little, and set his hands on one of the thorny coils. They began wriggling like worms, and retracted to form a doorway. I hastened after him, wincing at the chafe of my soiled skirts against my legs.

The forest we emerged into wasn't as ominous as the place

with the standing stones, but it still had an ill look about it that I hadn't noticed in the dark and couldn't easily explain. The green leaves were too glossy and glittering, almost as though a fever lay upon them, too. The sun labored to burn away the soupy mist I'd mistaken for clouds.

While we traveled, I couldn't shake my memories of last night. Whiffs of imaginary decay dogged my steps. Inspecting myself, I found a smear on my left stocking where the corpse had seized my ankle. It was all I could do not to stop and tear the stocking off right then and there. In the way of minor discomforts, now that I'd noticed it I couldn't put it out of my mind, maddened by the way it itched in the summer heat.

And with that thought, something occurred to me.

"The thane was from the summerlands too, wasn't it?" I asked Rook. "The one you destroyed the day we met. The temperature changed when it appeared, same as the Barrow Lord. But nothing like that happened with the Wild Hunt's hounds."

Reluctantly, he nodded.

I narrowed my eyes. "And what about the unusual number of wild fairy beasts you told me about? Were the rest of those coming from the summerlands as well?"

"Ah," Rook said. "A strange coincidence indeed, now that you mention it."

"I sincerely doubt it has anything to do with coincidence!" I grabbed fistfuls of my skirt and trundled up next to him, feeling dirtier and more disgusting by the minute. Good. He deserved it. "You mean the connection's never occurred to you before? Do you have any critical thinking skills at all?"

He stared straight ahead in full hauteur. "Of course I do. I am a—"

"Yes, I know. You're a prince. Never mind." I got the distinct feeling he'd never heard the term critical thinking before in his life. "Have any of the other courts been talking about it, then?" I pressed on.

He tore his crown off and ruffled his hair. "Why is this so important to you?" he exclaimed, vexed.

"Why is it . . ." I halted in my tracks. He turned around when he noticed I'd fallen several paces behind. "Why? Because a fairy beast from the summerlands probably killed my parents. Because one almost killed me, twice. Because they're going to kill more humans if nobody figures out what's going on. You know—just stupid, mortal reasons."

He paused. I clenched my fists against the unhappiness stealing across his expression. I didn't want him to feel bad and apologize, I wanted him to *understand*.

"We do not speak of such things," he said finally. "At all. Because we cannot. We cannot *think* of such things. Even this conversation puts you and me in grave danger."

Like bile, the forbidden words crept up the back of my throat. Shuddering, I swallowed them down.

Rook wasn't responsible for the fairy beasts. And while he was, to be fair, entirely at fault for dragging me into the forest in the first place, he had nearly died last night protecting me. This I couldn't deny. He drooped in his ragged clothes, and the crown shook between his fingers. He labored for breath. Arguing had obviously taxed him.

"I'm sorry," we both said at the same time, in identically grudging voices.

A startled smile tugged at the corner of his mouth. It was my turn to avoid his eyes. I took a deep breath, determined to address one more thing before we went on.

"We need to talk about what you said last night."

"I hate it when people tell me that," he replied. "It's never good."

"Rook. You aren't still taking me to trial, are you? You've changed your mind."

I'm not sure what reaction I anticipated. Perhaps for him to draw himself up and say, *You claim to know the mind of a prince?* Anything but the way he looked aside and uneasily toyed with his raven pin.

"I realize now that I—made a mistake," he confessed. "You did not intentionally sabotage me. What you did with your Craft was . . ." He struggled to find words, incapable of describing that which he didn't understand. "When I came to fetch you," he went on instead, "I told no one of my plans. We won't be missed in the autumn court. Once I have healed, I promise to return you to Whimsy."

The strength went out of my knees, and I steadied myself on a tree trunk. I was going home. Home! To Emma and the twins, my safe warm house filled with the smell of linseed oil, the work I already missed so much. And yet—back to the endless summer, and the way things were before—a life that crept along to the endless buzzing of grasshoppers in the wheat. I'd leave the autumnlands' wonders behind forever. My heart soared and plummeted by turns like a bird buffeted by a storm. If I felt like this too long, I'd tear myself apart. But what could I do? How could I stop?

And what exactly had finally gotten the truth through to Rook?

I studied him. His expression was impassive. But the way he ran his fingers over the raven pin, his eyes getting duller and duller, worsened the turbulence battering my spirits.

"What of you?" I asked. "Your reputation? What will you do next?"

He mustered himself and replied, "I will think of some—" Just like that he stopped. His jaw worked. "Let us not speak of it," he finished oddly. "Do you see that hill ahead? Once we reach the top we'll be back in the autumnlands."

I squinted. The hill looked no different to me than the forest behind us. While I puzzled over this, I realized why Rook hadn't been able to finish his sentence.

It had been a lie.

Nine

AS SOON as we crested the hill, it was autumn again. I turned a full circle. Gently swaying birches stretched into the distance across a forest painted in dreamy tones of white and gold. I took a step back, and another, but the summerlands didn't reappear.

"This doesn't make any sense," I said.

Rook didn't hear me. He'd leaned against the first autumn tree we'd come to and stood propped up like a scarecrow in his torn coat. His eyes were closed, and the relief on his face was profound. I was glad to see it, because after our last conversation his fever had seemed to sap his strength. He'd barely made it up the hill.

I waited for at least an hour for him to recover. I sat down, and tried lying down, but the leaves tickled my neck and I couldn't relax in such a vulnerable position. My fears and worries and longings and questions jangled around in my head, and the weight of my dirty, scratchy clothes and my own smell were apt to drive me mad now that I didn't have anything to distract me. Every time I glanced at Rook, he hadn't moved.

Finally I approached him.

"I hear running water nearby," I said. "I'm going to go find it. I'm thirsty, and I need to wash up."

I didn't expect him to respond, but his eyes opened halfway, and he regarded me as though in a trance. I fought back a shudder. It wasn't like being looked at by a person. His gaze lacked sentience, as though the forest, not him, stared through his eyes. Then he blinked and the impression went away.

"Follow me. It's safer here than in the summerlands, but you shouldn't wander around by yourself." He scrutinized me. "You are quite filthy," he added, as if only just now noticing it.

"Thank you. I'm in good company."

His indignation didn't stop him from replying inevitably, "You're welcome." After he'd bit out the reluctant words he swanned the rest of the way down to the brook and knelt on its mossy bank, reviewing his own reflection. I spied a patch of honeysuckles I could use for privacy—I wanted to rinse my clothes and let them dry a bit before I put them back on. A scrubbing would accomplish little in the way of comfort if my dress remained stiff as treated canvas with mud and horse sweat.

"I was without my glamour this whole time," Rook said behind me. He had a question in his voice. I turned and found him staring at the water, aghast.

"Well, yes." I wasn't certain what else to say. "Ever since you were injured by the Barrow Lord. Or no, a little after that—when you slew it and passed out."

"You've been looking at me!"

"Yes," I said again. Baffled, I went on, "It was hardly avoidable."

His expression hardened. "Stop this instant," he said in a cool voice.

I stood there a moment longer—out of sheer perplexity, not resistance. But the look he leveled at me was so hair-raising I wasted no time vanishing behind the shrubs.

"Don't look at me, either," I called back to him. "Bathing is private. Like peeing."

He didn't respond. Well, that would have to do. Glancing all around, I pulled off my shoes, shucked my dress and underthings, and clambered shivering into the brook. I'd washed in colder from the well back home, but the water had a bite to it, and I didn't waste time as I rinsed my hair and did my best to scrape some of the grime off with my fingernails. I dragged my clothes in with me and sloshed them around last, making a face at the cloud of dirt and horsehair they released into the clear shallows. Leaves floated along on the surface, twirling in the eddies I made. They were such marvelous colors I considered keeping one—here was a buttery leaf an almost perfect match for lead tin yellow, and here a vibrant orange one shot through with green—but I realized I wouldn't be able to decide on a single souvenir, let alone a dozen, and discarded the idea with a wistful twinge.

When I was finished I crept back onto the bank and spread my dress and stockings on top of the honeysuckle where they might catch some of the breeze. More self-consciously, I hung my underthings on a pair of lower branches. Then I folded my arms tightly over my chest and pressed up against the bushes, more exposed than I ever had been in my life before. I waited.

No sound came from Rook's direction. Misgivings started knocking on the back door in my head, an endless stream of unwelcome visitors. What if he'd passed out? Or vanished, leaving me behind? Worse, what if the Wild Hunt stumbled across us while I was naked?

I'd feel much better if I had a look. But dare I? For a time I couldn't will myself to put my back to the forest. I shifted indecisively, bare toes crunching the leaves, with my hair dripping all around me. Finally I gained the courage to crouch down low to the ground and peer through the honeysuckle.

The branches had a few gaps in them, no larger than coins, that afforded me a near-complete picture of the other side. Rook sat on a flat stone within speaking distance, but some length away from where I had left him, close to a bend in the stream. He'd taken off his shirt, though his trousers were still on, and his coat was draped loose on the ground around him. He was seizing the chance to have a wash too.

In some ways the ordinariness of it surprised me. Of course fair folk had to wash up from time to time. But he did it in such a regular way, cupping the water in his hands and scrubbing himself down with it, exhibiting no special speed or efficiency that I could determine. Perhaps it would have gone differently if he hadn't been injured. I couldn't picture another fair one, like Gadfly, doing this at all.

Feeling like some ill-behaved forest goblin hunkered down in the nude with my wet hair plastered to my shoulders and chest, I waddled over to a new spot and peeked through at a better angle.

The wound looked frightful, but better than before. The darkened veins had faded and receded, and the gouge's edges seemed to be closing. I suspected it wouldn't heal without a mark, however, because he had scars from older encounters: a long one across his forearm, and another going over his left shoulder. So his taste for battle hadn't been exaggerated by Gadfly or put on for my sake. Would his glamour hide those scars or leave them?

Much more importantly, why was I even asking myself that question?

I expected to be unnerved by his half-naked form, but the longer I watched, the more he struck me as merely strange as opposed to monstrous. At some point my mind had stopped trying to see him as a human and accepted him for what he was. There was something undeniably striking about his leanness and his angular face. His eyes still appeared cruel to me, but also pensive. The thrill I felt whenever he looked at me was as captivating as it was dangerous, like having one's gaze met unexpectedly by a lynx or a wolf in the woods at dusk.

Which was absolutely the last thing I should be thinking about. That was that. Time for this spying session to end.

But when I moved, a twig snapped beneath my heel. Rook paused, then looked over his shoulder straight at me through my leafy pinhole. I jerked upright, dizzy, heart thumping deep and muffled in my chest.

My clothes weren't dry but I seized them off the honeysuckle anyway, bracing myself against the cold cling of my damp underthings, my stockings, the dragging roughness of my dress as I pulled it over my head. I had just finished lacing up my shoes when Rook's footsteps approached, and knew he made himself heard deliberately for my benefit.

"Come along" was all he said, and with his face averted offered me his hand.

We barely spoke the remainder of the day. If Rook truly had caught me spying, he gave no indication of it aside from his silence. I was still growing used to this side of him. The smiling, devil-may-care prince I'd known in my parlor—he was real, too, but only a part of Rook, and the one I now suspected he preferred to show the world.

I tried engaging him in conversation once or twice, but he only gave me perfunctory replies and eventually I abandoned the effort. His pace was calculated as well: he walked at a speed that allowed me to trail behind him, but not catch up. By the time the daylight faded I had memorized every individual tear in his coat's hem as it swept over the ground.

Yesterday, I think I would have bullied him into acknowledging me whether he liked it or not. But I didn't have the heart for it now. He was no longer my captor. He was returning me home. And, I suspected, he was doing so at great personal cost, the scope of which eluded my mortal understanding.

The shelter he made for us that night was unlike both the rowan cathedral and the fortress of thorns. Slender yellow ashes and weeping willows sprang from his lifeblood, their branches trailing to the ground. A breeze sighed through the boughs. These were not perfect and elegant trees: some grew crooked or had knotholes, or hosted gatherings of toadstools on their roots. They weren't diseased like the ones in the summerlands. They were simply flawed, and seemed to vie cautiously for my attention, lonely and wary of rejection.

Without thinking I went to one and placed a hand on its

bark, and looked inside the hole in its trunk. The shadows were too deep for me to see anything. When I turned around Rook was watching me, frozen halfway in the middle of shedding his coat. It was the first time he'd willingly faced me since the brook.

"This is the sort of thing I like painting best," I explained. "The details, the textures—" I saw I was losing him. "Perfect subjects make for less interesting work."

Slowly he finished taking his coat off. "Then I hardly imagine you enjoy painting fair folk," he remarked aloofly.

"Rook," I said with a smile, perhaps a fonder one than I intended, "you can't just go around calling yourself perfect, you know."

His shoulders tightened. Somehow, I had struck a nerve. With a closed-off expression he handed me his coat. He'd removed the raven pin.

"The cold won't bother me. I'm aware it's ruined, but it should keep you warm."

Just like that the source of his frostiness revealed itself. I held his coat in my arms. Sympathy pierced me like a dart—a sharp, exquisite pain. Without willing my feet to move I found myself standing close enough that I had to tilt my head back to see his face. He tried to turn away, but I touched his shoulder. Marvelously, he stilled. He was a head and a half taller than I, and the forest leapt to obey his power, but with that one touch I might as well have clapped him in irons.

"It doesn't bother me, seeing you without your glamour," I told him. "You aren't unsightly." *You aren't ruined.*

He leaned down and put his face close to mine. The back of my neck prickled, and gooseflesh rose on my arms. His inhuman amethyst eyes moved across my features as though he were reading a letter, and then he made a soft, bitter sound and pulled away. "And yet you're frightened of me still."

I pushed his shoulder. It wasn't enough to move him against his will, but he took a step back. Color had risen in my cheeks.

"Only because you're deliberately being frightening!" He had put me off-balance and I was gripped by the sudden, defensive urge to return the favor. "I watched you at the brook, you know. And—and I kept watching." God, what was I saying? "If I had been frightened, or disgusted, I wouldn't have." I lifted my chin, though I'm sure the gesture came across rather differently on my diminutive frame.

He stared at me.

"Our true forms are loathsome to mortals," he said finally, as if I'd just declared the moon was made of cheese.

"It isn't as though we get a chance to see them very often. 'Loathsome' is a bit of a stretch. How many mortals have seen *you* without your glamour?"

Slowly, he shook his head. I took that to mean none aside from me. Not even the girl who'd given him the raven pin? Oh, Rook!

"Well . . ." I was running out of words to say. "That's that, I suppose," I finished awkwardly. "Thank you for your coat."

He inclined his head, and then stalked off, bringing to mind a tomcat retreating beneath an armchair to nurse his injured dignity. Still blushing hot enough I was amazed my red face didn't illuminate the clearing, I found a soft patch of moss, cleared it of twigs and leaves, and huddled down for sleep.

That night, I dreamed.

First I had the murky awareness that something was trying to infiltrate our shelter. The branches creaked, in one place and then another, as a being's weight stole across the canopy. Through my eyelashes I saw Rook asleep a few paces away. He lay utterly boneless, with one hand flattened against the ground. I recalled his trance when we'd first entered the autumnlands, and it occurred to me that if he was healing himself now, he might not awaken as easily as he would normally.

Weariness blurred my vision. Exhaustion lapped at my mind like warm dark water, sucking me back down in the undertow.

When I regained awareness a figure sat perched in the willow above Rook. It was tall and thin and clung to the branches like a cricket, with its folded knees drawn up past its ears. Its colorless hair floated. Its white face was angled down toward him, and it was speaking to him, even though he slept.

No, she was speaking to him. Hemlock was.

"It's only you now, Rook," she said. Her tone was pleasant, but her inflection had a pelting, hissing quality like rain lashing against a window during a storm. "Only the autumn court remains untouched, and look at you! You're too busy waving your sword about and collecting mortal pets to notice."

Responding to no sound I could detect, she abruptly broke off, tensed, and stared off over her shoulder at nothing. She silently watched the darkness for a time before she turned back to him.

"I am forbidden to speak of it, but you can't hear me, can you? Then I will tell you this: I no longer answer to the horn of winter." Her jade eyes were as unfeeling as polished gemstones. "Snow melts on the high peaks, and the Hunt has a new master. Try as I might, I cannot make a game of things now."

She paused to look over her shoulder again. "So I suppose

what I'd like to ask you is, what are we to do when following the Good Law isn't fair? It's a dreadful question, isn't it?" She spoke in a whisper now. A luminous fascination had entered her eyes, and they seemed to swallow up her face. "Rook"—she lowered her voice even further—"do you ever wonder what it would be like to be something other than what we are?"

I swear I didn't make a sound. But suddenly Hemlock looked around directly at me with her lustrous cat's eyes, and gave me a feral smile.

Down, down I sank, down into the dark. It was only a dream. I slept.

Rook had moved during the night. When I blinked against the morning light I found him facing me, close enough to touch, but still asleep. His glamour had returned. For all that I'd grown used to the way he looked without it, I knew him best like this, and was glad to see him restored. My gaze wandered over his eyebrows, arched slightly even in sleep, his long eyelashes, his aristocratic cheekbones and expressive mouth. Good health— or at least the illusion of it—burnished his golden-brown skin, and his tousled hair pillowed his head. I noticed an indentation in his cheek where the dimple appeared when he smiled.

He sucked in a breath trapped halfway between a muffled yawn and a sigh, and his eyebrows furrowed meditatively before he opened his eyes. At first hazy with sleep, his face showed dawning comprehension as he looked back at me, followed by acceptance of where he was and with whom. We lay there watching each other in silence for some time, listening to the breeze sigh through the trees, each time followed by the rustle of leaves falling.

"May I touch you?" he asked.

At that moment nothing existed beyond the clearing, beyond us, as though we drifted on a mirror-still sea with no land in sight. Soon we'd part ways. There was no harm in allowing myself this, just once. I nodded.

With a fingertip, he traced the curve of my jaw. His touch was so light I barely felt it. His hand brushed the collar of his coat pulled up around my neck, and a trickle of cool autumn air spilled into my warm cocoon. He traced all around the edge of my ear and up toward my forehead. His finger paused near my hairline.

Mortified, I realized a blemish had appeared there overnight. "Rook! Don't touch that."

"Why not?" he said. He lifted his finger and regarded my forehead. "It wasn't there yesterday."

"You aren't supposed to poke people's spots. It's embarrassing. It's—like when I was looking at your wound, I suppose."

"Your face isn't festering. Nor is it hideous."

"Thank you. That's nice."

He frowned at my amusement. Haughtily, he said, "Something about you changes every day. Isobel, you're very beautiful."

I harbored no illusions about my appearance. I was neither homely nor pretty; I occupied an unremarkable spot in between. But Rook couldn't lie. Despite his obnoxious tone, he really meant it. It wasn't so much of a stretch to imagine that fair folk saw humans differently than we saw one another. A flutter stirred in my belly even as I determined not to make too much of it. He was the vain one, not I. And I needed to keep my head out of the clouds.

His hand had wandered to my hair, and he spread it out on the moss, combing through the strands with his fingers until it gleamed as straight and smooth as it could get. It seemed impossible that someone who had lived for hundreds of years and hunted fairy beasts for sport could find this entertaining, but his expression was transfixed. I glanced at the trees, suddenly a bit afraid of how much I was enjoying his attention. How much time had passed? Surely we couldn't afford to linger like this. Shadowy anxieties flickered at the edges of my thoughts, some not unpleasant in the slightest, yet it surprised me how worrying about the Wild Hunt, getting home safely, and the possibility of getting attacked by more fairy beasts paled in comparison to the queasy anticipation of wondering what Rook and I might do if I allowed this to go on much longer. The whole world and its myriad possibilities shrank down to the tingling caress of his fingertips every time they brushed my scalp: all its beauty, and all its terror. Did other girls feel like this the first time they let a boy touch them? And not that I was humiliated by it, but—even at the age of seventeen?

His knuckles skimmed the nape of my neck. Well, that decided it.

"We should get moving," I declared, sitting up. The crisp outside air came as a shock as his coat slid away.

But Rook didn't move; he only regarded me indolently from the ground, with a look that plainly said he didn't much feel like going anywhere, thank you very much.

"Get up." I nudged his side with my shoe, hoping he couldn't sense how forced my composure truly was. "Come on. We can't lie about all morning like lumps."

He allowed my nudge to flop him over onto his back. "But I'm injured," he complained. "I haven't finished healing myself yet."

"You're looking very well to me. If you insist that you're in pain, however, I ought to take another look at your wound without your glamour on. The inflammation may have returned."

His eyes narrowed. Then he extended his hand. Unthinkingly I reached for it to help pull him up. But as soon as our skin touched he clasped his fingers around mine and pulled, and I landed on his chest with a thump. The coat drifted down after, settling neatly over our legs. Rook gave me a charming smile. I glared back at him.

"I'll use iron on you!"

"If you must," he said sufferingly.

"I really will!"

"Yes, I know."

I became conscious of the fact that his chest felt very solid, and I was straddling his slim waist. Our uneven breathing rocked us against each other slightly. Molten heat pooled in me again, ebbing lower.

I didn't use iron on him.

Instead, I leaned down and kissed him.

Ten

THIS IS *a terrible decision,* I thought. *I've gone completely mad and I need to stop this instant.*

But then Rook made a *sound* and parted his lips beneath mine, and I'm afraid that for a time I ceased listening to my brain entirely.

I lost myself in the hypnotizing press of give and take, the odd but intoxicating feeling of joining my mouth with his. Soon I felt Rook's palm slide down my back, and in one graceful, powerful movement he swept me up in his hands. I automatically tightened my legs around his waist and hooked my arms around his neck, boggling at how high off the ground he'd lifted me. It was almost like riding him as a horse again—a thought that made me turn red as a tulip. He took a few steps across the clearing, and a tree's rough bark pressed against my back. That touch was enough to jostle me partway back into reality.

Even though Emma had been careful to educate me on the specifics of this sort of thing (or perhaps *because* she had, quite frankly), a surge of nervousness warred with desire in the pit of my stomach. Noticing how rigid I'd gone, Rook drew back. He waited, his breath soft on my face. His lips were flushed, almost bruised. I wondered what I looked like and, recalling the pimple, instantly wished I hadn't.

"Um," I said. "I've never . . . that is to say . . ." I completely lost my nerve. "Are your teeth still sharp, technically? Because they don't feel sharp at all. I don't understand how that works."

He was breathing heavily, eyes unfocused. He frowned a little, coming back to himself as he processed my anxious carrying on. "I've never made a study of glamour's properties. All I know is that it isn't the same as shapeshifting, but it's more than a mere illusion. I won't harm you." My reluctance dawned on him. His shoulders stiffened. "If you'd rather not—"

I swooped in and silenced him with another kiss. I moved too fast and our noses bumped together, which hurt a bit, but he didn't seem to mind. My heart still hammered like a frightened rabbit's. By reflex I tightened my fingers in his hair, and again he made that noise—the one that pulled me taut as a bowstring inside. I flexed against him without meaning to, and both heard and felt his braced palm slide down the bark next to my ear.

Fascinated, I studied him. He met my eyes. I gave his hair a second, experimental tug. He let his head fall a little to the side, in the direction of my hand. Somehow I knew what that meant: he'd give me complete control if I wanted it. A rush of pure unadulterated *want* knocked the air out of my lungs and, ironically, knocked some sense into my brain.

"We can't do this!" I exclaimed. "We're stopping. Now. Oh, god."

I loosened my legs and gripped his shoulders to let myself down. He got the hint before I took an ignoble drop, and lowered me to the ground. His face had gone a bit gray, and his expression was stricken.

I demanded of him, "Have we broken the Good Law? Did that count?"

"No," he replied hoarsely. "Not unless—" He halted and shook his head. "No," he repeated, in a surer voice. He cleared his throat. "If fair folk and mortals broke the Good Law every time we—ah—kissed each other, suffice it to say there'd be few of us left."

"Sex really does turn people into imbeciles," I said, amazed at having committed yet another base human error to which I'd somehow thought myself immune. "Rook, we can't do that again. I'm really using the iron next time. That isn't a bluff."

White-lipped, he went over and claimed his coat from the ground. "Good," he said. And he seemed to mean it.

I tugged my dress straight, tightened my bootlaces, and yanked a bunched-up stocking back over my knee, wishing I had more to do to keep my hands busy so I didn't have to look at him. What I'd just done was so unlike me I could hardly believe it. The autumnlands' magic wasn't affecting me in some way, was it? I couldn't shake the feeling that something dark lurked at the periphery of my recent memories—an unsettling experience I'd forgotten somehow, like a bad dream. And as soon as I thought that, one of the shadows that had been haunting me all morning sharpened into focus.

"Hemlock!" I blurted out.

Rook whipped around with his sword drawn.

"No, not here. Not right now, at least. I think I saw her last night, or maybe I just dreamed about her." Already I'd begun doubting myself. The image of Hemlock perched in the branches was intangible, slipping away the harder I held on. "I'm not sure. If it had been real, I wouldn't have just rolled over and gone back to sleep."

He examined my face carefully. Part of his shirt had come loose from his trousers, and I bit back the urge to snap at him to tuck it back in.

"You are not prone to flights of fancy," he said. At least he knew that much about me. "Fair folk can deepen a mortal's sleep, if we wish, to move about unnoticed nearby. It is common for mortals to interpret such visits as dreams. But that would mean—"

"She's already found us," I finished slowly, apprehension weighing down the words.

In one clean arc he swept his sword through a stand of mushrooms, sending their caps flying. Then he stood with his back turned, leaning on the hilt, struggling not to project his defeat. Now I understood why Hemlock's actions exacted such a personal toll. He was already insecure about his suitability as prince, and the ease with which she tracked him through his own domain was yet another mark against him.

But I had witnessed Rook's power firsthand, and couldn't believe it was as simple as that.

"She tried to tell you something," I said, dredging up the details, frustrated that I could recall so little of use. "I think she was delivering a warning. She said it's only you now, and that she no longer answers to the horn of winter. Do either of those mean anything to you?"

"No, but there's an ill sound to both." He sheathed his sword. "Isobel, I . . ." The pause spun out into an agonizing silence. When he resumed, I could tell every admission cost him. "I was not lying, of course, when I told you I haven't yet fully recovered. I relied upon losing the Wild Hunt for several days at least. If we are attacked on the return journey—when we're attacked—I fear I may not be able to protect you."

I bit my lip and looked down. The heat between us had dissolved, a smoldering fire reduced to soggy ashes. "There must be another option."

"Revisiting the summerlands would be futile, if not perilous. The winterlands are out of the question, as is"—he hesitated—"my own court, given recent events. But Hemlock wouldn't dare accost us if we went straight to the spring court. We could stay several nights, and return to Whimsy along a safer route."

No human had ever visited a fairy court and lived. Or at least, none had ever done so and remained *human*. I was a master of the Craft, escorted by a prince, but I had to wonder whether I truly was a special case, or if every mortal deluded themselves into thinking they were an exception to the rule.

I took a deep, shaky breath. "I do have many patrons in the spring court."

Rook bowed his head in agreement. "If anything were to happen to me, Gadfly would honor your desire to return home. Of this I am certain."

"And once I'm back in Whimsy . . ."

"We shall never see each other again," he said, "for one reason or another."

A pain that had nothing to do with anything physical twisted in my chest. What would happen to Rook after we parted? I imagined him returning to the autumn court, walking down a long, dim hall, and taking a seat on a throne with a thousand eyes upon him—all searching for a sign of the human wrongness on his face, the wrongness my portrait had exposed. How long before he tripped, and his people bared their teeth and sprang upon him like wolves on an injured stag? How long would he last against them? I knew he wouldn't go easily. Or quickly.

But I was powerless to help him. I'd do well to remember that the only fate I had any control over was my own. Cold on the outside, aching on the inside, I nodded.

"Then let us go," he said, sweeping past me with his face turned away.

A sparkling fall day greeted us beyond the glade. We walked for hours with no sign of the Wild Hunt, encountering nothing more dangerous than the occasional acorn dropping from a tree over our path. Surrounded by the forest's peaceful beauty, with the sun warming our backs, it was hard to remain pessimistic for long. Even Rook's steps lightened the farther we traveled without incident.

"What are you smiling about?" I asked, bending over in another futile attempt to wipe the stickiness from the apples we'd found for lunch off my fingers, and watching him suspiciously.

"I just recalled the spring court holds a ball this time of year. If we haven't missed it, we might be able to attend."

"Yes, that seems like the perfect thing to do while fleeing for our lives," I said.

"Then we shall go," he concluded, pleased.

I snorted, completely unsurprised. "Fair folk are impossible."

"That's irregular, coming from a human who can't even eat a raw hare."

Hastening along behind him, trying to keep up with his long strides, I decided not to argue about the hare. I was coming to realize that the Craft was so enigmatic to fair folk I might as well have refused to eat meat unless it had been bathed in widow's tears under a new moon. Realizing that your own magic held more mystery to fair folk than theirs did to you was a peculiar experience. I felt like some sort of wizard with delicate and arcane indispositions, not an artist and a perfectly ordinary person.

We passed a mossy boulder with a squirrel perched atop it. I turned to have a second look, and both the boulder and the squirrel were gone. Scanning the forest around us, I realized that though it was made up of the same types of trees we'd been walking through before, they weren't the exact same individual trees. I looked forward, and looked back again. Yes—that ash with the overhanging branch had vanished. Straining my eyes, I thought I made it out a quarter of a mile or so behind us in the distance. With all the leaves in between it was difficult to tell for certain.

I remembered the old tales, and faltered.

"You aren't doing something with time, are you?" I asked.

He looked at me loftily over his shoulder, which meant he was confused by my question but didn't want to admit it.

"When I get back to Whimsy I'm not going to find that everyone I know died a century ago, or that I've suddenly become an old maid, am I? Because if that's the case you need to put it to rights." I said this firmly, trying to tamp down my rising alarm. "I just noticed the way we're traveling. Each few steps we take must add up to fifteen minutes or more of walking."

"No, the autumnlands are merely doing my bidding and hurrying us along. You mean to say you haven't noticed it until now?" I frowned. Indeed, I hadn't. "I give my word that time has passed normally since we entered the forest. What you're thinking of is an ensorcellment, and quite a nasty trick to play on humans. Which is precisely why it's done, of course," he added.

"You had better not have done that to anyone," I warned him.

"I haven't!" he said, with feeling. He proceeded to ruin the effect by continuing, "It's always seemed tiresome. All they do afterward is leak a great deal, and then come back to the forest to shout at you."

I shook my head. God, what a menace.

We walked on. One moment I was admiring a stand of fiery rowans, and the next I stepped into a different forest altogether. Everything was green. Not the rich simmering greens of summertime, but pale greens, lacy greens, delicate gold-greens, all layered up on the trees like icing and chiffon. Knee-high wildflowers parted around my legs. A bee droned sleepily past my face.

Delighted laughter bubbled up in my chest. We were in the springlands!

"Can we stop for a moment?" I called out. Rook hadn't paused and was now halfway across the clearing. "Only if it's safe, that is. This is wonderful. I'd like to try to paint it once I'm home."

He halted and gave me a furtive look.

"It's nearly as lovely as the autumnlands," I added loudly for the sake of his pride.

That seemed to mollify him. "There's a place over here to sit down." He ducked beneath some branches. When I caught up with him, he was sitting on the lip of a squat stone well half-way covered up by moss. Bluebells and feathery-looking ferns sprouted all around it. I sank down on the opposite side with my back turned to his, as that morning's events made keeping a distance seem wise, and considered taking my shoes off.

Then I looked at the well and forgot all about wiggling my toes in the ferns. The well was small, old-looking, and unre-markable in every way. I looked at it for a long time.

Rook said quietly, "I've brought you to the Green Well."

I shot up as though my buttocks had just landed on a bed of hot coals. A slushy sound filled my ears, and my vision darkened around the edges. Desperate to get away, I tottered over to a tree and leaned myself against it, breaking out in a clammy, crawling sweat. I'd never fainted before, but the feeling of being on the verge of it was unmistakable.

He spoke again with his head angled, not quite looking at me over his shoulder. My abrupt movement puzzled him; I don't think he saw the extremity of my reaction. "Nothing will happen unless you drink from it. But I understand the opportunity to drink from the Green Well is many humans' dearest wish."

I slid down the tree trunk and sat uncomfortably on its gnarled, jutting roots, wildflowers tickling my legs. He was right. Of those mortals who vanished into the forest, the major-ity sought the Green Well, hoping to find it on their own despite the insurmountable risk. Masters of the Craft toiled for years in pursuit of this end. Only perhaps one human every hundred years was bestowed with the honor. It was lusted after more than any enchantment, any glittering quantity of gold. And of all the things on earth, it terrified me most.

"It occurred to me," he went on, "that this might be an ideal alternative for you under the circumstances. You would no longer require my protection, or fear any of the forest's dangers. You could come and go in the autumnlands—and any other fairy court," he hastened to add, "as you please. And of course, you would live forever."

Somehow, I found my voice. "I can't."

This time he did look at me. Absorbing my expression, he stood up halfway. "Isobel! Have you taken ill?"

I shook my head.

A pause. "Are you starving to death?" he asked nervously.

I briefly squeezed my eyes shut, swallowing a painful laugh. "No. It's the Green Well. Rook, there's something you must know about me. My Craft isn't just something I do. My Craft is who I am. If I drank, I'd lose myself and everything I care about. I know it's hard for you to understand, because you've never been mortal, but the emptiness I've glimpsed within your kind frightens me more than death. I wouldn't consider the Green Well even as a last resort. I'd rather get torn apart by the Wild Hunt than become a fair one."

He sank back down, absorbing my words. I'd expected to offend him, but he only looked a bit dazed, as though something had struck him over the back of the head. Perhaps the effort to comprehend what I'd said left him reeling. From his perspective, after all, human emotion wasn't a blessing—it was a misery and a curse. Why *wouldn't* I want to be rid of it?

After a long hesitation, he gave a faltering nod. "Very well. I will not ask it of you again. But now, there is something else we must discuss before we continue on to the spring court. It's a matter of great importance."

"Please go on," I said. The frigid terror gripping me melted away bit by bit, leaving a trembling weakness behind. Seeing the Green Well and denying it aloud made it seem less threatening somehow. I had faced it, and emerged unscathed.

The ferns rustled. I looked up to find Rook pacing across the clearing. "Fair folk don't bring humans into the forest lightly. In fact, you will be the first mortal to visit the spring court in over a thousand years. To avoid suspicion, we must invent some explanation for why we're traveling together. But . . ."

"It can't be a lie, or else you won't be able to talk about it."

He glanced at me, and nodded tightly.

"I've always heard that the best lies are the ones closest to the truth. What will they assume first, seeing us together?"

"That we've fallen in love," he said, in an utterly neutral tone.

"And it wouldn't be your first time." He froze. "I saw what's in your raven pin—by accident, when you were unconscious. I'm sorry, Rook. I'm not going to pry, but it *is* relevant to our predicament. Naturally they'd draw conclusions, however far-fetched . . ." His stillness sank in. Dread resounded within me like the striking of a gong. My skin tightened and prickled.

"Are you in love with me?" I blurted out.

A terrible silence followed. Rook didn't turn around.

"Please say something."

He rounded on me. "Is that so terrible? You say it as though it's the most awful thing you can imagine. It isn't as though I've done it on purpose. Somehow I've even grown fond of your—your irritating questions, and your short legs, and your accidental attempts to kill me."

I recoiled. "That's the worst declaration of love I've ever heard!"

"How fortunate," he said bitterly, "how very fortunate you are, we both are, that you feel that way. We aren't about to break the Good Law anytime soon." I looked away from the raw anguish in his eyes. "The love must be mutual, after all."

"Good," I said to my hands.

"Yes, good!" He paced back and forth. "You've made it quite clear how you feel about fair folk. Now stop making me feel things," he demanded, as though it were as easy as that. "I must think."

My face felt hot and cold at once. His words rang in my head. This wasn't anything like how I'd ever imagined a romance would go, if I were to have one in the first place. God, how close we'd come to disaster. If only our sentiments for each other had overlapped . . .

But would it have mattered? I was no longer certain that what I'd felt for Rook back in the parlor truly had been love. It had felt like it at the time. I'd never experienced anything like it before. But I'd hardly known him, even though in my feverish infatuation I'd felt as though we'd been confiding in each other for years. Could you really love someone that way, when all they were to you was a pleasant illusion? If I'd been aware he would kidnap me over a portrait, I dare say I would have changed my mind.

And yet—I did feel *something* for him. What was that *something*? I picked at my emotions like a snarled knot and came no closer to finding an answer. Was I enamored with what he represented—that wistful fall wind, and the promise of an end to the eternal summer? Did I only want my life to change, or did I want to change it with him?

Frankly, I had no idea how anyone knew if they were in love in the first place. Was there ever a single thread a person could pick out from the knot and say "Yes—I am in love—here's the proof!" or was it always caught up in a wretched tangle of ifs and buts and maybes?

Oh, what a mess. I planted my face in my skirts and groaned. I only knew one thing for certain. If even I couldn't figure myself out, the Good Law wasn't about to do it for me.

Rook's shadow fell over my tumbled hair. "Your behavior is extremely distracting," he announced. "I need to come up with an idea soon, or we'll be stuck here overnight."

My reply came out muffled by fabric. "Whatever it is, it should have to do with Craft. That's the one thing we can count on to properly distract them."

Belatedly, it occurred to me that Rook wouldn't know where to begin. He didn't possess the barest inkling of what Craft entailed. I snuck a peek at him through my hair, and found him standing over me looking predictably frustrated, a muscle flickering in his cheek as he clenched his jaw.

That left solving things entirely up to me—which, I had no doubt, would turn out far better for both of us in the end. I mentally arranged our problems like dabs of paint: my presence in the forest, Rook's company, and even the dilemma of his portrait, news of which might have already reached the spring court. And like blending a new color, I began to see that something not only satisfactory, but perhaps even extraordinary could be done with them.

"Listen," I said, lifting my head. "I have an idea."

Eleven

MY PLAN required some discussion to ensure that Rook could say the necessary lines. We rehearsed it as we walked, and he was well pleased with how it sounded. I was more than a little pleased myself. I felt the glowing satisfaction of having negotiated a particularly twisty enchantment, or stretched and framed a month's worth of new canvases in advance. My world was in order again, and finally I had some measure of control over what happened to me next. Moreover, there was a chance I might even put my accidental sabotage to rights.

"Do you really think it might repair your reputation?" I asked, lifting my skirts to step through a meadow of nodding yellow cowslips. Whenever the breeze changed directions it brought a different fragrance—some I could identify, and others I'd never smelled before.

"At this point, I doubt anything can," he replied with a

crooked smile. "But the portrait . . . yes, I believe so. I'm relieved I'm no longer on the receiving end of your schemes. You're a great deal more devious than you look."

Try as I might to block it out, I heard an echo of Rook's confession in everything he said since leaving the well behind. Now that I knew to look for it, I perceived the warm admiration in his tone. While our mood might have lightened, the perfumed air hung heavy with tension. I forced out a laugh, focusing on my steps through the tall, tangled flowers.

"I'm not devious, I'm just practical. But I suppose fair folk don't have much to do with the latter."

He frowned, trying to figure out if I'd insulted him.

"Look," I said quickly, hiding my amusement as I waded over to a great mossy stone, "this blossom's as large as my hand. I wonder what makes them grow so large?"

As soon as I bent down and plucked the flower, a trouser leg appeared next to me. It was made of shimmering rose-gray silk, and another, matching trouser leg followed. I started back and fell on my rear in time to watch Gadfly finish stepping out from the space between the two halves of the cracked boulder. This was made even stranger by the fact that—and I was completely certain of this—he hadn't emerged from the other side. Somehow, I'd stumbled upon the entrance to a fairy path.

"Good afternoon, Isobel," he said pleasantly, straightening his impeccably tied cravat. He didn't seem at all surprised to find me sitting on the ground in front of him, alarmed and clutching a cowslip.

As the shock wore off, I found I was terribly happy to see him. The homesickness I hadn't had time to indulge in these past few days struck me like a runaway carriage. I'd spent years with him in my parlor, and though his pale blue eyes betrayed not the slightest genuine warmth, his face was more familiar a sight than anything else I'd lain eyes upon since leaving home.

I nearly exclaimed his name, but caught myself at the last second. My manners had deteriorated appallingly during my time with Rook.

"It's wonderful to see you, Gadfly," I said, standing up to curtsy. "Did Rook inform you of our arrival?" If he had, it was news to me.

He swept me a bow, then sent Rook a pointed look. "Does our dear Rook ever bother with common courtesy? No, I simply knew you were coming. Very few things escape my attention in the springlands—even the plucking of a flower."

I looked at the cowslip guiltily.

"Do keep it," he urged, "as a welcome to my domain."

While I digested his curious words he swept past me and walked a circle around Rook, who withstood the inspection with a lifted chin and a set jaw. Comparing them, I was oddly proud to note that Rook was several inches taller. His dark, tousled hair and striking eyes set him apart like night from day in contrast to Gadfly's refined pastel pallor. Though by far the younger of the two, he was in every way Gadfly's equal.

"Those clothes are at least fifty years out of fashion," Gadfly was telling him. "No one wears copper buttons in the spring court. If you insist on staying we'll have to find . . ."

Whatever he said next, and whatever Rook said in reply, was lost to me as I finished digesting that phrase—*a welcome to my domain.*

I cleared my throat. Gadfly looked around. "Sir, are you the spring prince?" I asked.

He smiled. "Why, yes. None other! Surely I've mentioned that to you before?"

"No, I can't say you have."

"How remiss of me. I'm so forgetful with mortals—I simply assume everyone already knows." While Gadfly spoke, Rook studied him with an unreadable expression. "Well, fear not, Isobel. Your manners are beyond reproach. I always felt welcomed as a princely figure in your home. Now, before I forget another detail, would you care to tell me why you're roaming about in the forest, and in such distinguished company?"

"Actually—" I glanced at Rook. I was grateful we'd planned on having him explain, because the revelation about Gadfly's rank had left me quite speechless.

"Let's discuss it as we walk," he suggested, yanking his coat straight and tightening his sword belt, rather crossly, I thought. I wondered if he'd taken Gadfly's criticisms to heart. Then he set off through the meadow, leaving us to catch up.

"He's a singular fellow, isn't he," Gadfly said.

How could I possibly answer that without giving anything away? I settled for the blandest reply I could think of. "Indeed, sir. I find all fair folk to be quite singular."

"Oh, how I wish that were so! But we're all the same, I'm afraid." He gave me a smile as subtle and chilly as a spring thaw. "Most of us. Now, Rook—you were saying?"

Pacing along in front, Rook was clearly growing tired of all the cowslips. "As you know," he said impatiently, "Isobel is the most distinguished Crafter in Whimsy at present. The portrait she painted for me was unlike anything we've ever seen in the autumn court."

"So I heard," Gadfly replied. It took a monumental effort of will not to look at him and gauge his reaction.

"It shocked us, myself most of all. At first I imagined it to be an act of sabotage for which Isobel should stand trial. But on the way to the autumn court I discovered that she had no harmful intentions. She merely painted a human emotion on my face, and skillfully, without understanding what she had done." This was all true—in a manner of speaking. "Now, Isobel is interested in replicating her newfound Craft."

"Human emotions, Gadfly," I said to him, my confidence swelling the further we got without slipping up. "You've sampled everything Craft has to offer—tea cakes and china, silk suits, books, swords. We keep coming up with different versions of the same old things, but I think what I'd like to try is completely new. I could put true joy on your face. Wonder on someone else's. Laughter, or wrath—even sorrow. Rook has informed me your kind will find this most diverting."

"So I've brought her to the spring court, where she might demonstrate first for her most dedicated patrons," Rook finished grandly. "If the results are satisfactory, I do believe such Craftsmanship deserves a just reward. I propose that should she choose to take it, Isobel's payment will be a trip to the Green Well."

My smile radiated innocence. *A trip to it,* not a drink from it.

"Something completely new," Gadfly mused in a faraway voice. Briefly he looked much older than his apparent age. The bees stopped droning in the honeyed air, and all the songbirds stilled. I held my breath along with the rest of the world. "Yes. Yes, I think that's just the thing. Isobel, Rook, I would be delighted to host you. For as long as you're in the spring court, you will want for nothing."

We reached the court much sooner than I expected, and I almost walked straight in without realizing we'd arrived. Birch trees wider than a man was tall grew around us, soaring to impossible heights. Craning my neck, I saw that their branches were woven together much in the same way as Rook's shelters, with songbirds and jewel-bright hummingbirds flitting among them. The only tree that stood apart from the rest was an old, knotted dogwood in full bloom, elevated on a mossy knoll. It had grown into a strange shape, and puzzling over this, I realized it was no normal tree, but in fact a throne.

As soon as I drew that conclusion, the forest around me changed. Silvery laughter filled the air, and with a shimmer like steam escaping a teapot, brocade chairs, silken pillows, and picnic blankets unfurled across the flowery meadow. Previously unseen, dozens if not hundreds of fair folk watched us approach from various states of repose. My knees turned to water, and I had to force myself to keep walking. I'd never seen even a fraction this many fair folk in a single place at once. Worse, they weren't watching us after all. They stared at me, and me alone: the first mortal to enter their court in over a thousand years.

As we neared the throne, a girl rose from a blanket—she seemed to be having tea, but all the teacups were empty— and pelted toward us, her long blond hair flying, the many layers of her periwinkle-blue gown frothing up and down like waves. When she reached us, she startled me by seizing both my hands. Her skin was cold and flawless as china. Were she human I would have guessed her age at around fourteen.

"Oh, a mortal! Gadfly, you've brought us a mortal!" she cried in a simulacrum of rapturous delight, revealing that all of her little white teeth were as pointed as a shark's. "We simply must introduce her to Aster, she'll be ever so pleased! Are you going to drink from the Green Well?" She shifted her attention to me. "Please say yes, please say yes! We can be the best of friends. Of course, we can still be best friends if you don't, but you'll die so quickly it would hardly be worth it!"

Gadfly's hand alit on her shoulder. "Isobel, this is my"—he searched for words—"niece, Lark. Please forgive her excitability. This is her very first time meeting a mortal. I trust she'll be on her best behavior, with you as our honored guest." This was clearly more for Lark's benefit than mine.

I gave her an awkward curtsy, which was difficult with her still clinging to my hands. But apparently it counted, because to my relief she let go and curtsied back. My fingers felt as though they'd been immersed in ice. "It's a pleasure to meet you, Lark."

"Of course it is!" she said.

"And you already know Rook," Gadfly went on pleasantly.

"Hello, Rook," said Lark, without ever taking her eyes off my face. "Can you turn into a hare for me again and let me chase you about?"

Rook laughed. "That was a child's game, Lark. You're a young lady now."

"You're no fun. Poor Isobel, she must be ever so bored with you. Can I put her in some new clothes?" she asked Gadfly, whose smile was acquiring a fixed quality.

"In a moment, darling. For now, Isobel and I must discuss her Craft. Why don't you have a seat beside the throne and think about the dresses you'd like her to wear? Remember, she cannot use glamour, so it must be a *new* dress." He inclined his head meaningfully.

"Oh, fine!" She collapsed next to the throne in a tragic heap of blue chiffon.

"Now," Gadfly said, arranging himself elegantly on the dogwood's platform, "what will we need to provide you with so you may work your Craft? I'm afraid we have no materials similar to what I've seen in your parlor. I can send for supplies from Whimsy, but my court is terribly busy preparing for the masquerade, and it may take some time to have them delivered."

I resisted glancing at the fair folk around us, none of whom were doing anything more productive than nibbling on shortbread.

"Let me think, sir." What *could* I use? "First I'd need a substitute for canvas or paper. Perhaps sheets of bark, thin and pale in color, sturdy but flexible enough to straighten out without breaking. Birch bark might do well, and there looks to be plenty of it." Was it my imagination, or were the branches on Gadfly's throne moving? "And then," I went on, unnerved by the idea that his dogwood might have taken offense, "I think I can gather natural pigments myself. I used to do so often as a child."

"Excellent," he said, tapping a spidery finger against his lips. "And a chair, and a stand for you to put the bark on?"

"That sounds very good, sir." I hadn't the slightest idea what I might use in place of a brush or pencil, but I'd figure something out. I'd use my fingers if I had to. "Because of the difference in materials, the portraits won't look like the ones I usually do, nor will they last as long. But if you're pleased with the work, I would be happy to do them over in oils. Using my normal method, that is," I added, aware that he might not understand.

"*Now* can I dress her?" said Lark's voice from the ground, where she was still collapsed in the same, piteous heap.

Gadfly raised his eyebrows at me.

"Er," I said. "Yes, I suppose. Though I should—"

"You're going to try everything on!" Lark exclaimed, her cold hand closing around my wrist like a vise. Before I knew it I was being dragged through the laughing picnickers with little hope for escape. I glanced over my shoulder at Rook, who watched me go intently, and had the comforting thought that he'd find some excuse before long to make sure I didn't suffocate in last century's silk bustles.

Lark towed me toward one of the giant birches, which had thick vines winding up it like a spiral stair. She mounted this dubious-looking feature without hesitation while hauling me behind. We went higher and higher, the fair folk on the ground receding to the size of toy soldiers. I found that if I paid close attention to where I stepped on the knobbly roots, didn't look down, and held on to the bark with my free hand, I could resist the urge to vomit on Lark's chiffon. She chattered at me gaily the entire time without seeming to mind that I didn't once reply.

At the top, we emerged into a leafy labyrinth. It reminded me a bit of a hedge maze, if instead of hedges there were arched bowers of white, wickerlike branches filled in with pale green leaves. The ground felt springy but otherwise solid. I wouldn't have minded walking across it if I hadn't known about the long drop beneath. Items of Craft lay jumbled all along the pathways, climbing the walls in teetering stacks of furniture, cushions, books, paintings, and porcelain wares. Jewelry dangled glittering from upended chair legs; spiders wove glistening webs over atlases and bronze coatracks.

"This way!" Lark cried. She whipped me around with nearly

enough force to dislocate my shoulder and took off down one of the corridors. Racing behind her, I frequently had to hop sideways to skim through the narrow aisles, and suspected I rendered a few spiders homeless along the way.

She said, "I keep my dresses in the Bird Hole. We name all our rooms, even though they aren't really rooms, because that's what mortals do."

"Oh, how nice," I replied faintly, filled with dread.

As it turned out, however, the unpropitious-sounding Bird Hole looked more or less like the rest of the labyrinth, except that it was a dome-shaped room protruding from one of the corridors and had songbirds roosting in it, which flew off in a melodic explosion when we entered. Blossoming vines shielded the far wall like a curtain. Lark finally released my abused wrist to go root around in it, vanishing up to the waist.

"Here," she said, thrusting a pile of chiffon through the curtain into my arms. "Take off your boring old brown dress and put this on. It might be long on you because you're short, but you can change it, can't you? And then put it back the same way afterward?"

It took me a moment to understand what she meant. "I don't do that sort of Craft, unfortunately. I can sew a bit—mend tears, and that sort of thing—but I'm not a tailor."

Lark straightened and stared at me without comprehension. Her large, widely set blue eyes gave her the look of an inquisitive sparrow. If not for the teeth I would have found her countenance very charming.

I tried, "Some fair folk have different types of magic, don't they? Magic that's unique to them or a small number of your kind, such as Rook being able to change his shape, for example."

"Yes!" she exclaimed. "Just like how Gadfly knows things before they happen."

I filed that information away for later. "Well, that's also how it is with mortals and the Craft. My specialty is making pictures of people's faces. I can do a little with food, but not much with clothes, and nothing at all with weapons."

"Who needs weapons anyway! If I were a mortal I'd want Craft to make dresses. Please won't you hurry up and put that on?"

I regarded the pink fabric grimly. "I suppose. Hold it for me while I get ready?" I handed it back and stripped off my dress. For the lack of a better place to put it, I laid it out on the ground, and then struggled into the new dress with Lark's "help," which involved an unnecessary amount of poking and prodding. All the while I thought of the iron ring hidden away in my pocket, and wished I'd thought to put it in my stocking instead.

"You look much better," she said gravely when we were finished. "Except pink isn't your color. Take it off again!" She dove back to the closet.

I was stepping out of the wads of fabric when a rustling sound came from the wall. I turned to find a raven poking its beak through the branches. It angled its head this way and that, snatching at the leaves and tearing them off to make room for itself, cocking a demanding purple eye in our direction. Relief swept through me, chased by the prickling awareness that I stood there in my undergarments. I snatched my arms against my chest just as Rook popped his head the rest of the way through. Stuck halfway in and out of the wall, he made an irritable burbling sound in his throat.

I couldn't help it—I laughed. It was hard to remain self-conscious in front of a bird.

"All right, hold still," I told him. I went over and slipped my hand in next to his feathers, and pulled the branches aside. He flapped down to the floor. With a self-important air, he strutted across the room and tugged on the hem of Lark's dress.

"Stop!" she said. "I'm busy. I won't break her, I promise."

Rook and I exchanged a look. She'd just given her word, whether she meant to or not, but I had to wonder if it counted for much given how unlikely she was to understand how, exactly, one went about breaking a mortal.

She spun around. "This one." Her face glowed with satisfaction.

Oh, god. It was a Firth & Maester's. I took it reluctantly, as one might a queen's diamond necklace, and held it close with my knees pressed together, overwhelmingly mindful of Rook standing just a few feet away. "Lark, I don't know about this one. I have to go tromping around in the woods looking for berries after we're done, and I'd hate to damage it."

"Why would you care about that?"

"Well, because then it's ruined. Wouldn't Gadfly be upset if he had to replace it?"

"You're silly. Watch!" She fetched another dress from inside the vines. Involuntarily, I recoiled. It looked like it had served as a wedding dress long ago, but its once-white fabric was soiled and graying, riddled with moth holes. The ribbons dangling from the waist were so rotten one of them dropped off when Lark pulled it against herself. But as soon as the dress touched her body, it unrolled new lengths of snowy satin. Lace restored itself like blossoms unfurling, and the ribbons spooled down to her toes, pristine. Just like that the dress looked freshly sewn, without the slightest trace of decay.

Seeing my expression, Lark shrieked with laughter, showing every one of her pointed teeth. Then she stopped laughing all at once, as though she'd shut the lid on a music box.

"That's what he meant when he told me to get you new ones," she explained. "But we can only make them look exactly how they did when they were made. So I can't change its shape if I want to, or add anything on." She sized me up. I could tell she was about to ask about my sewing skills again, so I swiftly donned the Firth & Maester's dress before she had a chance.

It was made of gorgeous sage-green satin. The bodice was embroidered with tiny songbirds in silver thread, and a cream-colored satin ribbon marked its raised waistline, beneath which an additional layer of sheer muslin draped over the green underskirt. I felt diaphanous and shimmering, like a dragonfly's wing. Ordinarily I'd never wear anything half this fine without a petticoat underneath, and the sleek fabric slid unfamiliarly over my bare legs, a touch as silky and subtle as water. It looked terribly at odds with my stout leather half-boots peeking out beneath the hem, but that was one aspect of my wardrobe I refused to compromise. I never knew when I might have to run.

"Perfect for berry picking," I joked weakly.

"What about you?" Lark demanded of Rook, who was watching me with a cocked head. Warmth flooded my cheeks, and I resisted the urge to fold my arms again, even though there was nothing to hide. "Has Gadfly changed you out of those dreary autumnlands clothes?"

Wind shook the Bird Hole, and Rook materialized beside us looking rumpled and cross. "Yes, that was his first order of business, unsurprisingly. But these colors don't suit me at all."

"Don't be a spoilsport! Black and brown and whatever else you had on suit everyone poorly. I think you look awfully fine."

"I believe we must agree to disagree about fashion," he replied with dignity. "Also, it wasn't brown, it was copper."

"Copper!" she repeated, and gave another shriek of laughter, though the source of her amusement eluded me.

To be perfectly frank, Rook could trail about in a bedsheet and still look magnificent. But he did look better in his own clothes—the fern-green jacket Gadfly had scrounged up for him didn't match his darker complexion or his hair, and fit too tightly across the shoulders. His embattled cravat showed signs of restless clawing; I doubted it was long for this world. But, I thought wryly, at least we matched.

"Are the two of you finished? I've been ordered to bring Isobel back down for introductions once she's dressed. And you can help introduce her, of course," he added to Lark, who was summoning a pout.

"Oh, all right!" She seized his arm.

Rook lifted his other elbow meaningfully, and I smiled and shook my head. "We'll never make it through those corridors if we're promenading arm in arm. I'd impale myself on a coatrack."

"Just do it, Isobel!" Lark cried. "We aren't going *that* way."

What other way could there possibly be? Certain I was about to experience another fairy strangeness I'd rather go without, I took Rook's offered arm. I observed how delicate my hand and wrist looked resting on his sleeve, and conceded it was possible to see how fair folk got so vain, parading around in Firth & Maester's and constantly discussing which colors looked best on them.

Rook looked down, his gaze stripped bare.

He really is in love with me, I thought. My heart leapt forward like a startled deer. Seeing a confession of love in his eyes was nothing like hearing it declared aloud. This was a look that would make time stop, if it could. Soft and sharp at once, an aching tenderness edged with sorrow, naked proof of a heart already broken. Here I stood in a dragonfly dress, holding his arm, and he knew our time was almost over.

A thousand wings unfurled inside me. I chased after them, trying to silence them, stuff them back down where they'd do no harm, but I might as well have been in the middle of a whirling vortex of butterflies, attempting to capture each one by hand. I became conscious of the heat of Rook's skin through the fabric of his silk jacket, and that ever so slightly, my hand had begun trembling.

He couldn't say anything in front of Lark, and he didn't need to. I saw everything I needed to know reflected back at me in his eyes.

What was I feeling? How could I be certain?

Love between us was impossible. I forced myself to confront what would become of us if I allowed this feeling to take flight. There were only two options: drink from the Green Well, or condemn us both to death. Meeting his gaze, I let the resolve show on my face. I could permit neither. I was stronger than my emotions. If I lived a thousand times, not once would I destroy my own life and another's for love. A storm gathered in my breast; the butterflies fell fluttering weakly to the ground.

With a sharp intake of breath, Rook looked away.

According to my head, I'd done the right thing. But my heart yawned dark and hollow with the emptiness his averted gaze

left behind. I wondered if my head and heart would ever rec-
oncile, or whether I'd just cursed myself to relive this moment
for the rest of my years, half assured I'd made the only choice
available to me, half always whispering *if only*, the whole of me
filled with bitter regret.

The Bird Hole creaked. The floor shivered beneath my feet,
and the walls' wicker branches began twining about like thread
in a loom, weaving, tumbling, bowing outward. I clenched
Rook's arm by reflex. Lark howled devilishly at the look on
my face. All around us the room transformed, and a panicked
thought gripped me: during that single intimate moment, had
Rook and I broken the Good Law after all?

Twelve

THE WICKER floor cascaded downward, starting at the tips of my shoes. Slender birch supports rose from the ground to meet the newly forming stairway at intervals, creating elegant arches above and below, their branches fanning out as banisters.

In mere seconds I stood at the top of a broad, sweeping stair grander than that of any palace, stretching down five stories or more. At the bottom a crowd of fair folk awaited, arranged around a semicircle of open grass to which I assumed we were about to descend. Gadfly knelt in the middle of it, his hair glinting silver in the sun. As I watched he stood, reviewed the tip of his index finger, and then discreetly brought it to his lips, sucking away the blood. He had done all of this, it seemed, with little more than a single drop.

My pulse raced stumbling along. Though my worst fear hadn't come to pass, I now possessed ample material with

which to replace it. There were even more fair folk gathered here than there had been in the meadow before, and as grand as Rook looked beside me, I was the one they'd truly come to see. All of them were dressed to perfection in the delicate pinks, greens, blues, and yellows of a spring garden, resplendent in silver embroidery and mother-of-pearl buttons, with jewelry that glittered as brightly as their immortal eyes. I knew if I walked among them for hours, I wouldn't find a single chipped nail or hair out of place. And I also knew that each and every one of them could kill me as easily, and as casually, as dropping a teacup.

Gadfly inclined his head to us.

One foot in front of the other. That's all it took. Yet the descent seemed to stretch on for minutes rather than seconds, and the crowd waited in complete silence, the only sound the susurrus of my gown's fabric slithering over the steps behind us. The closer we grew, the more unnatural the multitude of fair folk looked. The flawlessness that only nagged at me a little in the presence of one or two of their kind amplified to a sensation of dread when I was confronted by so many, as though I were beheld by an army of living dolls.

As soon as my first shoe touched the grass, a delicate chime of laughter, sighs, and whispered conversation rippled outward through the crowd. And so the introductions began.

When Gadfly turned around, scrabbling ensued among the fair folk in the front. A woman with arresting hazel eyes emerged victorious. She adjusted her hat back into place with a queenly smile as she swept forward, placing her hand in Gadfly's. She wore a lilac dress with a high lace collar that strangled her slender neck, and the flaw in her glamour, unnaturally sharp

cheekbones, was more subtle than most. Like many of the other fair folk present, she was fair-skinned—a common spring court characteristic, whereas the autumn and summer courts tended toward richer complexions like Rook's, every shade of sunlight-gold and acorn-brown and deep umber.

"Isobel, I'd like you to meet Foxglove," said Gadfly. I curtsied deeply. "Foxglove, this is Isobel, though you already know her by reputation." She curtsied back.

I knew her by reputation too. She was the fair one who'd stolen Mrs. Firth's vowels. I had always counted myself lucky that she'd never come calling on me.

"I am *utterly* thrilled by your visit," she said, leaning close enough that her breath tickled my hair. It had a sweet flowery aroma over a base note of some rich and deadly spice. "I've followed your work ever since it began appearing in the courts. I would so love to have a portrait done while you're here."

My jaw already ached from smiling, and the ordeal had only just begun. "Thank you. It would be my pleasure."

"You're a darling," she replied, with hunger in her eyes.

Fair folk came forward in an endless stream. Soon my knees creaked from curtsying and pleasantries numbed my brain. The whole time Rook and I stood side by side as if we were strangers, never meeting each other's eyes. Many of the fair folk I greeted were current or former patrons, like Swallowtail, who loudly engaged me in a conversation about his past commission as others in line peered jealously over his shoulders. All of them were familiar with my Craft.

As the afternoon dragged on, I grew increasingly impatient. I needed time to gather supplies before dusk. More importantly, I needed to send word of my situation to Emma—in writing—

now that I was at last in a position to do so. News delivered verbally by a fair folk messenger, if indeed Gadfly could spare one from a tea party, would only leave her stewing until the sun came up, trying to figure out if I was really dead or injured and they'd figured out some twisty way to make it sound otherwise.

So I was distracted, wondering how I could escape before it grew too late, when Gadfly pulled forth another fair one and introduced her as Aster.

"I think you will be particularly delighted to meet our Aster," he said, with an extra veneer of enthusiasm. "She was a mortal once, like you, and drank from the Green Well. When was that, Aster?"

"It must have been some centuries ago now—though it seems like just yesterday," she replied in a soft, wispy voice, like willow branches stirred by a breeze.

My attention snapped back into focus at once. Had I not known, I wouldn't have been able to tell Aster apart from the rest. She was perhaps a little less tall, but not remarkably so. Flowers were woven into her wavy, waist-length black hair. Her skin looked starkly pale in contrast, which only accentuated her glamour's flaw: she was inhumanly gaunt. Her collarbones and ribs protruded from her chest above her gown's neckline, and her shoulders looked as fragile as a bird's bones. She watched me closely with brown eyes nearly as dark as mine.

We exchanged curtsies. "It's a pleasure to meet you, Aster. I hope to drink from the Green Well one day myself." The ability to lie had never seemed as useful or necessary. "How do you find being a fair one?"

She gave me a flickering smile that didn't reach the rest of her face. "It's lovely, you know. There are so few things to worry about—I hardly ever have cares these days. I remember getting sick, or the way I used to feel pain, and there's so much . . . less of it now." Her smile faded and came back.

"That sounds wonderful." I was aware of everyone watching me, and made sure my expression didn't change. "The forest is so beautiful compared to Whimsy."

"Yes," she said. "Oh, yes."

"Were you a master of the Craft?" I inquired.

Her wan smile lit her face like the striking of a flint. "I was! One must be to drink from the well, of course. Let's see—I was"—she faltered horribly—"you know, I seem to have forgotten the name for it. Ha ha! How strange!"

My skin crawled, a thousand many-legged insects skittering from my scalp all the way down to my toes. I desperately hoped the fair folk couldn't see my hair standing on end. "Perhaps you could describe it to me," I suggested, "and I'll find the name for you."

"Well, I made words. I made words for books, the ones that tell stories that aren't true. Isn't that odd? I used to do that myself!"

"You were a writer," I said.

Her pupils swallowed up her eyes. For a heartbeat I had the terrifying notion she was about to leap at me and tear my throat out. Then I saw her hands fisted so tightly, gripping the fabric of her dress, that her knuckles bulged white and her fingers looked fit to break. "Yes, that's it. I was a writer. Ha ha! A writer! Silly me—one does forget such things. We all forget things from time to time."

"Yes, we certainly do." I kept my voice steady with an effort. "May I ask, did you also have the pleasure of visiting the spring court before you drank from the well?"

"Oh, no," she said. "How splendid that would have been. I only came here afterward, once I'd transformed."

How many fair folk had Aster met before she made her decision? How much had she understood about the consequences of her choice? I couldn't continue my line of questioning without risking suspicion. But it seemed to me that she might not have known what was in store for her, not truly, the same as everyone back in Whimsy.

"I see," I replied. "It was a pleasure to meet you, Aster."

"I'm so glad we had the chance to talk. I do hope you follow in my footsteps. It would be lovely to have you here in the spring court, just lovely." Her fingers gripped and loosened. "Perhaps we might speak a second time before you return to Whimsy, so you can remind me of that word again. Oh, it's amusing how forgetful I am."

My smile felt carved onto my face as she took her leave. Rook shifted beside me, but I dared not look at him. I was chilled to the marrow of my bones. The wintry calls of the Wild Hunt's hounds rose again in my ears, and I saw Hemlock's white, wild-eyed face receding into the darkness. I recalled the hunger tearing forth from behind the polite, cold smile of every fair one I had ever painted. How was it that we had ever come to admire the fair folk—even hope to become them?

"Gadfly," Rook said cheerfully, "I believe Isobel has had enough for the day. You know how mortals are, hardly able to stand up for an hour or two before they collapse from exhaustion. If we're to have any hope of seeing her Craft tomorrow, she will require her remaining energy for—well, whatever it is she needs to do this evening." I heard, rather than saw, his charming half-smile.

"Good gracious. We mustn't interfere with her Craft!" Gadfly raised his voice. "Ladies and gentlemen of the court, you will simply have to wait. We will convene again at supper."

Unhappy exclamations engulfed me. Murmured conversation followed. Numbly, I took Rook's offered arm and allowed him to lead me away from the bottom of the stairs. Lark gamboled after us, waving at her friends, who watched us go with resentful scowls, which to all appearances Lark enjoyed immensely.

"Now we have you all to ourselves," she said, coming around to take my other arm. Rook grimaced, struggling to contain his frustration. He couldn't speak freely in Lark's presence—but her company was a blessing for the same reason. We couldn't be seen alone together too often without drawing suspicion.

I nodded at him, hoping it would tell him everything he wanted to know. I was all right. I was grateful for his intervention. But it didn't make him look any happier.

Lark swung our arms back and forth. "You're awfully quiet, Isobel! You really must be exhausted. What's it like?"

"What's what like?"

"Being exhausted, of course."

Even after spending years in their company, fair folk still had the capacity to surprise me. "It makes you want to sit down, I suppose, or go to sleep. Anything that doesn't require you to move or think."

"So it's like having too much wine," Lark said knowingly.

I raised my eyebrows, thinking that if Gadfly were human, someone would need to have a talk with him. "Yes, but without the good parts. And, um, most of the bad parts, really," I added, recalling my first, and last, experience with Emma's holiday brandy.

Lark shrieked straight into my ear. "That doesn't make any sense at all," she said once she'd recovered. "What are we going to do now? Please don't take a nap, it would be ever so dull."

"No, I'd like to get started gathering materials for pigments. Do you think the two of you could help?" I shot Rook a sideways glance. "Or is that chore beneath a prince?"

Finally, he smiled—a real smile this time, dimple and all. "Ordinarily I'd say so, but I find I can't pass up the chance to get stains all over Gadfly's wretched clothes. It may not matter to Lark but it certainly does to him. So tell us what to find, and we are at your service."

They took me some distance from what I had begun to think of as the spring court's throne room, to a place that looked more like normal forest, and sat me down on a stump. There I described to them what I needed. Blueberries, blackberries, elderberries, mulberries—any berries they could find. Wild onions and apple bark for yellow; walnut shells for brown. For black, I could use soot.

"But what are the eggs for?" Rook asked indignantly, looming above me at his full height.

"I need something to bind the pigments into paints. Typically one uses linseed or spike lavender oil, but egg yolk is a readier alternative." Seeing his expression, I added, "Just don't collect raven eggs, for heaven's sake. Oh, and get fresh ones—I can't have chicks popping out of them."

"I'll eat those for you," Lark assured me, the very image of a proper young lady.

"You'd get along with my . . . never mind." God, how could I sit here enjoying myself while my family waited at home, think-ing me dead or worse? Rook glanced at me, but fortunately Lark didn't notice anything amiss.

"Let's see who can get them first!" she cried, and vanished. A bush's leaves trembled nearby as though something had whipped past them at a high speed.

"Isobel," Rook said softly. "When you spoke to Aster—"

Lark's voice interrupted from far away. "Hurry up!"

He hesitated, torn. I glanced around to make sure we were alone, then took his hand. Right away he looked down at our intertwined fingers as though they contained the secrets of the universe.

"Go on," I said. "I'm the one who came up with this plan, remember? Right now I could really use your help."

Conflict played over his features. But Lark called for him again, and he didn't linger.

That evening the fair folk gathered to watch the preparations for my Craft. We'd set up in the same clearing so we didn't have to go back and forth, and it wasn't long before the court arrived, more ethereal lords and ladies appearing unnervingly from thin air whenever I turned my back. Fascinated, they watched me grind up the berries, shells, and bark on a flat stone, then scrape them into a collection of porcelain bowls and teacups Lark had brought from the labyrinth. I cracked the tiny songbird eggs, strained the whites out with my fingers, and mixed the yolk and pigments using a twig. A campfire's sticks popped and shifted nearby, producing the charred wood I'd need for soot.

Pigments were expensive. Before gaining the fair folk's patronage I'd only used charcoal along with whatever colors

I could make myself, and as I worked, my childhood experiments came back to me. Blackberries made the deepest, richest red. Elderberries dried with an ocher tint. Mixed with walnut shell, mulberries created a pleasant medium brown with wine-purple undertones. And blueberries often went on pink, only to darken to a deep indigo over the course of a day. Perhaps ironically, green was the most difficult of all colors to achieve from nature—I would need to experiment with the yellows cooked from onion skin and apple bark, and see what they looked like mixed with my blues.

So absorbed was I that for a time I forgot my audience, focusing on the rapture of color alone. The sun slanted lower and lower, casting a golden edge on all my makeshift tools and feathering my hair with light.

Finally I finished crushing the charred wood from the fire. "I think I'm done," I said, meaning to address Rook and Lark, but found I spoke instead to an entire crowd of fair folk clustered around me.

"Marvelous," Gadfly declared, as though I were a court alchemist transmuting lead into gold, while I sat looking up at him with egg slime all over my fingers. He offered me a square of peeled birch bark, and I wiped my hands off on the ground before I took it.

"Thank you," I said. "This looks like it will do nicely. Would it be all right if I requested a favor?"

Gadfly inclined his head. "I did tell you you would want for nothing."

"If I write a letter to my family in Whimsy, may I have it delivered? Even by bird, if that's something that can be arranged. The earliest date possible would be ideal," I added hastily, aware that otherwise it might arrive at the front door of our abandoned, tumbledown cottage a hundred years late.

"Certainly. I give my word that your letter will reach your home by sunrise two days hence."

"And my aunt Emma will receive it?" I pressed, sensing another loose end.

He gave me a knowing smile. "Never one to forget a detail. I promise it shall be delivered directly into Emma's hand. Now, I confess I've never had the good fortune to watch writing Craft!" And with that he seated himself next to me cross-legged to watch.

"Oh. Er, I'm happy to demonstrate," I replied, trying to ignore his close attention. He peered at the bark in my hand as though I were about to wave my hand and transform it into a dove. I reached for the soot bowl but halted halfway with a sinking realization. "I haven't anything to write with," I said to myself aloud, casting about.

Wind stirred my hair, and Rook hopped onto the stump beside me in raven form, twisting his head to preen his tail feathers. Just when I was about to shoo him off, he seized the longest feather and yanked it from his body. This he handed to me with courtly aplomb. It was warm, and the end of the translucent shaft contained a bead of his amber blood.

I turned the feather in my hands, running my fingertip along its silky edge, to buy myself a little time. I wasn't certain why I felt so touched by the gesture. The feather was one of many, and Rook could grow it back in an instant. When I could stall no longer, I cleared my throat and dabbed its tip on the ground to clean it.

That was, perhaps, a mistake.

Right away the grass bulged and a sapling pushed forth from the wildflowers, rapidly straining upward into a young tree, unfolding branches like a stage prop. Vivid scarlet leaves burst forth in glorious bloom. Its foliage spread across the spring glade triumphantly, and a bit obnoxiously, in what struck me as a truly Rooklike fashion.

"Have a care!" Gadfly exclaimed. "I won't see you defacing my court, Rook. That's terribly unsightly."

Rook spread his wings and released a series of belligerent croaks. I hid a smile.

"Thank you," I whispered to him, rolling the feather's stem between my fingertips.

Gadfly soon forgot the offense as I began scratching out my letter in wet soot. Fair folk might not be able to write, but they could certainly read, so I needed to be careful about what I revealed.

Dear Emma, March, and May, I wrote. *I am safe and well. It pains me to think of the distress my disappearance must have caused you. The truth is that I have been on an unexpected adventure*—I knew Emma would understand how I felt about being on an "adventure"—*and haven't had the opportunity to write you until now. Presently, I'm demonstrating my Craft in the spring court. I was brought here by Rook, the autumn prince, who spirited me away quite suddenly. I look forward to seeing you all again soon. With love, Isobel.*

This would give Emma more questions than answers, but I was running out of room on the little square of bark, so it would have to do. I waited for it to dry, then handed it to Gadfly.

He brought the letter close to his face, examining it with remote fascination. "So simple an act," he said eventually, "and yet, do you know that if a fair one were to attempt what you have just done, he would crumble to dust?"

"I've—heard that, yes."

Gadfly's pale gaze flicked to me. "Make no mistake, it's a small price to pay for the power and beauty of immortality. Yet it does make one wonder, doesn't it? Why do we desire, above all other things, that which has the greatest power to destroy us?"

A chill brushed my spine. Never before had I known Gadfly to wax philosophical about anything more profound than lemon curd. I resisted the urge to look at Rook, wondering if he shared my unease.

"Craft itself doesn't harm you," I pointed out. "You wear it and eat it every day without consequences."

"Ah, yes. Still." He summoned a faint smile. "Some consequences go unseen. One day, you might discover that Craft has the power to undo my kind in ways you'd never imagined. That sounded quite depressing, didn't it? I do apologize." He winked at me. Then he clapped his hands and stood.

Only then did I realize the letter was gone, vanished from his grasp too quickly for me to detect. He'd given his word, I reminded myself, shaking myself free from the lingering oddness of our conversation. Emma would receive it. She'd read it soon, and still fear for me, but at least not think me dead.

"Who would like to help Isobel convey her Crafting materials to the throne?" Gadfly asked, as if mustering a group of schoolchildren. Immediately I was surrounded by a tittering crowd of fair folk lifting the bowls and examining them. At first I was concerned they might upset some of my pigments, but that worry faded when I saw them handle the vessels as though they were enchanted goblets, liable to explode or turn anyone nearby to stone if dropped. Rook, apparently, had done enough helping for the day, because when I stood he flapped over my shoulder until I gave him permission to perch there, and then sat regarding everyone with an upturned beak.

We walked back in a procession like something out of a tapestry—me at the very front, wearing a gossamer gown with a prince riding on my shoulder in animal guise, and a fairy host parading behind. The setting sun lit everything aglow, so that even the insects rising from the disturbed wildflowers looked like motes of gold suspended in the air.

When we reached the throne room it became clear work had been done in my absence. A long table was set up along the birch-lined path to the throne, caparisoned in white cloth and draped down the center with an embroidered runner that must have measured forty feet or more. Its pale green and silver silk matched the chair cushions and the designs on the fine china place settings. But the food put it all to shame—glittering mounds of grapes and plums and cherries, stacks of frosted pastries, roast goose and partridge still gleaming from the spit.

"Who's done it all?" I murmured to Rook. "Does everyone take turns at playing servant, or do the squirrels and hares come pouring out of the woods to set everything up while you're gone?"

He let me know what he thought of my teasing by flipping around and flicking his tail at my nose.

The table was so impressive I didn't notice the smaller addition until we drew nearer. A brocade chair had been set up a few paces away from the throne, and before it an easel. The easel was decorative, meant for displaying works rather than painting them, but it would serve its purpose. I found the amount of birch bark Gadfly had acquired for me a great deal more daunting. It was piled higher than the chair itself, evidence of his expectations.

"I fear it will be quite late by the time we've finished supper," Gadfly said, drawing up beside me. "Perhaps you would grace us with your Craft tomorrow morning?" And he pulled out the chair at the head of the table.

Thirteen

I DEARLY wished I could have refused the honor. But it would be impolite, and all glittering eyes were upon me. I curtsied, and as I sat, Rook took wing from my shoulder and transformed next to me in time to push my chair back in. Gadfly deferred to him with a smile, while I wondered if that had been at all a wise thing for Rook to do.

The fair folk came forward and took their seats. Lark sat on my left, and Rook on my right. Gadfly went all the way down the table and sat last at the foot, directly across from me, half obscured by the delicacies mounded up over the long distance. With a rustle of silk and muslin, everyone else descended to their places.

The feast that followed was bizarrely fascinating. Rather than using spoons, forks, or ladles, the fair folk simply took what they wanted using their fingers. So beautiful were their forms, and so delicate their movements, that the practice didn't strike me as repulsive. No servingmen circled the tables—if a fair one wanted something too far away to reach, he either stood up and got it himself or had it passed to him, hand to hand, with the risk it might get eaten capriciously by someone else along the way. Wine bottles went around and we all poured ourselves a glass. My tastes weren't refined, but I took one sip and knew the vintage was worth its weight in silver. Wine was one of the few things we didn't make in Whimsy; it was imported from the World Beyond at great danger and expense.

I selected pieces of fruit and pastry the same way as the fair folk, but when it came to eating the goose, which glistened with honey and spices, I took up my knife and fork. As I carved the meat I felt I was being watched. By the time I looked up several fair folk were wielding silverware, carefully watching my example, and a few others examining their utensils curiously. It was obvious most of them had never dined with silverware before. Why, then, did they arrange their place settings this way?

Because that's the way humans do it, I thought, with the smallest prickle of unease.

The conversation went from my Craft to other human works. The fair folk discussed clothing and swords. I fielded a number of baffling questions, and had to explain again that being a master at one Craft didn't automatically reward me with expertise in the others. As the feast wore on, my hope of overhearing even a scrap of useful information about the other courts, the summerlands, and corrupted fairy beasts crumbled beneath the barrage of small talk.

As the sky darkened to night, fireflies came out in such numbers they glittered in the trees like stars. A few fair folk summoned ethereal lights in different hues that hovered above the table. When I grew cold, Rook was quick to offer me his borrowed jacket—and seemed very glad to be rid of it. Whether the colors suited him or not, the cut of Gadfly's tight-fitting waistcoat certainly flattered his form, and it was an effort not to stare at him in shirtsleeves. The cravat was long gone, leaving his collar open at the throat.

Over time, a strange pattern revealed itself. A smiling fair one passed a dessert or fancy up the table in my direction, only for Rook to intercept it before it reached me. The fifth or sixth time this happened he even had to reach all the way across the table, stretching over a wheel-sized mound of grapes, to snatch it out of Lark's hand. He sent me a troubled glance as he regained his seat, bracing his hand on the armrest. By this time he'd had quite a lot of wine, and I thought it was beginning to show, an observation which made me equally conscious of my own condition. The presence of so many fair folk was, admittedly, easier to endure after a few glasses.

I leaned toward him, trying to ignore the way the lights swung when I moved, and murmured, "Are they enchanted? Poisonous?"

"Not as such," he replied in a tone of discomfort.

"Then why?"

Our eyes met. "It would be better if you did not know," he said, with such a miserable look I didn't press further.

But Rook couldn't spot all of them, and eventually I discovered the reason for myself. Lark came hurrying back with a handful of tartlets, ate one herself, and handed me another. When I touched it, it changed. The pastry withered and fuzzed gray with mold. Whatever filling had been inside dribbled out as an unidentifiable black sludge, reeking of decay. Even worse, the deflated morsel squirmed in my hand; it was full of maggots. I threw the pastry shell to the table, missing my plate, and shot upright amid a noisy clatter of crystal and silverware, shoving my chair back with the backs of my legs.

Just like that the evening's magic shattered. All the fair folk stared at me from up and down the table, and though I knew it had to be my imagination, their eyes looked catlike, glamourless in the shivering lights. Gadfly's were so pale they glowed like a candle flame shining through quartz. My breath quickened. Then Lark, gazing up at me in stupefaction, gave a raucous laugh and snatched the spoiled pastry off the tablecloth. As soon as she took it, it wasn't spoiled anymore—it looked a bit squashed, but otherwise exactly the same as it had before. She stuffed it into her mouth.

An amused titter went around the table, and the tense feeling in the air evaporated. Slowly, I sank back down. I looked at my plate to make sure I hadn't imagined the entire thing, that it wasn't some cruel trick they had played on me. I couldn't say whether I was more relieved or disgusted to see the maggots still writhing away on the china.

A muscle moved in Rook's cheek. He exchanged my plate for his own, bending close enough that his hair brushed my still-raised arm. Afterward, he retrieved a handkerchief from the front pocket of the jacket he'd lent me and gave it to me in silence. I wiped off my fingers, but it wasn't the mold or maggots making my stomach revolt. I had touched mold many times before, and would many times again. I'd handled my fair share of spoiled food. And of course, I'd watched March eat all sorts of things.

No, it was the knowledge that all around me sat empty

people in rotting clothes, nibbling on flyblown trifles while they spoke of nothing of consequence with fixed smiles on their false faces. What would this feast look like with all the glamour gone? I imagined fresh grapes gleaming next to a dish of pudding turned brown as mud, swarming with larvae. Clotted fluid pouring from a bottle, imbibed without protest. The wine soured in my gut, as if it too had spoiled and festered.

My simmering nausea threatened to boil over. I swallowed several times as saliva flooded my mouth.

"I didn't realize fair folk could project their glamours," I said to Rook, desperate for an explanation, a distraction. "Lark couldn't change the dress until she held it."

"It is an uncommon ability. The illusion isn't as complete as a glamour—if a mortal touches it, it falls apart. Foxglove is the one doing it now, if I'm not mistaken."

Foxglove looked up the table at us, hearing her name spoken even in Rook's low voice. She smiled.

"Does the illusion affect the"—I hesitated—"the taste, at all? For you?"

"Ah," Rook said. "No. But generally, we care more about the way it appears." At least he had the good sense to look embarrassed. "This is the main point of contention between the winter court and the rest of fairykind, if you had wondered," he went on impulsively. "They believe that surrounding oneself with human things, all of this, even wearing a glamour, is a perversion of our true nature."

"And how dispiriting their lives must be," said Gadfly behind us. "I do so enjoy being perverse. In fact I rather think it is my true nature."

I would have jumped if not for the wine slowing my reflexes.

I was certain that a split second ago, Gadfly had still been at the opposite end of the table. I looked over my shoulder, unease sloshing in my head as I turned. Rook and I hadn't been behaving too familiarly toward each other, had we?

"Thank you for your hospitality, Gadfly," I said, fumbling for the first polite remark that came to mind. "The feast is lovely."

His spidery fingers alit on the back of my chair. "And yet it isn't quite, is it? Isobel, I'm sorry you encountered one of our less . . . immaculate dishes. I thought Rook up to the task of watching over you."

Beside me, Rook frowned. An inexplicable urge to defend him seized me. "He has done as well as anyone possibly could," I replied. It came out more forcefully than I intended, and I added quickly, "Truly, I'm fortunate to have been waited on by a prince in the first place."

"Yes, of course," Gadfly said, glancing between the two of us.

Shit. I plastered on my politest, most vacuous smile, refusing to give him anything else to go on. Let him think me charmed by the attention of a handsome fairy prince, and nothing more. Not that there *was* anything more. Rook's feelings were the ones that needed hiding, not mine.

"I do admit, sir," I continued, "that the incident's left me feeling unwell. If I'm to rise early and begin my Craft at a reasonable hour tomorrow morning, I think I ought to retire before midnight."

"Very sensible." Gadfly's fingers drummed out a thoughtful rhythm, too close to my cheek for comfort. "Lark, would you please show Isobel to a room? Our best, of course."

Rook seemed about to protest, or perhaps offer to help me

instead, so I bumped his knee under the table as a warning. I had no doubt he'd find his way up eventually, but it needed to be more discreet than escorting me upstairs in full view of the court.

Lark wobbled upright and insinuated herself around my arm. "I have sooooo many nightgowns," she said, towing me toward the tree stairs.

"I want to come!" exclaimed one of her friends, who had been introduced to me as Nettle.

Lark whipped around and hissed at her. Nettle sat back down. Lark smiled prettily, tightening her grip on my arm.

When we reached the tree's base and began our ascent, the feast's lights glittered like a whole city behind us. Weaving up the vines behind an equally unsteady Lark, I feared for my life nearly as much as I had during the Barrow Lord incident. Somehow we reached the top unscathed. Enough starlight filtered through the labyrinth's leaves to see by, and the corridors sparkled like a diamond mine with fireflies.

"Would you mind if I fetched my things from the Bird Hole?" I asked. The ring had lurked at the back of my thoughts all evening, and after the feast's strained conclusion I couldn't bear going without it any longer.

"I don't know why you care about your boring dress, but that's where I keep all my nightgowns, so we have to go there anyway. You'd better not wear it to bed!"

"I won't," I assured her. But I'd certainly keep my iron close.

By my estimation I tried on nearly a dozen silk nightgowns, all of them flimsier than a slip and nearly see-through, though I found I didn't really mind—the final, conclusive sign that I'd had too much to drink. Lark settled on a green one, deciding this was to be my signature color. It gathered beneath the bosom and had a questionable number of ribbons for sleeping in, unless perhaps one used a hammock and needed to be tied down during high winds. But it was stunning. I wished I had a mirror to see myself in. No, I wished I could see what Rook's face would look like if he saw me wearing it, how different it would be from the way he'd gazed at me in the dragonfly dress. I stepped back from the thought immediately, my face burning, but no matter how hard I tried to ignore it, the fizzy glow of the idea wouldn't fade.

Finally Lark permitted me to gather up my things and led me through the twinkling labyrinth toward another room. I stopped dead in my tracks at the doorway.

The room contained a four-poster bed, and dozens of Gadflies stared at me from within. Some polished, some dusty, some hanging slightly askew, the portrait frames hung on almost every square inch of the room, depicting Gadfly in different fashions across the centuries. They were secured in place by leafy vines, so that they appeared partially grown into the walls. A few were my own work—perhaps eight in all. I hadn't seen most of them in years, and felt a shock when I spotted them, as if recognizing the faces of old friends in a crowd. In the blinking firefly light, their eyes seemed to move.

"Surely I can't sleep in Gadfly's room," I said.

There was no resisting. Lark tugged me inside. "Of course you can! Gadfly only sleeps once a month, during the new moon. The only other reason he comes in is to look at his portraits. Since this is your Craft, he'd be very pleased to have you stay here."

That made sense in the bizarre way of fair folk, and no

doubt Gadfly thought it a great privilege to spend a restive night being stared at by all his faces. A flurry of laughter rose up from the feast below, and Lark gave a disconsolate pause.

"If you'd like to go back down, I won't blame you," I said. "I won't be good company once I've gone to bed."

She grasped my hand. "Oh, are you certain? Absolutely certain? I just can't bear the thought of you being lonely up here all by yourself."

I smiled. "I won't be lonely. I can hear everyone down below, and I'm so tired I'll fall asleep instantly."

"You're wonderful." Lark clasped my hand to her chest. "I knew we'd be the best of friends. I'll see you tomorrow, Isobel!" And she released me and pelted from the room.

I shivered, stuffing my hand into my armpit to warm it. Then I put my clothes down on the covers, sat, unlaced my boots, and slipped beneath the blankets—a fine goose-down coverlet with soft sheets beneath. For some time, I watched the doorway. When Lark didn't reappear I stole my hand out to feel around in my dress pocket. I held my breath as I blindly searched the folds, imagining what might have happened if a fair one had discovered the iron. But presently my fingertips bumped its reassuring shape, and I twisted beneath the sheets to slip it into one of my stockings in the dark.

Conversation and laughter drifted up from below, almost comfortingly human. Yet I could not, would not fall asleep. Above and all around me, Gadfly's smile shifted subtly in the winking firefly glow. At the periphery of my vision, the changeable light made his eyes seem to move, and sometimes even blink. I had the feeling of being watched without the luxury of knowing for certain that it was only a feeling. And it occurred to me I hadn't checked under the bed—a child-ish notion—but it wasn't difficult to imagine a fair one lying down there in the dark, spidery fingers folded over his chest like a corpse, smiling to himself as he prepared to leap out and surprise me . . .

Wishing it were safe to wear my ring, I clenched my hand so tightly my nails dug dents in my palm.

It felt like over an hour passed; it might have been less. Something clattered loudly in the hallway.

"Wretched teapot!" Rook's voice exclaimed in vexation.

Just like that, my fear melted away. My chest shook with laughter at the image of Rook staggering, drunk and affronted, through the labyrinth's crowded hallways, being assaulted by falling teapots. "Rook," I whispered, trusting he would hear me, "are you all right out there?"

A mortified silence. Then, coolly: "I haven't the faintest idea why I *wouldn't* be all right."

"That's true," I said. "You slew a Barrow Lord, you shouldn't have any trouble with a kettle."

He came into the room, wrestling with Gadfly's green waist-coat. When he'd gotten it off he cast it aside onto the floor like a piece of rubbish. Then he strode right over and, in one smooth motion, insinuated himself into the bed next to me, facing me, under the covers, with the bold and unselfconscious vanity of a cat sitting down on an open book.

I lifted myself on an elbow. My skin prickled with the awareness that his bent leg was almost touching mine—that I could feel his body heat across the narrow space beneath the linens. Recalling my state of dress, and my dangerous thought from earlier, I drew the blankets close.

"What are you doing?" I asked. "You can't sleep here."

"Yes, I can. In fact, I must. I can't let any harm befall you, so it's best I stay close."

"You could offer to sleep on the floor, like a gentleman."

He appeared horrified by the suggestion.

"And I'm not certain you're in any state to protect me," I went on, sensing a lost cause. "Just now you were almost assassinated by a teapot."

"Isobel." Rook looked at me gravely. "Isobel, listen. The teapot is of no consequence. I can defeat anyone, at any time."

"Oh, is that so? That's the truth?"

"Yes," he replied.

I grappled with exasperated fondness. Despite how annoying he was being, I found it shockingly difficult to resist smiling. "Then you must be very drunk."

"I am not. There may have been a lot of wine, but I'm royalty, you know. I'm the autumn prince. Therefore, I'm only a little drunk." With that he closed his eyes.

"You can't sleep here. You really, really can't, it's too—"

The room's leaves trembled as someone came racing up the hallway. "Oh, no," I groaned. "Quickly, get under the bed, or transform—"

Wind lifted the covers, and a soft, slithery maelstrom of feathers caressed my arms. When it settled Rook crouched indignantly in raven form among the tousled bedclothes, wings akimbo, as though his body had transformed automatically on my suggestion without his agreeing to it. Before he could change his mind, I snatched him beneath the covers and clasped him against my stomach.

Right as I finished, Lark peered around the doorway. She

stared at me for a moment while I pretended to sleep, then giggled and raced away again.

"No," I said, when Rook began struggling. "If you're going to stay, you must be subtle about it."

He kicked his legs and nibbled my fingers, trying to free himself so he could transform again. I saw that more extreme tactics were necessary.

"What a pretty bird you are," I crooned.

His struggling slowed, then stilled. I felt him cock his head.

"What a lovely bird," I repeated in a syrupy voice. "Yes, you're the loveliest bird." I stroked his back. He made a pleased muttering sound in his breast. Soon his smug silence indicated that he was quite content to remain as he was, so long as I continued my praise.

I knew I wasn't truly safe now, but Rook's presence, such as it was, came as an undeniable comfort. The day's exertions drew over me like heavy wool. Rook's heart beat against my fingertips through his soft feathers, and my eyes sank closed as I murmured drowsy endearments to the spoiled prince nestled against my stomach, warm within a nest of blankets.

Wink, wink, wink, went Gadfly's eyes overhead. A hundred of him watched us with unknowable smiles as we drifted off to sleep.

Fourteen

THE LINE of fair folk waiting for a portrait stretched so far down the tree-lined approach to the throne that I couldn't see the end of it. No evidence of last night's feast remained. Try as I might, I couldn't spy a single grape or crumb on the mossy lawn. The entire evening might as well have been an illusion.

Presently Foxglove sat across from me, wearing a smile that suggested her tight collar was slowly asphyxiating her. I wondered how she had achieved the coveted first place in line, and then decided not to think about it too closely.

Queasiness curdled my stomach. Formulating my grand plan had been one thing; executing it was another. What if Foxglove saw the results and flew into a rage as Rook had? She had no reason to, I told myself—the context was completely different—but the fact remained that if they turned on me, I had only my wits and one iron ring for protection, now a hard lump inside my tightly laced boot. *And,* I thought . . . *and Rook.*

I knew, with the same unshakable certainty that sunrise came at dawn, that Rook would defend me from the other fair folk even at the cost of his own life. The thought was not romantic. Rather, it was grim. If this scenario ever came to pass, I couldn't think of any way it might end without both of us dead.

I spared a glance toward where he sat near Gadfly's throne. He looked elegant but uncomfortable on the brocade chair that had been brought for him, bent over restlessly with his elbow resting on his thigh, half-listening to whatever Lark was prattling into his ear. He caught me looking, and our eyes met. I noticed, for no particular reason, that a lock of dark hair had fallen over his cheek. Quickly, I returned my attention to my work.

For Foxglove's portrait, I had chosen human joy. It seemed to me that what passed for joy among fair folk came in two varieties. The first was something akin to the self-righteous, frigid gladness a cheated-on wife might feel upon hearing that her husband's mistress had taken a fatal fall down a flight of stairs. The second was a vain, selfish, and indulgent pleasure: a rich nobleman calculating that his silver mine had earned so much money he could survive on caviar alone for the next three centuries, were he to live long enough to enjoy it.

And so as I inked Foxglove's features in blueberry pigment with the tip of Rook's quill, I gave her the swelling, radiant joy of being swept up in a lover's arms; of seeing a beloved figure coming down the road after months apart, and recognizing his silhouette against the morning light. Without the crisp and glossy perfection of oil paint on canvas there was something raw about my work, less beautiful, less realistic, but *stronger.*

A stray line by Foxglove's mouth that I couldn't correct suggested she was holding in a smile. Laughter welled up behind her crinkled eyes. Working in this imperfect medium made it easier to transmute humanity, the court alchemist turning gold back into lead.

When I was finished, I rose and curtsied. Foxglove approached to take the sheaf of bark from the stand. All around, the court held an indrawn breath. No one spoke, and I sensed an unusual stillness from Gadfly's direction. Though only a heartbeat passed, a lone heartbeat in which Foxglove expressionlessly scanned my work, the pressure built and built in my chest until I felt like screaming.

"Oh, how quaint!" she exclaimed in a high, clear voice like the ringing of a fork against a crystal glass. She turned the portrait just long enough for the waiting fair folk to have an unsatisfying half-second look, and then whipped it around again to resume her own perusal. The quality of her smile had changed. She had an empty look in her eyes. While the court whispered gaily behind her, the prior tension diffused, she stood there frozen, staring at a version of herself that felt human joy. No one noticed the oddness of it but me.

No one but me and Gadfly, I corrected myself, and Rook, glancing toward the throne again. They too watched Foxglove closely.

Lark's words came back to me: *Just like how Gadfly knows things before they happen.*

Earlier that morning, he had declined the honor of sitting for my first demonstration. I hadn't made anything of it at the time, but now I wondered. Was he waiting for something? Something he had seen?

Movement fluttered in the corner of my eye. I looked back in time to see Foxglove walking briskly out of sight, the portrait held in front of her as though she'd unwillingly been given an infant to hold for the first time in her life.

Finely, almost imperceptibly, the feather shook between my fingers. I held my breath, seeking calm.

Swallowtail approached next. His flaw was his hair, which was spider-silk blond and so impossibly fine it floated about his head like milkweed fluff. He looked to be between Lark and Rook in age, and his large eyes and youthful features lent themselves well to an expression of human wonder. He dashed away clutching his portrait when I was finished and went down the line boastfully showing it to everyone, particularly those who had several hours left to wait.

The day stretched on. Each portrait was a single stepping-stone, the sum of which would form a path home. I lost count of how many portraits I did, marking them only by the emotions I used: curiosity, surprise, amusement, bliss. The pigments dwindled in their teacups.

Throughout it all I felt Rook watching me, and firmly avoided sorrow.

Every fair one reacted differently to seeing themselves transformed. Some laughed, as if at a delightful joke. Some flinched and giggled skittishly. Most of those, I observed, were younger-looking fair folk. Others, usually the older ones, stood and stared like Foxglove. And a few more went and sat down, gazing quietly into the distance, with such an inhuman expression I couldn't begin to guess at their thoughts. Though fair folk ceased aging once they looked about like Gadfly, it seemed to me these were the oldest ones of all.

Painting straight through the day was as arduous as running a marathon. My right elbow ached from being held for hours in a bent position. My buttocks and knees became sore from sitting. My fingers—cramped around the quill—first grew stiff, and then painful, and then numb, joints spasming whenever I straightened them. Most of all, my face hurt from smiling. My frozen expression must have eventually become rather horrific, but none of the fair folk appeared to notice.

After a time, many of those who had had their portraits done gathered for games on the lawn. I was relieved to find myself no longer the sole focus of attention as the courtiers played shuttle-cocks and ninepins nearby. A spirited atmosphere overtook the gathering. Behind me I heard, rather than saw, Rook shift in his chair. My smile grew genuine as I imagined how much it taxed him to stay put for so long.

Finally he exclaimed, "I must say I don't see the point of sitting here any longer!" and trotted off to beat Swallowtail at lawn billiards. He then lost a game of blind man's buff to Fox-glove, but rallied and defeated everyone shamelessly at both ninepins and shuttlecocks. Lark fluttered behind him like an inquisitive butterfly as he proceeded to win every match in his path.

The fair folk played at a human speed, I noted with interest. Perhaps this was the only rule that provided a challenge. On several occasions, I saw a feathered projectile fly past a player at a distance they surely could have reached with little effort.

Rook had left his coat behind. Every time he twisted his body, an inch or two of his white shirt showed beneath his tightly fitted waistcoat, accentuating his slimness. His rolled-up sleeves put his muscular forearms on display, and the faintest

sheen of sweat gleamed on his throat above his unbuttoned collar. Having seen him slay fairy beasts without perspiring, I recognized the exertion of holding himself back. With each swing,
each strike, he struggled not to flaunt his power like a war-horse
prancing stiffly in a flimsy parade harness.

Without warning, heat rushed through me. The morning
before last—had he broken a sweat then, too? I remembered the
way his hands had felt lifting me as though I weighed nothing,
running down my sides, pressing me against the tree . . .

With burning cheeks, I finished contouring the lines of my
subject's hair, whipped it off the easel, and passed it on. He ran
off laughing at the expression of befuddlement on his portrait's
face and settled into a game of ninepins. My next subject sat
down, smoothing her skirts over bare, bird-frail knees.

The heat died like coals dashed across winter flagstones.

It was Aster.

"Good afternoon, Aster." I scraped up the last of my reserves
addressing her as though nothing was wrong—as though merely
looking at her didn't make my skin crawl. "Do you have anything in mind, or would you like me to choose an emotion for
you?"

"Oh, you choose, please. I'm certain you can choose better
than I." She gave me a wan smile. But her eyes . . . her eyes were
ravenous. Twisted in swaths of muslin, her hands trembled. I
knew what she wanted, and I wasn't sure I could give it to her.
Or, more importantly, whether I *should*.

She wanted to see herself mortal again.

I dipped Rook's quill. A bitter smell of crushed acorns rose
from the bowl as I made my first line in dark ocher. I felt as
though I were pouring a glass of water that I was about to show,

from the other side of prison bars, to a person dying of thirst. In that moment, I hated the Green Well more than I ever had before. I hated that it existed, and that people wanted it. I hated that I had sat on the edge of it and not felt the vileness radiating from its mossy stones. How dare it look the way it did, an evil thing, a hollow thing, surrounded by ferns and bluebells and singing birds. Had Aster had any way of knowing the eternal horror to which she was agreeing? The tip of the feather quivered with the force of my anger.

I outlined her features in bold, violent strokes. The ink spattered as I worked, giving the sense that her portrait was coalescing onto the page from particles of darkness. Her sharp chin, hollow cheeks, and overlarge eyes took shape beneath my hand, raw in form, but true. I changed the angle of her face so that it was slightly lifted; her eyes gazed directly at the viewer. *How dare you?* they blazed. Her mouth was shut, but her upper lip curled. *How dare you do this to me? Where are your consequences?* She looked as though she were about to spring forth from the page to enact vengeance—to wrap her fingers around someone's throat. *I shall deliver them to you!*

Thus I gave Aster my rage. Ugly rage, human rage, the rage she deserved to feel but could not, because it had been taken from her forever.

When I finished, I was breathing heavily and a strange energy buzzed through my veins, as though my blood had been replaced with a howling wind. As I met the eyes of Aster's portrait, a thrill sparked through me. She was alive on the page in a way even my Craft rarely achieved. She was real again.

I needed to stand. The gale force within me demanded movement. I rose painfully from the chair, unable to feel my thighs or buttocks, my knees creaking. I brought the portrait to Aster, who watched me approach with polite confusion. The bark shook in my hand. At the last moment, I remembered to curtsy. Across the court, dozens of elegant forms bobbed obligingly back.

"I needed to get up," I explained in a harsh voice. I cleared my throat. "Mortals' bodies aren't designed to sit in one place for long periods of time."

Murmurs of understanding rippled through the line. Everyone had been observing me, trying to make sense of my actions. Yes, of course; mortals were so fragile . . .

I handed Aster her portrait.

She studied it. A curtain of long, dark hair fell over the side of her face, so I couldn't see her expression. Finally she raised a finger and traced the still-wet ink, smudging it. She dragged the smudge all the way across the bark, to the edge of the canvas, pressing hard enough that I thought she might crack my work in two. When she reached the edge and released it, the bark flipped up to its original position. She turned her stained fingertip over to look at it.

"I remember," she whispered. And she angled her head just slightly toward me, enough for me to catch a glint of her eyes through her hair.

A bell might as well have tolled through the clearing—a bell only I could hear. In Aster's eyes rage, true human rage, struggled like a fire guttering wildly in the night. Gooseflesh rose all over my body.

So quietly I almost didn't hear her, she said, "Thank you."

The spell broke. She stood up, her expression blank, so blank I almost wondered if I had imagined that angry spark, but I knew I couldn't have made it up or mistaken it. She wandered onto the lawn with her portrait dangling limply from her fingers, apparently without a care in the world. But when she sat she kept the portrait angled downward against her lap, like a secret she was determined to keep.

I steeled myself and turned around.

"Sir," I said to Gadfly, "my Craft has wearied me, and I'm running low on pigment. May I take a break?"

He clapped his hands together. "Of course, Isobel. You needn't even ask, you know. You're the guest in our court, and deserve every courtesy I can offer." The fair folk waiting in line sighed as one, whispering their disappointment. "Now, now," Gadfly chastised them before his attention sprang back to me. "Would you like someone to escort you through the forest? Rook, perhaps?" He suggested this without a hint of guile.

I glanced toward the game of shuttlecocks and found Rook standing there watching me, chest heaving with exertion, his game forgotten. A birdie whizzed past his head, ruffling his hair.

"No, I'll do quite well on my own." I spoke evenly, hearing my own voice as though it came from someone else speaking around a corner. "I plan to remain close by, and I wouldn't wish to trouble the prince over something so small."

I had no way of knowing whether Gadfly's question truly was innocent. If he were to suggest anyone to accompany me, Rook was the natural choice. But I couldn't shake the scrambling paranoia that he *knew*. Perhaps that he had even seen something—something in the future—

I smiled at Gadfly and curtsied my leave. Then slowly, deliberately, I gathered up the teacups and walked away toward the glen, where the top of Rook's autumn tree spread its scarlet leaves in the distance. I felt Rook's gaze searching me, but I didn't once turn to look.

I had to accustom myself, after all, to leaving him behind.

Fifteen

AS I SLOGGED through the undergrowth, I assured myself Rook would be all right. He was probably already languishing insufferably after having beaten everyone at shuttlecocks for the dozenth time over. But why did he have to be so utterly, stupidly transparent? He might as well have I'M IN LOVE WITH ISOBEL! written across his face for everyone to see.

With a frustrated shout, I yanked my boot free from a vine's ensnaring tendrils. Even the delicate spring foliage had started to feel less friendly. Fleeced with clouds, the blue sky beamed as harmlessly as Gadfly's smile, and squirrels bounded along the branches above me, shaking loose showers of white petals. But if I had learned anything from fair folk, it was not to trust the way things appeared.

I cleared the thicket and sat down on the same stump as the afternoon before. A breeze rattled the leaves of Rook's tree, and a few twirled downward, scattering across my lap. I picked one up and traced its edges. Its color stuck out like a sore thumb, much like Rook himself.

Things weren't going entirely as I'd expected. I shouldn't have let myself get so carried away with Aster. There was no mistaking that she had felt real anger, human anger, as impossible as it seemed. Not only that—my portraits had affected some of the others, too. I'd been painting fair folk for years, and never once had I seen such reactions to my Craft. Foxglove had felt something, I was sure of it. Perhaps she had experienced emotion. Or perhaps she had caught a glimpse of what it meant not to, and found herself confronted by the emptiness of her existence, the hollowness of never having once known joy. I wasn't certain which possibility was more alarming—or more dangerous.

All I knew for certain was that I couldn't fail. My life wasn't the only one at stake.

I realized I had torn the leaf apart, stripping it down to its fibrous veins. I flung away the pieces and put my face in my hands. My eyes prickled. My heart ached. Even if everything went perfectly according to plan, and I was working myself up over nothing, I faced a future I was no longer certain I could bear.

"I wish you were here, Emma," I mumbled, wanting nothing more in that moment than my aunt's embrace. She would know what to say. She would reassure me that I wasn't a terrible person because there was a part of me that didn't want to go home. Perhaps she could even convince me that I could live with myself after I buried my heart in the autumnlands and left it behind forever.

"Who's Emma?" a cheerful voice asked, right next to my ear.

I nearly jumped out of my skin. "Lark! I didn't know you were there."

She sat perched on the edge of my stump like her namesake, smiling at me with her hands cupped around a pile of freshly picked blueberries. When she saw my face, her smile vanished. "You're dripping!"

"Yes, I've been crying." Seeing her raised eyebrows I added, "It's what mortals do when we're sad. I miss my aunt, Emma."

"Well, stop now, please. I've brought you some blueberries—Gadfly told me you were out of things for your Craft. Here." She poured the blueberries onto my lap, in the basket my skirts created between my legs. At the last moment she snatched a few back and stuffed them into her mouth.

I felt strangely touched. "Thank you, Lark. That was very thoughtful."

"Yes, I know. I'm simply full of thoughts, but no one cares to realize it, and everyone treats me as though I'm the silliest creature in the spring court."

"I don't, do I?" I asked, concerned.

"No. And that's why I like you so much!" She sprang to her feet. "Come along now, let's find more berries."

With a wet laugh, I plucked one of the blueberries from my lap and popped it into my mouth. Its ripe, tart flavor burst sweetly on my tongue.

A black-eyed raven alit on the uppermost branch of Rook's tree.

Lark grinned, showing each and every one of her sharp, purple-stained teeth.

I knew I shouldn't have eaten that berry—shouldn't have *considered* eating that berry—even before the world spun in a kaleidoscopic wash of color. I plummeted downward as though a hole had opened up in the earth beneath me. The sky receded, growing smaller and smaller, surrounded by a warm, soft, rumpled darkness that I first grasped at frantically as I fell, then recognized with senseless horror as my own clothes.

I thrashed, smothered by fabric on all sides. My body wasn't working the way it should. My face, my limbs, my very bones had taken on an alien assemblage that sent terror jittering up and down my spine. As I strained for any sense of what was going on, two long appendages swiveled on the back of my head. For some reason I sniffed, and my flexible nose twitched in response. My heart beat so rapidly I couldn't identify the feeling at first—it was like a trapped wasp buzzing madly in my chest.

I kicked free of my clothes and hopped through the shoulder-high grass, half-blinded by the sun, finally grasping the nature of my transformation. Lark's enchanted berry had turned me into a rabbit.

Her shriek rang out behind me, stabbing my tender ears. Impossibly, my heartbeat kicked up another notch. I thought my heart might burst as I raced toward a hawthorn bush that loomed above me higher than the tallest bell tower in Whimsy, and broader than a house. The forest had grown so dauntingly large it hardly bore looking at. I needed to get somewhere dark, safe, and enclosed, *right now*.

"Run, run, run!" Lark laughed. "I'm going to catch you, Isobel!"

With a dreadful unspooling of my memories I recalled what she had said to Rook the day before. *Can you turn into a hare for me again and let me chase you about?* I thought of the way

Rook had been ignoring her in favor of paying attention to me instead.

I skidded under the bush, sending dirt and platter-sized leaves flying. My fur slid sleekly beneath branches that hung mere inches above the ground. I zipped forward, aware Lark must have seen me disappear under this bush, and judging by the sound of her laughter, she was already following.

There—a hole! But as I approached the burrow dug into the hawthorn's roots, I shrank from the rank odor emanating from its depths. My instincts screamed *Danger!* Somehow, I knew the thing that lived in this hole would eat me if it got half a chance.

"Oh, you're a quick one! I think I've lost you!" Through a space between the leaves I watched Lark's gigantic feet stomp over to the bush across from mine. She bent and looked under it, her golden hair cascading down in a shimmering wave as huge as royal tapestry.

It was obviously a game to her. Surely she didn't mean me any harm. By the sound of it, she used to play this game with Rook often. Yet if she caught me, would she understand I was a mortal rabbit, not a fair one in rabbit form? Might her fingers go around my little ribs and squeeze them just a bit too hard? I shuddered, recalling that if fair folk caught rabbits they ate them raw.

And what if she was truly upset with me for stealing Rook's attention from her?

Before I had a chance to think about it too hard, she whipped around to stare directly at me. "There you are!" She bared her stained teeth again and scuttled forward bent at the waist, her arms extended, fingers curled into greedy claws. I spun and zoomed off, targeting a stand of honeysuckles. They weren't as dense as I'd have liked, but I lost her by leaping behind a log coated in a thick growth of spiraling ferns. I couldn't help but eye them as I passed. Perhaps, if I escaped, I could double around and try nibbling on some later . . .

"Isobel, Isobel!" Lark sang out sweetly. "Where have you gone, Isobel? You know I'm going to find you. I can hear you! I can smell you!" The ground shook, and great crashing sounds came from behind me as she thundered into the honeysuckles. "You're just a silly hare!"

A silly hare! A silly hare! The words ricocheted between my ears, losing their meaning as my whole being narrowed down to a single primal urge: survival. I lived to run. Emerald light and leafy shadows whipped past, my body bunching and stretching straight as an arrow with every stride. I dodged to avoid stones and roots in my path. If I zigged one way, then zagged another, the beast lumbering behind me would get confused and fall behind.

I froze on top of a boulder to look back. My nose spasmed with the effort of getting enough air, flaring red. Heat evaporated from my ears. The pursuer had stopped to look under a log. Mightily, it flipped the log with its upper appendages. Even from a distance I heard soft bark crumbling, tender ferns uprooting and tearing. One of my ears rotated of its own accord to better take in the sounds. Then the pursuer straightened. *Danger!* I dove from the boulder and streaked across the clearing. One of the stumps in the clearing seemed familiar to me: it had fabric draped over it, and teacups beside it. I was unsettled by the sight, as I might be by seeing a hawk's shadow pass over the ground.

And then, from an angle I did not expect, a predator descended.

No! No! No!

I was caught!

I kicked my feet and twisted, screaming, showing my teeth. Giant hands had seized me, and now lifted me. The sun flashed in my eyes—the world soared dizzyingly—and the grip that held me was too firm for escape. I drummed my feet against the creature's chest, but he cradled me so close I couldn't move my legs, and lifted some of his clothes to press my face inside.

Enclosed darkness. Muffled sounds. I stopped struggling, thinking that perhaps the peril had ended. In the sudden quiet only my heart galloped on. The sound of it filled my ears and shook my body in swift, rhythmic pulses.

"Lark," the creature said. He didn't shout. I sensed he didn't have to. His voice was like a cruel wind, stripping everything in its path to the marrow. *"What have you done?"*

A petulant voice answered. "You don't play with me anymore, Rook! No one pays attention to me except for her! And you're trying to keep her all to yourself—it isn't fair!"

Nose twitching anxiously, I burrowed farther into my captive's garments. That voice was *Danger!* But the smell of the creature that held me, a crisp leaf-smell, a night-air smell, was *safe*.

"You little fool. Did you ever pause to consider what would happen if she escaped from you? Look." One of the warm hands left my back. I trembled. "She's already forgotten what she is. She would have lived out the rest of her short years as a common hare."

A foot stomped. "I wouldn't have lost her! I take care of my things! Rook, why are you being like this? You're being awful, just *awful*. I'm going to tell Gadfly how awful you are."

"Tell Gadfly if you like," my captor said, "but I don't think he'll be pleased to discover how impolitely you've treated his guest."

"Fine!" But the voice sounded uncertain. "I'm going right now!"

"See that you do," my captor said, coldly.

Footsteps charged away across the grass. With my ears flattened against my back, I couldn't hear well enough to determine whether the predator had left for certain. Even so, I wasn't afraid. I trusted my captor wouldn't expose me until the harm had passed.

He lifted me from the darkness and held me up at face level. I regarded him calmly with my hind feet dangling. I detected no one else in the clearing, no hawk-shadows, no fox-smell.

"Isobel, do you recognize me?" he demanded. A shadow had fallen over his face, and his smell acquired a bitter edge. He was angry. Even then I still thought to myself, *Safe*.

I wiggled my nose.

He sighed and cradled me against his chest again. "I'm going to turn you back. Try not to struggle, as I haven't had a great deal of practice with this sort of magic. That is to say," he added quickly, "I'm perfectly capable of doing it—I am sure you've noticed I excel at all enchantments—but it would be best if you remained still. So, please try."

I sat obligingly in his arms, wiggling my nose.

At first, nothing happened. Then, just as I thought it might be a good idea to settle down for a nap, the world turned inside out, flipped over, and threw me down again as though I'd just spent a few seconds as a toddler's spinning top. Everything shrank. My body became heavy and fleshy and slow. I blinked in a daze, orienting myself. Red leaves whirled across the clearing, and the trees swayed in a subsiding wind. When the wind gusted its last breath the autumn tree stood naked, bare-branched, without a single leaf left.

I wasn't touching the ground. My feet hung in the air, and warm arms supported my shoulders and the insides of my knees. Rook. That was Rook, holding me.

I wasn't wearing any clothes.

Before I could find my voice and ask him to set me down, he dropped me like a hot coal. I landed in the wildflowers with an undignified *whump*. Horrified, I squashed my legs together, hunched inward with my arms clamped over my chest, and stared up at him. He looked as aghast as I did.

"Why did you just—" I began, at the same moment he blurted out:

"You stopped being in peril, and I couldn't touch you any longer! Are you all right?"

"No." I'd just been turned into a rabbit! "But I will be. Thank you for coming to my rescue. Couldn't you have set me down a bit sooner?"

He averted his eyes. "I was distracted," he replied with dignity.

Oh—right.

When he started shrugging off his coat, I forestalled him by speaking. "I'm going to put my dress back on. Just . . . don't look." I stood and skulked over to the stump, conscious that lately I was doing an awful lot of sneaking about in the forest nude. Sporting a blush that spread all the way down my neck, I slipped back into my underthings, today's Firth & Maester's, and finally my stockings and boots and hidden ring, while Rook waited for me, gazing determinedly at a fixed spot away to the side. "Are they going to miss you back at the court?" I asked, hoping to dispel the tension, or at least refocus it to a more pressing topic.

"Undoubtedly." He paused. "Isobel . . ."

I smoothed my skirts. The ground suddenly became very interesting to look at. "Yes, it was supremely idiotic of me to eat something Lark gave me. I shouldn't have gone off on my own, either, but I'm worried the court—Gadfly especially—will grow suspicious if we spend more time together." The leaf I'd torn up had blown into one of the teacups. "And I needed to get away. You noticed it too, didn't you? What was happening back there?"

When I glanced up, Rook's expression told me he would have brought it up himself if I hadn't first. "Yes. Your Craft is affecting us somehow. Isobel, I've never seen anything like this before."

"If I keep demonstrating, do you think it will put us in danger?"

"As I said, this is—new. My kind hungers for your work, all the more for its difference. I cannot honestly say that I believe there to be no risk, but I do think it would make the court suspicious if you stopped now, with everyone expecting you to continue. If, perhaps, we stay for just one more day, and leave after the masquerade ball tomorrow night . . ."

A long pause elapsed, neither of us looking at the other. Our alliance had progressed far past the point of mutual survival; we both wanted to buy ourselves more time together for decidedly unpractical reasons. It was no use pretending otherwise, and yet we left those words unsaid.

"But I'm almost healed," he went on decisively, forcing himself to finish. "If you would like to leave today, even right now, we can."

I squeezed my eyes shut, cursing my foolishness. "After tomorrow night, then."

His gusty sigh of relief wasn't subtle. I aimed a wry smile at him, but something else drew my attention. "Your pin's gone! It isn't in your pocket, is it? It must have been torn off when you dropped me."

He patted at his chest in alarm and then ducked to hunt through the wildflowers. This wasn't the leisurely search of someone who'd lost a pocket watch or a handkerchief. Rather, he clawed at the ground with a wide-eyed desperation that could be inspired only by the loss of a priceless and irreplaceable treasure. When he found it, he gripped it tightly in his hand. He moved his thumb to the hidden clasp. But then he stopped himself, remembering I was there, and started to put it in his pocket instead.

My heart hurt for him. It was painful to watch Rook reduced to this over something so small. He cared more about that pin than most people cared about everything they owned in the world.

"Who was she?" I asked.

On his knees, he stilled.

"I just—I'm sorry. You don't have to answer that. I suppose I only wondered whether—how the two of you escaped the Good Law."

I thought he might be angry with me. Instead, he looked at me as though I'd torn his heart from his chest. His eyes dulled with shame and despair. He put the pin in his pocket.

"I was in love with her, but we never broke the Good Law," he said.

"How is that possible?"

I wished I hadn't asked. His misery was terrible to see. "She didn't love me back."

Silence reigned in the meadow. After a time, a squirrel started gnawing on an acorn overhead.

He resumed haltingly. "She was—fond of me, but she knew she could not be anything more. We decided it would be best if we never saw each other again. She gave me the pin as a good-bye present. I stopped visiting Whimsy, and more time passed than I realized." He looked at the ground. "When I returned, I found that her great-grandchildren now lived in the village, and she had died long ago of old age. Until your portrait, I never came back." He drew in a breath. "I know it's—wrong, that I care so much about the pin. I can't explain it. It's—"

"It isn't wrong." My voice was so soft I barely heard myself speak. "Rook, it isn't. It's just human."

He hung his head. "What has happened to me?"

I couldn't stand it any longer. I went to him and pulled him into an embrace. He was so tall I felt I barely accomplished anything; I had my arms wrapped around his middle like a child. But after a tense moment he stumbled into my touch, as though he were too crushed by despair to stand on his own.

"You aren't weak," I said. I knew no one had ever told him that before in all the long centuries of his life. "The ability to feel is a strength, not a weakness."

"Not for us," he said. "Never for us."

There was nothing I could say to that. My words of comfort were in vain. I could say nothing to reassure him, not truly. Because here, in the forest, his humanity would be the death of him. Perhaps not now—perhaps not for hundreds of years—but in the end, no matter what, he faced murder at the hands of his kind. I steeled myself against the tears stinging my eyes and the hard, painful knot swelling in my throat. It seemed terribly, unimaginably unfair that I was going to leave him here to die alone. The unfairness of it howled within me like a storm, tearing everything apart.

He pulled away. I must have lost track of time, because I felt cold without his touch.

"It was arrogant of me to assume that I could protect you from every ill at the hands of my kind." His voice sounded empty. "I barely arrived in time to save you."

"It wasn't your fault."

He shook his head. "If something like this happens again tomorrow, whose fault it is won't matter. You might be killed."

And here I was, deciding to stay an extra night despite the danger. An extra twenty-four hours was nothing. Yet, it was everything. I might live more tomorrow than I did all the years of the rest of my life combined. How much was I willing to risk for it? The old me, the one who'd hidden Rook's sketches in the back of her closet, would never have asked that question. But that was the problem with the old me, I was coming to realize. She'd accepted that behaving correctly meant not being happy, because that was the way the world worked. She hadn't asked enough—of life, or of herself.

"Is there a protective charm you can cast on me?" I asked. "Just until we part."

His expression shuttered. He spoke carefully. "There is only one way to safeguard a mortal from fairy magic. No other fair one would be able to enchant you or influence you while it lasted, but it's more than a mere charm. For it to work, you would have to tell me your true name."

Rasp, rasp, rasp, went the squirrel, a harsh and grating sound. "You speak of ensorcellment."

"Yes. I understand if you won't allow it. But if you asked it of me, I would use it only to keep you safe. I would never manipulate your thoughts."

"If you did, I'd have no way of knowing."

He dipped his head in assent. "You would have to trust me. I give my word."

If he had been any other fair one, I'd have been combing through his words in search of a trick—the lie of how he planned to hurt me twisted into truth. But god help me, I wasn't. I believed him. I closed my eyes and breathed in and out in the darkness, turning my judgment inward. Keeping my true name a secret was among my most deeply held principles. Trusting a fair one was madness.

I was tired of it all. Perhaps it was time to stop keeping secrets and become a little mad.

This time, both my heart and my mind screamed the same truth.

I opened my eyes to find Rook studying me, gaze shadowed by the hair falling to frame his face. His lips thinned. Reading my expression, he gave the slightest nod. "We'll think of another way—"

"Yes," I said.

He inhaled sharply. "What?"

"I trust you." Fierce conviction flooded me like morning light, searing away every doubt. "I know you. I'll take you at your word. But," I added, "if I begin paying you too many compliments while you have me ensorcelled, I will become suspicious."

He didn't seem to have quite grasped my answer. I don't think my weak joke even registered with him. He bent a knee, bringing our faces to the same level. "Isobel, before you decide for certain, you have to know this would unbind me—I would be able to touch you again when you aren't in danger."

"Good. I don't want you dropping me again."

He gave a startled laugh, dangerously close to a sob. He looked at me as though I were life's greatest mystery. "You mortals are terribly strange," he said, in a tight voice.

"Coming from you, I'm beginning to suspect that's a compliment. Is there anyone else around?" He shook his head. He didn't take his eyes from my face, but I had faith that he didn't need to look to know. "Then hold still," I said.

There is magic in names. Mine had only been spoken aloud once before in all the world's history. I was the sole living person who knew it. The sound, the shape of it would never leave me, even though by all rights I shouldn't remember it—my mother had whispered it into my ear just after I was born, a tiny infant still red and wrinkled from the womb. This is how it went. I leaned forward. I placed my lips so close to the shell of Rook's ear that when I spoke, in a breath quieter than a whisper, quieter than the folding of a moth's wing, the warm air stirred his hair.

And so, I gave him my true name.

Sixteen

THE NEXT day the court buzzed with talk of the masquerade, which would begin at dusk. By the time the shadows lengthened I had not only completed a portrait for nearly all the fair folk in the spring court, but had also heard an exhaustive account of what each one was wearing, who had stolen fashion ideas from whom, and several deeply alarming suggestions of sartorial revenge.

The more portraits I finished without incident, the more I relaxed. By the time I'd reached the last fair one in line, I was cautiously prepared to believe my plan had succeeded. More of my subjects had had peculiar reactions to their portraits, freezing to stare at their faces or spending the rest of the afternoon in a state of distraction, but mercifully, neither they nor any of the onlookers seemed to catch on—for once their utter ignorance of human emotion worked in my favor. I was intrigued to note that just like yesterday, a clear pattern had unfolded. It was always the older fair folk who were the most affected by my Craft.

Of the ensorcellment, I felt nothing. The absence of my awareness of it was its most disturbing feature. I poked and prodded at the back of my mind as I might a loose tooth, knowing the tooth was loose, yet never detecting a wiggle. At times, I even wondered if Rook had applied it successfully. But he seemed certain, and there had been a change in the glade after I told him my name, a sort of sigh, as though all the trees and ferns and flowers had let out a breath at once.

And it was an ensorcellment, after all. If I was able to sense it, it wasn't doing its job.

I stifled a groan when I stood, hoping my legs would recover in time for the dancing. My final subject was a tall, grave-looking fair one named Hellebore, who took his portrait with an amused bow. He examined it as he wandered off. Before long he pressed the back of his sleeve against his mouth, stifling an errant chuckle. He laughed again. Then he stumbled. And then he slumped against a tree, giggling helplessly, struggling for breath. His mirth wasn't controlled, inhuman—it verged on hysterical.

I'd drawn him laughing.

Skin crawling, I knelt to tidy up my workspace, needlessly ordering the teacups and remaining strips of bark. Hellebore had walked far enough away that with luck, no one would notice and make a connection.

And then I caught sight of Foxglove. She'd paused in her game of ninepins across the lawn, observing him with narrow suspicion. When his laughter overcame him and he toppled to the ground clutching his stomach, she turned sharply to stare at me, nostrils flared and shoulders rigid.

"Isobel," Gadfly said from his throne.

I braced myself and raised my head. He wasn't smiling; his expression was serious, in a mild, pleasant sort of way. This was it. My very last portrait, and everything was over.

But he only went on, "I believe Lark has something to say to you."

A teacup slipped from my unsteady grasp, knocking against its neighbors with a quiet clink.

Lark minced over from where she'd been standing next to Gadfly, half hidden by the throne's flowering branches. Her face was impassive as she sank into a deep curtsy in front of me. Then, to my surprise, she burst into tears.

"I'm—I'm s-sorry I turned you into a hare, Isobel," she stuttered out between gasps. Huge, woeful droplets dripped down her cheeks and off her chin. She sniffled noisily. Disquieted, I wondered if she was imitating me, the only example of weeping she'd ever witnessed. It wasn't a flattering impression. "I only—I only wanted someone to play with."

Was Hellebore still laughing? Was Foxglove still watching me? Had anyone else noticed? I couldn't risk looking. With an effort, I forced my attention to remain solely focused on Lark. Despite what she'd done, I really did feel sorry for her. "I forgive you, Lark."

"Can we still be friends?" she wrung out piteously.

"Yes, of course we can." I added for appearances' sake, "But please don't play any more tricks on me."

"Oh, good!" Her messy tears vanished instantly, leaving no trace of wetness or splotchiness on her porcelain doll face.

Because, of course, she hadn't specifically said she was sorry because she had almost hurt me, or because she had frightened me. More likely she was only sorry for turning me into a hare because she'd been caught and punished for it.

"Come along, then," she said. "The ball's starting soon, and you need a costume. I already have one picked out. You'll adore it. It's—"

Someone slapped away the hand she'd reached out to me. At first I thought it was Rook. But instead Foxglove stood beside us, wearing her frigid, strangled smile. Lark's expression went blank. She swiftly pulled her hand to her chest, but not before I spied a long, thin cut, like the swipe of an animal's razor-sharp claw, fading from the backs of her knuckles.

"I think you've spent quite enough time with our dear Isobel. Don't you agree, darling?" Foxglove's smile thawed unconvincingly as she turned it on me. "Lark's so young. She means well, but she isn't the best company for a mortal girl. I, on the other hand, have dealt with humans many times. And I have an extensive wardrobe, filled with hundreds of dresses accumulated over a long, *long* lifetime." Her eyes flicked back to Lark, relishing the fruits of her well-aimed blow. "Do come with me instead."

My stomach churned at the thought of being alone with Foxglove. I'd have better chances locked in a room with a starving tiger. But what would she say if I denied her in front of the whole court?

"No." Nettle stepped forward. "Why don't you come with me? I've only just started visiting Whimsy, but everyone's already talking about my enchantments."

So fleetingly and savagely I almost missed it, Foxglove's face contorted into a hideous frown.

More fair folk joined in. Soon I stood in the middle of a loud, grasping throng, over a score of immortal women vying for the privilege of lending me a mask and gown, like greedy children arguing over a toy they would sooner tear apart than share. I searched for Rook, but when I caught a glimpse of him between two fair folk's bodies, he had already taken his leave and was halfway across the clearing. Gadfly walked beside him with a fatherly hand on his back, the other brandishing a cravat in the air.

We had arranged the ensorcellment for situations just like this one. I was immune to all fairy magic but Rook's, and if anyone attempted to harm me physically, he would sense it. But faced with the claustrophobic press of so many people clawing at me at once, I couldn't quell my rising panic with logic.

Why was this only happening now? Lark had laid claim to me without any competition whatsoever on my first day in court. I glanced toward her, only to find her missing. Unlike Rook, she was nowhere to be seen.

My breath caught in my throat. I did know the answer: Lark had shown weakness. Like predators, the fair folk had seen her stumble, and they had pounced. Now it was simply a matter of who would take her place.

High overhead, between the fair folk bending over me, a branch bounced as something landed in the canopy. I glimpsed a scrap of shiny black before the heads closed in again. Had that been a raven's feathers, or just a flash of the blood-dark garnets studding Foxglove's hair? I couldn't see. I couldn't hear. And I wasn't getting enough air—their feral animal perfume was suffocating. Light-headed, I tensed my muscles to charge through the mob, to escape the cramped onslaught of smell and noise and unwanted touch no matter the consequences.

"Stop." A soft, wispy voice spoke. Barely anyone noticed. Its owner stood at the edge of the crowd, hands knotted into fists at her side.

"Aster," I gasped. I strained toward her, but couldn't get anywhere with so many fingers grasping at me, so many bodies crowding in close.

She noticed, and gave me a small nod. "Stop," she repeated, turning back. "Leave Isobel alone now, everyone. I will be the one to prepare her for the ball. *I will be the one to prepare her for the ball!*" Her voice rang out like a gunshot. All heads turned, and everyone went silent. For a second, only a second, a hot ember of true anger flared in her eyes. I think I was the only one capable of recognizing it. But even though the fair folk couldn't put a name to what they saw, it affected them still. They shrank back, uncertain.

Yanking my hands from the two fair folk who gripped them, I managed a clumsy curtsy. "Why do you think you should be the one, Aster?" I asked. My voice rasped, dry and desperate. I hoped they couldn't sense my fear. "Please tell me."

She raised her chin. "I drank from the Green Well. None of you can say the same. Tonight, the privilege belongs to me." And she held out a fragile hand.

My scrabbling fingers met hers. For some reason, it startled me that there was nothing human about her steely grip. She pulled me free of the throng, toward the stair. The other fair folk sighed wistfully. "Oh, dear. Perhaps next time . . ." "It would have been such a pleasure . . ." "I'm ever so fond of your work . . ." I suppressed a shudder as each one purred their regrets at me while I stumbled past, their breath caressing my cheeks like feather plumes.

Aster silently led me up the stair. And while we went, I counted. One raven, watching us silently from the banister. A second peered out of the dogwood throne's flowers. A third flickered across the clearing, as liquid as a shadow, and a fourth and fifth hopped bright-eyed along a branch. None of them showed signs of dispersing. If there was a sixth—

But Aster's hand tugged on my wrist, and I couldn't stand there exposed on the stair's landing. Together we passed into the labyrinth. Whether it was my imagination or otherwise, the unfamiliar bend she chose looked stranger, wilder, its clutter less friendly. I didn't recognize the rocking horse positioned at the corner, its paint peeling and faded with age. I stepped on something, and would have turned my ankle if not for Aster's hand steadying me. It was a carved bird figurine, partly enveloped by the floor. We passed a giant church bell grown over with bark, sticking out of the wall at an angle. Farther on, a doll's hand protruded from the leafy ceiling. The collections of Craft must have lain here so long untouched that the labyrinth had begun enveloping them, where they would remain for eternity, forgotten.

Finally Aster drew me around another corner and stopped. She peered back the way we had come, with the hushed alertness of someone listening. "We were not followed," she murmured to herself.

"I must thank you," I said, "for coming to my—"

She turned, eyes wild. "Do not thank me!" Each syllable of her fraught whisper struck me like a slap across the face. I froze, stunned.

With a trembling hand, she tucked her hair behind her ear. A smile plucked at the corners of her mouth. She darted another look behind us. "Come along," she said, as though nothing had happened, and pulled me into the room waiting beyond. "I must prepare you for the masquerade."

Thoughts awhirl, foreboding yawning darkly in the pit of my stomach, it took me a moment to process what I had stepped into. I stood in a chamber completely lined with books. Stacked books stretched up the walls like bricks and paved the floor like cobblestones. Gilt titles winked at me from scuffed spines. A musty smell of leather and yellowed paper filled the room.

"You've collected all of these?" I breathed. "Have you read them all?"

Aster hesitated. Her free hand fluttered uselessly, then alit on a book. She slid her fingertips down it, but didn't pull it from the wall. "They are Craft." She spoke softly. "The words—they don't always make sense, but I need them anyway, you see. It's as though there's something I'm looking for. I always think, once I have just one more, it will be enough . . ." Her words dwindled.

"But it never is," I said.

She didn't seem to hear. "Follow me. We cannot take too long."

Her hand fell from mine. Glancing repeatedly over my shoulder, I trailed her into the next room. The sun must have tipped behind the trees, because gloom had fallen over the labyrinth, leaving its contents vague with shadow. My heart skipped a beat when I mistook the figures lined up beyond the doorway for fair folk standing in rigid expectation, waiting for us. But they were only mannequins arranged in two long rows along either wall, wooden faces devoid of expression. Aster had brought me to her wardrobe. She made a gesture, and an amber fairy light appeared above us, drifting upward toward the ceiling. A standing mirror on the opposite side of the room reflected its illumination, shifting over my uncertain countenance as I looked around.

"We are similar in size," she said. "Most of these should fit you, I think. Do you have a preference for green?"

"No. I don't have much of a preference at all, really. That must be an odd thing for an artist to say, but I'm not in the habit of painting myself." I paused, recalling her portrait session. "Why don't you choose for me?"

Her shoulders tightened. She thumbed the nearest gown's gauzy train, absently evaluating its texture, then released it without interest. "You look lovely in green, but it's a spring color. When you drink from the well, I don't think you'll belong in our court."

I slipped along the other row, tracing silk and lace, never taking my gaze from Aster. "Why do you say that?" I asked.

"Oh, I don't know. It's just a silly feeling."

I kept my tone light. "Can I ask—why did you rescue me down there? I might be mistaken, but these past few minutes, I've received the impression that it was for a reason. That perhaps you wanted to tell me something."

She halted, hand paralyzed in midair between two dresses. I was right. A deep, resounding note of dread tolled within me. Something was about to go terribly wrong.

"He knows," she said.

"About my Craft?"

A quick, dark-eyed glance. "He knows you have broken the Good Law."

No, I thought. Then, *yes.*

Because suddenly it was quite clear to me that I was in love with Rook, and it had happened as most quiet, perfect, utterly natural things do: without my even noticing. We had stood together in a glade, and I had trusted him enough to tell him my true name. I turned the strange, marvelous thought around in my head. I loved Rook. I loved him. It was the best thing I had ever felt. And it was the worst thing I had ever done.

I'd doomed us both to death.

Nothing around me changed, though it seemed there ought to be some tangible proof that everything was about to be over. I didn't collapse to my knees or cry out. I just stood there breathing as usual, trying to comprehend the scope of what was happening, my thoughts measured and calm.

Who was "he"? Gadfly? I supposed it had to be. He'd probably seen this coming from a mile away. Despite our history, perhaps he'd even enjoyed watching my mortal folly unfold. The thought gave new meaning to the way Lark and Foxglove and Nettle and the others had fought over me—fought over who would dress me up in the last gown I'd ever wear.

Quickly as a striking snake, Aster whirled around and seized my arms. Her bony fingers dug into my flesh like claws. Her eyes glittered. "So that is why you must leave the masquerade. Make your entrance, but the moment Gadfly turns his back, you must flee to the Green Well and drink before he catches you. You must. I will help you."

I might have only imagined it. But when Aster grabbed me I thought I felt a twinge of alarm that wasn't my own, a ghostly, faraway sensation shivering across me like ripples spreading outward across the surface of a pond. *Rook?* I asked, but received nothing back.

"Isobel," Aster was saying.

"No." I shook my head. "No, I cannot. The story Rook and I told the court—it was a lie. I will never drink."

"You must."

"If you could turn back time, if you could do it all over again, would you make the same choice?"

The light left her eyes. Her grip loosened, and she turned away.

"I could show you a way out of the court that no one watches," she said. "But no matter where you go, they will find you."

Emma. The twins. They would have gotten my letter this morning, never knowing I was to die the same night. I shook my head, over and over again.

"I can't ask you to endanger yourself on my behalf for nothing." A cold fog crept around me. There was one thing left I could do—one thing left to try. "I will attend the masquerade. I need a moment alone with Rook."

Aster said nothing. She thought I was already dead, and perhaps she was right. She moved ahead down the aisle, halting in front of one of the last gowns. "This one," she said, and lifted it from its mannequin.

I'd never seen a dress like it. Deep red roses were embroidered in lace over its inner layer of nude, faux-sheer fabric. The roses clustered over the bodice and scattered downward across the flowing skirt, coming apart as though swept away by a breeze. On the other side the dress had been left unadorned, creating the illusion of a low-cut back. Once, it might have taken my breath away. Now there was no beauty in the world, no pleasure, that could shake me from the bleak understanding of what awaited me.

Mechanically, I shed my clothes onto the floor. I stepped

into the gown, almost tripping, my body made clumsy and slow by dread. While I crouched to gather the fabric up around my ankles, I paused long enough to brush my hand against my stocking, reminding myself of the ring's presence. A laughable defense. But it was something.

I straightened.

"Oh," Aster breathed. She took me by the shoulders and guided me to the mirror.

When I moved, the lace bodice remained stiff and fitted, but the skirt rippled around me in almost impossible swirls, shapes that reminded me of a famous painting of a maiden drowning in a lake at dusk, sinking into shadow as her dress billowed weightlessly after her. Stepping up to the figure reflected in the glass, I almost didn't recognize myself. I'd been wearing Firth & Maester's since I'd arrived, but never once had I seen what I looked like in a mirror. The gown's rich scarlet accentuated my fair complexion and emphasized my dark eyes to a startling degree. I appeared less frightened than I expected. My eyes just stared, and stared, and stared, like pits swallowing up the light, out of a face as blank as the mannequin that had worn the gown before me.

"Jewelry," Aster said to herself. "And a mask. I know of a mask that will match, if I can find it . . ."

She drifted away. A latch jingled, followed by the sound of a chest creaking open. While I waited, my hands rose of their own accord to unfasten my hair and rake through the tangled snarl. Indifferently, I watched myself braid it back up into a messy bun, which I held in place until Aster handed me a pin to secure it. I had the vague idea that if I looked composed—if the fair folk did not sense my fear immediately—I might buy us more time. All I needed was a moment with Rook.

Aster's pale fingers descended, placing a delicate circlet atop my braids. It was a slender piece fashioned from gold filigree, studded with tiny leaves. I swept my eyes over my reflection, seeing it anew. Autumn colors. A coronet to match Rook's. She was being kind, I supposed, in the only way she knew how. Giving me dignity in my last moments, unlike Foxglove or any of the others, who I now suspected would have tormented me like cats with an injured mouse, smug with foreknowledge, before they conveyed me to the ball. Perhaps until I pressed her Aster had hoped to spare me from knowing entirely, to allow me a swift and merciful end.

As she stood next to me in the mirror, there was a hint of sadness to her distant expression, shivery and faraway, a glimmer of moonlight at the bottom of a deep, deep well. At her waist, she held the stick of a half-mask. A rose mask to match the gown, an expressionless, flourishing bouquet with holes at the blossoms' hearts for eyes.

"You look like a queen among mortals," she said. "You will be the most beautiful person at the ball."

I tried summoning a wan smile but didn't succeed. It was very likely I would never smile again. "The most beautiful human? I can hardly hold a candle to Foxglove."

"No. You surpass us all." Beside me she looked colorless and frail. "You are like a living rose among wax flowers. We may last forever, but you bloom brighter and smell sweeter, and draw blood with your thorns."

Carefully, I took the mask from her hands. "I can see how you were a writer once."

Aster looked away.

I lifted the mask to my face, concealing my expression. Gazing at myself, I could only think one thing. I knew Aster was thinking the same. I did look like a queen, but my dress was a funeral shroud. She had made me beautiful to go to my death.

Seventeen

WHEN ASTER and I returned to Gadfly's stair, the throne room had transformed. Spider-silk garlands looped between the branches, their dew sparkling in the moonlight. Night-blooming flowers shivered on every bough, aglow with fairy lights flickering within them like votives. They bathed the clearing in an ethereal glow in which nothing seemed quite real. Not the tables laden with wine, sweets, and fruits, or the musical flocks of songbirds that swooped low before darting back into the canopy. And certainly not the fair folk, who had stepped straight out of a storybook. Moonlight shimmered on the jewels in their hair and set cold fire to the silver embroidery on their coats and dresses. They danced in pairs without music, a strange, silent waltz furling and unfolding across the clearing below, vignettes glimpsed through eyeholes in my mask. And all of them as faceless as I was: birds and flowers, foxes and deer,

their smiles sharper than candlelight striking the curve of crystal glasses.

Everyone was dressed in the pale colors of the spring court, aside from me—and Rook. I picked him out immediately where he stood at the foot of the stair beside Gadfly. Tonight he looked every inch the autumn prince in a sweeping wine-colored coat trimmed with thread-of-gold. His crown winked from his tousled curls, and a raven mask covered the upper half of his face. Reading his easy manner, his smile and the relaxed set of his shoulders, and noting that his hand didn't stray near his sword, it struck me with grim horror that he did not know; Gadfly had not told him. I was in love with him, and he didn't know.

The realization weighted my feet like shackles. Each step required an effort, even with Aster's hand supporting my elbow.

No one noticed us until we were halfway down. Then the entire ball stilled. A hush fell over the clearing. Everyone watched, expectant. I halted, trying to muster the courage to continue. Was this how Rook felt? Always on guard, always trying to hide any sign of weakness that could have the fair folk leaping at his throat in seconds? Without the mask, I would be doomed.

A rose petal tumbled down the step next to my feet, followed by another. Barely suppressing a flinch, I looked over my shoulder to see where they were coming from. Rose petals were strewn in a path behind me all the way up the steps, scarlet against the white woven birch, but I saw no one responsible for their presence.

"The dress is enchanted," Aster whispered, leaning in. "Petals will appear wherever you step. But they aren't real—watch."

A breeze blew, scattering the petals, which vanished like shadows as they stirred. The sight was captivating, and awful. My path through the masquerade would be marked like a wounded animal leaving bloodstains on snow. An appropriate comparison, all things considered.

I forced myself to continue. Finally, well concealed beneath the gown's loose, flowing hem, my boots touched the ground. Gadfly took my hand and kissed it while, next to him, Rook studiously tried not to react. For the first time I was grateful for his ignorance. If he'd known, he would have drawn his sword against Gadfly then and there, and it would all have been over before we'd had a chance.

"What a delight it is to have our very first masquerade with a mortal in attendance," Gadfly said. His swan mask's snowy feathers covered almost his entire face, leaving only slivers of his jawline visible, but I heard the smile in his voice. "And what an intriguing dress Aster has chosen for you. Why, you and Rook make quite the matching pair! Of course, it would be a shame if he kept you all to himself this evening. I must insist on having the first dance."

My stomach swooped with vertigo, as though I were still descending and had just missed the stair's final step. I forced a smile over clenched teeth. Gadfly kept talking, but I didn't hear a word, hoping my polite nods would suffice. Rook shifted impatiently. With so many eyes upon us, I despaired of the chance of speaking to him alone.

Perhaps there was a way to warn him before Gadfly swept me away. Briefly, I pressed my eyes closed. I conjured up the sensation of cold, clawlike hands wrapped around my throat, squeezing, suffocating the life from my body. Dizziness. Terror.

Death. Throughout it all, I didn't let the smile fall from my face. Hopefully it only looked to Gadfly as though I'd modestly lowered my eyes at one of his flowery compliments. More likely it looked as though I had indigestion.

When I looked up, I found Rook scrutinizing me. He'd felt it. Framed by the mask's dark feathers, his eyes pierced me with shock and concern. I watched his expression change. First confusion, seeing there was nothing wrong with me, followed by dawning understanding. He ran his hands down the front of his coat, assuring everyone he'd only gotten a peculiar look on his face because he was worried he'd forgotten something. He patted at his sword belt and checked his sword. No, he hadn't forgotten his sword after all. There it was! Beaming, he adjusted the lay of the sheath against his leg. God, he was a terrible actor—what did I expect from someone who couldn't lie?—but his meaning was clear. Message received. He would be on his guard.

". . . and that's how I ended up with the entire wagon of turnips, and Mr. Thoresby was forced to return my second-best waistcoat. But enough carrying on," Gadfly was saying, quite oblivious, or at least pretending to be, as he admired one of his own cuff links. "I could talk about myself forever, couldn't I? Let's take a turn. The night isn't getting any younger, after all, and it appears everyone is waiting on us."

As though I were extending my neck to the guillotine, I held out my hand. I had no other choice. He gallantly took my arm and escorted me to the center of the glade. The other fair folk stood at a respectful distance, having paused the waltz in preparation for their prince's entrance. He placed his free hand on my waist, and at last I had to lower the mask to rest my own on his shoulder. Skillfully, he swept me into the ebb and flow of movement as everyone resumed dancing together. The courtiers flowed around us with inhuman grace, whispers of muslin and silk in passing, but aside from that—silence.

"You look very fine this evening, Gadfly," I said without feeling.

"Yes, I know," he replied. "Yet I can't deny it's wonderful to hear my suspicions confirmed."

Within the holes of his swan mask, laugh lines appeared around his eyes, which I had never seen at home in my parlor. Perhaps they hadn't existed before now: an artful deception, like that single strand of hair he'd allowed to escape from his ribbon on the fateful day I'd learned of Rook's commission, or spending years as my patron without ever letting slip to anyone that he was the spring prince. His mask was tied with a pale blue ribbon, so that he could watch my face while I saw nothing of his.

"I hear you and Aster spoke of the Green Well," he went on.

Mouth dry, stomach in knots, I scrambled for a way to draw things out, to maintain my innocence of my fate, to deny Aster's involvement.

"You needn't lie to me, Isobel. I have a rather unique gift, even among my kind. But you already know that, don't you?"

And that was that. There was no use pretending any longer. "Lark told me," I said, the whispery rhythm of the waltz receding as blood roared in my ears.

"Just so. None of this was set in stone, of course. The future never is. It's like a forest, you see, with thousands upon thousands of paths running through it, all branching off in different directions. Some things can change, up until the very end. Yesterday I wasn't certain whether we would do this version, or the version in which you chose not to tell Rook your true name and returned home none the worse for wear, and then due to the fact that I was dancing elsewhere with Nettle, instead of here, with you, a passing nightingale spoiled my lapel as it relieved itself overhead. Which is why I wore my least favorite suit and still ordered the lemon creams specially, just in case." He gave a rueful sigh. "Alas. We'll never get to eat the lemon creams now. But at least Swallowtail will have ruined that offensive yellow jacket of his."

A bird trilled sweetly across the clearing. Somewhere among the dancers, a young man gave a shout of consternation.

"How long have you known?" My voice throbbed with terror and rage, snarled together in a choking tangle. "How long have you been waiting for this?"

He favored me with a look. *You can do better than that,* the look said. "I haven't been waiting at all. I have traveled with you the entire way, lighting your path, ensuring that you selected the one necessary fork in the road out of hundreds. In retrospect do you not find it peculiar that I was your first patron, or that Rook came to you to have his portrait done after so many centuries in hiding?"

"You utter bastard," we both said together, Gadfly speaking over me in cool counterpoint. He shook his head, disappointed but unsurprised, and said: "That one was a given."

I thought I might be sick.

Clumsily, like someone reaching out in a dark room, a warm rush of assurance bumped against me. It felt unmistakably of Rook. He was testing the bond between us, aware something was wrong and doing his best to comfort me. He didn't know, I thought. He didn't know I'd condemned him to death. Soon,

I'd have to tell him. I swallowed, pushing his presence away as best I could, and before the sensation vanished I received one last pang of unhappy surprise from him, as though I'd slammed a door in his face without warning.

"You are empty," I said, my throat working, "and cruel."

"Ah. Yes, now that is true. Would you like to know the greatest secret of fairykind?" When I didn't answer he continued, "We prefer to pretend otherwise, but truly, we have never been the immortal ones. We may live long enough to see the world change, but we're never the ones who changed it. When we finally reach the end, we are unloved and alone, and leave nothing behind, not even our name chiseled on a stone slab. And yet—mortals, through their works, their Craft, are remembered forever." He turned us gracefully through the crowd without missing a step. "Oh, you cannot imagine the power your kind holds over us. How very much we envy you. There is more life in your littlest fingernail than in everyone in my court combined."

Was that truly all it was? Was that the reason why fair folk condemned mortal emotion—because those few of them who felt it only served to remind the rest of what they couldn't have? And thus love, the experience they envied most bitterly, became the deadliest offense of all.

"That's why you've done this?" I whispered. "Jealousy?"

"I am wounded by your low opinion of me, Isobel," Gadfly replied, not sounding wounded at all, and in fact sounding as though he cared so little about others' opinions he might not even recognize what they were upon their delivery to him. "No, I am playing a longer game, a little deeper in the forest, farther along the path. And now I won't keep you any longer. Time runs short, and I'm certain you'd rather be dancing with Rook."

He wove us around the other dancers, steering us toward where Rook stood out like a sore thumb, unwillingly requisitioned into a dance with Foxglove. Gadfly maintained an expectant air, but I had nothing left to say to him.

"Fear not," he said to my silence. "This business will be unpleasant while it lasts, but it will be over soon enough." As his silk glove slipped from my shoulder, he brought his mask close to my ear. "Remember: for all my meddling, your choice is the one that matters in the end. Hello, Foxglove! Rook! May I steal this dance?"

Rose petals swept around us as we switched partners, disappearing with a ghost of heady fragrance. If I survived this, I thought, I'd never want to smell roses again.

"I felt—" Rook began, but I cut him off with a sharp jerk of my head. I meant to wait until Gadfly and Foxglove had moved away from us to speak. Yet I found, as the seconds passed, that I couldn't say the words. I didn't know how to say them. They were too vast and terrible to fit on my tongue.

Around and around we swirled. Lights glittered across Rook's hair and the gold thread on his coat. Courtiers flowed past us, whirling but never touching, like flowers spinning on the surface of a lake. A wolf mask turned to stare at me as it passed; I felt countless eyes upon us, waiting for the first sign of the hunt's climax. Two prey, one alert, the other unsuspecting, about to be flushed from a thicket toward a bloody end.

"Isobel? What is it?"

"I must ask you to do something for me," I said.

He replied quickly, "Anything."

I forced myself not to look away. "You must use the ensorcellment to change what I feel."

Rook almost missed a step. "What are you saying?"

Nearby Foxglove tilted her head back, her silvery laugh splitting the masquerade.

"I'm saying that I—"

"No. Don't." He looked at me as though he were marooned and I were a ship he was watching sail out to sea, farther and farther away.

A sickly odor of decay reached my nose.

"Rook, I'm sorry," I said. "I love you."

Our next turn brought the tables into view. A fair one lifted a pear to her lips, only for the fruit to blacken in her hand, oozing through her fingers, swollen with maggots. She ate it anyway, wearing an expression of sweet delight as juice and pulp dripped down her chin. On all the platters, the fruit had turned rotten. Dark putrefaction spilled over the china, soaked the tablecloths, and dribbled to the ground.

"When?" he asked, his lips barely moving. The lower half of his face was masklike itself, ashen against his dark curls and high collar.

A songbird dove down, tearing a butterfly apart in its beak. Whirling in circles, the revelers grew sallow and feverish in the fairy lights' multicolored glow. Animal masks snarled. Flower masks boggled at us, inscrutable. They spun dizzily and with delirious abandon, no longer playing at being human, parodying a mortal ball like a nightmare masquerade.

"Yesterday. But I didn't know until . . ." I couldn't bear to speak of it. "Please. We're almost out of time."

"I can't do it," he said.

A raven croaked overhead.

"You have to!"

He released my waist to pull on the trailing end of the ribbon holding his mask in place. It tumbled to the ground, lost among the dancers. "I gave my word," he said, stripped bare.

We took one step forward. Another back. Turned. I tasted the words like poisoned wine. "Then it's over."

"Isobel," Rook said. He stopped moving, so that we alone stood still. "I have never met anyone more frustrating, or brave, or beautiful. I love you."

A sob caught in my throat. Standing on my toes, I closed the gap between us and kissed him; I kissed him fiercely, bruisingly, as a cacophony of mocking wails and scandalized shrieks rose from the fair folk looking on. This was what they had been waiting for.

A whisper of sound. Suddenly we stood alone, as though the courtiers had vanished like specters into the night. But no—they were still there—I caught the grotesque shapes of masks peering out at us from the bushes, from the trees, from every shadow, their hidden owners crouching in stiff anticipation like mantises waiting to strike.

And we weren't completely alone. A slender, white-haired figure clad in black armor stood at one of the tables. Her back faced us. I hadn't seen her arrive; perhaps she'd already been standing there for some time. She picked up a spoiled pastry, examined it, and flung it away in disgust.

A horn blast echoed through the forest. I felt it in the ground, reverberating up through my bones. Two other blasts answered its call, but those deep bellows did not belong to horns. In the misty darkness between the trees, a pair of towering shapes moved. They were so tall, crowned with branches, that I might have mistaken them for giant oaks had they not shifted, revealing themselves as massive thanes, both at least half again as large as the one Rook slew the day we'd met. Hounds leapt out of the woods as though fleeing from them, pale flames in the night, to boil sinuously around Hemlock's legs, overturning the table as they vied for her affection, utterly ignored. Steam rose from their lolling scarlet tongues.

The horn sounded again. Only then did she turn.

With the movement, it was as though she pulled a dustcloth from the throne room. The air rippled, and the birches grayed and sagged, bark peeling, riddled with beetle holes. The moss underfoot atrophied to an unhealthy yellow-green, and flowers shriveled in the damp heat that rose from the earth, rank with the stench of decomposing vegetation. The summer court's corruption had reached the springlands—or it had been here all along.

"I am here to enforce the Good Law!" Hemlock cried in a clear voice. What she said next made the trees groan and whisper and all the waiting ravens take flight in a nervous, silent cloud. "By the order of our sovereign, the Alder King."

Eighteen

HEMLOCK HALTED only a few paces away, her open hands held out to the sides as though to show us she didn't have a weapon, or as if she were prepared to embrace us. Given the wicked claws on the ends of her long, knotted fingers, I didn't try to guess which.

Rook eyed her up and down, and in one smooth, contemptuous motion drew his sword. He angled his body in front of me. I seized the chance to bend and work the ring out of my stocking, and slipped it on while he spoke. "How long have you been the Alder King's servant, Hemlock?" he spat. "I was unaware the winter court had fallen so low. Bending the knee on ceremony is one thing. Carrying out orders on his behalf is quite another."

Even with Rook between us, Hemlock's unsettling, luminously green gaze fixed on my face. "Do try to be more polite,

Rook," she said. "Have a look around. Myself, Gadfly, even the winter prince—none of us do what we like now." A smile twitched across her features. "I did tell both of you silly fools to run. I told you I'd be after you."

Rook's sword sang through the air. It moved so swiftly I didn't see it strike, or see Hemlock raise her arm to block it. They stood locked together, the blade lodged in her armor, Rook's coat billowing around him as the wind settled. Her smile hardened. She dug her heels in, and her arm shook with the effort of holding him at bay. But Rook and I were outnumbered. We knew it, and so did she.

She crooked one finger, beckoning the courtiers forward. "Make yourselves useful, please, and seize them. Do wipe your faces first."

The fair folk swarmed from the forest. Before I could react, they tore me away from Rook. Dozens of hands grasped my clothes, my arms, my hair, sticky from their feasting on putrid fruit. They jerked me this way and that, as though pretending to dance with me—leering faces spun around me like a carousel. I lashed out with my ring, and someone gave a bloodcurdling scream.

"She has iron on her finger!" the fair one exclaimed. The voice was familiar—Foxglove. "Take it from her! Take the whole hand if you must!"

An arm struck me across the back, slamming me to the ground. Gulping air in hoarse gasps, I pulled my arm underneath me and lifted my chin just enough to see that Rook had been overpowered too. Gadfly stood behind him with his elbow wrapped around Rook's throat and his other hand squeezing Rook's wrist, which no longer held a sword. Mask gone, he looked calm and amused as Rook thrashed with bared teeth in his grip. Their height difference was such that Rook was bent backward, unable to find footing, while Hemlock's hounds snapped at his kicking boots.

We had scored only two small victories. A chunk of bark armor hung loose from Hemlock's forearm where she stood aside, nursing it. Sap dripped down, sharp with the smell of winter pine; the bark was already growing back over the wound. And Foxglove sat on the ground across from me, holding a hand to her cheek. An angry weal stood out on it where I'd struck her, already melting away to flawless skin behind the furiously trembling cage of her fingers.

I knew her command had been serious and the fair folk wouldn't hesitate to follow it through. I tugged the ring off and flung it away, past the pool of rose petals spreading around me like a bloodstain. The iron wouldn't do me any good now.

"You wicked, nasty creature," Foxglove hissed, yanking me to my feet. I hadn't seen her get up. I stifled a cry as she wrenched one of my arms out of its socket—tingling, lightning-bright sparks of pain shot through my shoulder, numbing me to every other sensation. I tripped forward, pushed from behind, barely managing to stay upright. The circlet hung askew on my head.

"No," Aster's wispy voice said nearby. "Don't hurt her—don't hurt them more than you have to, please—" Her touch alit on my arm before someone swatted it away.

"I'll reach down her throat and tear her heart out if I so choose," Foxglove snapped. "What is wrong with you, Aster? You would seek mercy for those who have broken the Good Law? This human wielded iron against me."

Aster's answer seemed to come from afar this time. "I'm sorry . . ."

"And stop looking at her like that," Foxglove added, vehemently. I thought she was still addressing Aster until she went on, "How disgusting. Have some dignity, and die like one of your own kind."

I raised my head to find Rook watching me, his agonized affections written plainly on his face. Some fair folk stared in revolted fascination. Others cringed away, unable to bear the sight. But Gadfly looked down at him, and then over at me, with a subtle, almost regretful smile shading the edges of his mouth. I was reminded of his many portraits, a hundred versions shifting in the firefly glow.

"Foxglove, while I appreciate your enthusiasm, let us not begin tearing hearts out quite yet," he said. "Now that our masquerade has been cut so tragically short, I find myself unprepared for the evening's diversions to end." He sent a quelling look at Hemlock, who had started forward. "Oh, I insist. This is still my court, after all, isn't it? Well, then—that's settled. First, we shall take them to the Green Well. And we will give Isobel one last chance to save the prince's life, and undo all the harm she has inflicted."

The clamor that followed drowned out my scream. I slumped in Foxglove's grasp, stars bursting across my vision.

"Now, everyone," Gadfly said. "It's only fair. And I promise it will be a memorable spectacle." As Rook twisted against him, shouting incoherently with fury, he gave a cheerful wink.

The fairy host drove us forward, across the glade, through thickets and meadows, past the riven stone and the bluebells. The moonlight frosted everything like a dream. My head hung, but from time to time I caught glimpses of the thanes keeping pace with us on either side, colossal shadows striding through the wood, terrible in their immense and silent majesty. Hounds leapt among the fair folk like nobles' dogs in a hunting party. And of course, Rook and I were the game. Perhaps it was fitting that the place where Rook had confessed his love to me would be the place where we died.

When we reached the Green Well it was just as I remembered it, even in the dark. The squat circle of mossy stones filled me with the same lurching horror as before, but Foxglove propelled me inexorably forward when my body stiffened and my steps shortened into halting, balking scuffles. She didn't stop until the tips of my boots stubbed against the rocks. She tore the circlet from me while I writhed in her grip, and thrust my shoulders forward over the edge. Freed from its braids, my hair fell loose over the well's shadows.

Gadfly brought Rook up short across from me on the other side. It was grimly satisfying to see that Rook had clipped his nose at some point on the short journey over. Blood smeared his mouth, and ferns and flowers sprouted around him where some of it had dripped to the ground.

"Isobel—" Rook began.

Hemlock stalked into view, kicking aside the overgrowth as it spread. She drove an elbow into Rook's gut, and he doubled over, silenced. A few fair folk jeered. That was when I knew our death would be many things, but it wouldn't be swift.

Swallowtail came forward with a winning smile. He stole Rook's crown, placed it on his own head, and strutted around pretending to swing a shuttlecock racket as everyone laughed. Emboldened, another fair one approached, seized the lapel of

Rook's coat, and ripped the garment half off him. The raven pin went spinning into the flowers. Rook staggered. Then he lunged at the offender, only to go sprawling when Gadfly lifted a foot and neatly swiped his legs out from under him.

A sob caught in my throat. Rook climbed back to his feet, his clothes torn and his chest heaving. I never could have imagined him so humiliated.

"Do what you will with me," he said, "but don't make her watch. Let her go."

Gadfly sighed. With a fatherly hand, he brushed twigs and leaves from Rook's hair. Rook didn't react. His head was lowered, hiding his face. I ached with the knowledge that if anything like trust existed between fair folk, he had felt it toward Gadfly.

"It takes two to violate this particular tenet of the Good Law, I'm afraid," Gadfly said.

"She is ensorcelled."

"Ah, but her will remains her own. It seems you love her so much that you've resisted enthralling her." This time, no one jeered. The whispers sounded unsettled, confused. "And in any case, as both you and I know, the breach of the Good Law occurred beforehand."

"Do hurry up, Gadfly." Hemlock's smile looked pasted on. "I hate to keep the king waiting."

"Then kill me!" Rook snarled, twisting around to face Gadfly. "We can hardly break the Good Law if one of us is dead. What is a mortal's life to the Alder King? She will have returned home, married, borne children, perished, and turned to dust before he takes his next breath. She is noth—" He drew up short with a painful gasp, caught in a lie. "She is nothing to him," he said instead, anguish wracking his words. "Kill me and be done with it!"

"Rook, stop!" I shouted. I might as well have been a bird twittering for all the attention the other fair folk paid me. Only Rook reacted, flinching as though I'd struck him.

"I suppose we *could* do that." Gadfly paused. "But it wouldn't be fun at all, would it? And it isn't as though we aren't giving Isobel a choice in the matter."

Unceremoniously, he released Rook, who had been leaning so heavily against Gadfly's restraint that he fell, catching himself on his hands and knees. He threw one arm over the edge of the well and pulled himself up to meet my eyes, panting, though I could tell he wanted to look away; it took everything he had to look at me.

"I was not strong enough to protect you," he said, at a volume pitched to me alone.

"It's all right," I said. "It's all right."

We looked desperately into each other's eyes. It wasn't.

"Now, I apologize for spoiling the moment, but Hemlock has a point—we're dallying. So." Gadfly pulled his gloves off, one after the other, and slipped them into his pocket. "Isobel, Rook is quite correct about one thing: the two of you only violate the Good Law in the state you're in presently. That is, both alive, a mortal and a fair one, and in love. Ah," he said at my expression. "Yes, if either of you could stop loving the other, we would have to release you. Go on, give it a try if you like."

All these years, how hadn't I realized what a monster Gadfly was? But god, I had to at least make the attempt. I squeezed my eyes shut so hard lights exploded across the insides of my eyelids. I thought of Rook stealing me away in the dead of night; his arrogance; his tantrums; how foolish I was for loving him. I imagined Emma tucking March and May into bed alone. Yet my traitorous heart wouldn't surrender. I could no more change my feelings than I could command the sky to rain or demand that the sun rise at the stroke of midnight.

I released the breath trapped in my chest with a sound that was half a gasp, half a scream. Gadfly knew. Damn him, he knew that for me, not being able to rein in my own heart was the greatest torment of all.

"But there's another way." His mild voice insinuated itself into the following quiet. "It is not a crime for two fair folk to be in love." Someone snickered. Love among fair folk—a grand joke indeed. "All you must do is drink of the Green Well, and you will save your own life, and Rook's. The two of you can be together for eternity."

I shook my head. "I don't believe you. Perhaps you'd let me live, but not Rook, not for long."

"Oh . . . I've had a bit of wine, I'm in a generous mood." I opened my eyes in time to see Gadfly nudge Rook with his boot. Rook seemed to have given up entirely; his forehead rested on the well's stone edge. "He will have to have his power stripped from him, of course, remaining a prince is out of the question, but—I would see to it that he lives. No doubt a part of him wouldn't want to, after that. He has always been proud. But he would do it for you."

I was trembling so hard my hair shivered around me. "No," I whispered.

"No? Truly? You value your mortality so highly that you would condemn not only yourself to death, but Rook as well?

He has so many thousands of years left to him. And they say my kind is cold."

My gaze fell on the raven pin, glinting among the bluebells. "I will never become like you," I said. "Never."

Gadfly smiled down at me sadly. "What of your family?"

I raised my head, trembling now with rage as well as fear. How dare he.

"Surely," he went on, "it would be a comfort to your aunt Emma, and your little sisters March and May, if they could see you again. Just imagine how much you could help them as a fair one."

"Do not speak of my family."

"Ah, but I must. Are you truly willing to leave them with no final word of resolution, no body for them to bury? Your dear aunt is so alone. Your memory would haunt her forever. She would blame herself for everything that has happened. Believe me—I know."

"You are deliberately tormenting me. Emma would never . . . she wouldn't . . ."

She wouldn't want me to make this choice. I slumped in Foxglove's grip, gazing again at the cold sparkle of the raven pin on the ground, almost close enough to touch. Gadfly had planned every excruciating moment of this awful charade. He knew I would never drink of the Green Well, no matter what he said to me, and that my torture would be the utmost spectacle. He held my fate suspended like a magician's caged dove, ready to collapse the bars upon me and crush me at any moment. And yet . . . and yet . . . the choice remained mine, and mine alone. Gadfly might see every path through the forest, every possible split in the trail—but what about the impossible? What if I left the path and charged blindly into the wild wood, to a place where none of his visions had ever led?

I thought I knew why Foxglove had torn the circlet from my braids. I hoped I was right, because I was about to take the biggest gamble of my life, and I wasn't fond of surprises.

"I will drink," I whispered. Foxglove's fingers loosened on my wrists, whether to allow me to move or out of sheer shock, I didn't care. I dropped to my knees and groped my way over the ground, fumbling clumsily in my pain and desperation, until I'd pushed an elbow over the well's stone lip, scraping myself on the rough edge. I cried out softly as the touch jostled my dislocated shoulder. Gadfly watched me, utterly still, his eyes narrowed. How far had I already deviated from his path? Agreeing to drink was the last thing I would ever do. And of course, I wasn't done yet.

I stretched my good hand down into the well, cupping my fingers. The water felt like any other water, but the mere awareness of what it was sent cold shocks racing through me, and my breath shivered in and out as I lifted the shimmering palmful, which reflected the moon in broken fragments. And then, abruptly, I stopped. My arm had simply . . . stuck. My fingers were pressed together tightly, but water still trickled away, the puddle at the center of my hand dwindling.

What if just touching the water was enough to begin a transformation after all?

Rook said my name.

I raised my fearful gaze and found him watching, tensed as if prepared to spring forward. I saw the anguish of his indecision. He did not want me to make this choice, knowing that for me it was worse than death. But he also didn't want me to die. There was nothing he could say that wouldn't betray me in one way or another. In the same stroke, I understood what had happened to me.

"Release me," I told him gently. "Trust me."

Rook bowed his head. The ensorcellment's paralysis faded. I clenched my teeth and raised the cupped water until my breath sent ripples shuddering across its surface.

Then I looked over it straight at Gadfly. I turned my hand, letting the water dribble back into the well. I raised my other arm high, though my shoulder screamed with agony, though I barely felt the metal object clenched within my fist, caked with dirt and grass.

In Gadfly's own words, I was about to discover whether Craft had the power to undo the fair folk in a way I'd never imagined. Until now.

"Go to hell," I told him, and hurled the raven pin into the Green Well.

Nineteen

THERE CAME a collective gasp, a strange sound in the meadow's silence, like a flock of birds all taking flight at once. Several fair folk lunged toward the well with their hands outstretched. But though they reacted with unnatural speed, none of them was fast enough to catch the raven pin before it descended, twirling and sparkling, into the well's murky depths.

A tremor shook the ground. Instinctively everyone backed away, except Gadfly, who didn't move. He simply stood and watched. He looked terribly old and strange, like a statue of himself. Perhaps he was replaying the things he'd said to me back in the clearing, recalling the moment he'd furnished me with the idea that Craft could destroy the Green Well.

The stones wobbled, and then loosened, tumbling inward one by one. As each row crumbled more stones shoved up to take its place, pouring from the earth in an endless fountain. The percussion of clattering rocks drowned out every other sound, and chalk dust billowed like smoke. Rook reached my side, and we staggered away together just as the clearing heaved, throwing everyone to the ground. I felt, rather than saw, the final eruption of stones. One as large as a wagon wheel rolled past us, leaving a trail of crushed ferns and bent saplings behind.

When the air cleared an immense cairn sat where the Green Well had been, a brooding tumble of rock that already looked a thousand years old. Regardless of what happened to us now, I took a fierce satisfaction in knowing that the hateful thing was ruined, that no mortal would face its torment after me. No one would meet Aster's fate ever again.

The place where Gadfly had stood was buried beneath enough rubble to crush a man ten times over. He was gone.

Foxglove was the first to react. *"She has destroyed the Green Well!"* she howled, scrambling toward us on her hands and knees. Rook dealt her a blow across the face with an outswung forearm, flinging her aside. Her head struck the cairn with a wet, hollow crack. Moss surged over the stones, covering them halfway, followed by a riot of purple wildflowers springing up between the cracks. Of Foxglove's body, nothing remained. She was dead. I'd just seen a fair one die.

The other fair folk descended upon us. This time it was Hemlock who seized me and hauled me to my feet. It took four to overwhelm Rook; he threw each of them off before they managed to subdue him together, restraining his arms in wary tandem, shooting glances at Foxglove's remains over their shoulders.

Amid the exclamations of horror and wordless keening, one

person laughed. Senses dulled by pain, it took me a moment to identify the source. Aster lay on the ground, running her hand across the moss in front of her, as though feeling it again for the first time after a long imprisonment. Tears streamed down her face, and she laughed and laughed deliriously. I stared at her without comprehension until I realized what was different. She was human again.

"That was awfully clever of you, mortal," said Hemlock into my ear. Her mouth was so close I heard her lips part to speak. Her breath brushed against my face, cold as frost. She smelled more frightful than any other fair one I'd encountered: I had a vision of endless, ice-locked pines, and mountains rising in the distance with snow dusting their peaks, and wolves leaping through the drifts with fresh blood soaking their jaws. Her armor's rough bark scraped against my back. "Or, it wasn't clever at all. It's ever so hard to tell sometimes. Hold still."

I expected her to kill me there on the spot. I wasn't prepared for her to seize my dislocated arm and wrench it back into its socket with a brutal twist. I was so taken by surprise I didn't even cry out. The pain in my shoulder faded to a dull throb.

"There you are. I simply cannot stand the sound of humans whimpering. Come along, everyone! Stop moaning. Get up."

At Hemlock's call, the trees surrounding the clearing thrashed, snapped, and rustled. A thane stepped forth, bowing its head to free its antlers from the branches. Its glamour streamed from it in ragged pennants. One moment it was a handsome stag of majestic proportions; another it was a monstrous forest growth skittering with insects, its eyes dark knotholes weeping rivulets of decay. When it turned and looked at me I felt something else, ancient and implacable, gazing through it.

"This mortal has just earned us an audience with the Alder King," Hemlock finished. And she whirled me around before I'd processed the words, marching me back the way we had come. The fair folk picked up and followed us, clutching their disheveled clothes, gazing around wide-eyed. They left Aster behind as though they'd forgotten she even existed.

At first I had not a clue where Hemlock meant to take us, until I spied the riven stone in the distance. Rook lurched upright nearby. He'd thrown off two of his detainers and made it halfway to us by the time they managed to get him down again. One received an elbow to the chest for his trouble. Rook thrashed beneath them, spitting out dirt. "Do not take us this way," he said to Hemlock. "You know mortals aren't meant to walk the fairy paths."

She aimed a dangerous smile down at him. "Do you propose we keep the king waiting?"

"The Huntsman always strove for a clean kill. A fair death."

The smile froze in place. "She used to," she replied, so low I barely heard it. Then without another word she dragged me forward. The others heaved Rook, resisting, to his feet.

"Isobel," he panted.

I couldn't turn far enough in Hemlock's grasp to look at him. "What's going to happen?"

"I cannot say. Some mortals fall ill, and others go mad. Do not dwell on the things you see. Keep your eyes closed if you can."

Most of the other fair folk reached the riven stone before we did. They slipped into the space between the cracked boulder and simply didn't emerge on the other side. I strained for any hint of what was about to befall me, but saw nothing other than a perfectly ordinary stone.

"Do be dears and watch him closely," Hemlock said to Rook's detainers over her shoulder. "He is still a prince, with a prince's power, and I shall be quite cross if he attempts something on the way. Put this on him." She tossed a crumpled-up handkerchief to Swallowtail, who cried out and almost dropped it.

"This is iron!" And indeed, gleaming coldly within Gadfly's monogrammed linen was my own ring.

"Oh, cease your whining. You needn't touch it yourself. Just slip it on, quickly now."

"But—"

Hemlock's smile widened. Swallowtail hurriedly seized Rook's sword hand and crammed the ring onto his little finger, the only one it would fit. Rook braced himself, his chin raised defiantly. At first he didn't react. He stood glaring at Hemlock, proud despite having his arms twisted behind his back and his glamour melting away, hollowing the planes of his face, making a wild, feral tangle of his hair. I had grown used to his false appearance again, and felt a visceral shock at the sight. Just as I began to hope that he could somehow bear the iron's touch, a muscle moved in his cheek. He wavered on his feet, listing forward drunkenly. A moan tore from his throat, a deep, raw, almost animal sound.

I couldn't bear seeing him in such agony. I jerked toward him, but Hemlock used my own momentum to swing me around and shove me bodily through the riven stone.

I did not have time to close my eyes.

The first thing I saw, staring upward, was stars. There were too many of them. Pinwheels of light, burning cold and vast, spiraled in a black void without end. The longer I stared, the more I felt I'd never truly been aware of the night sky before, nor had I possessed an accurate understanding of my own insignificance in the face of its enormity. The void between the stars wasn't empty as it first appeared, but rather filled with more and more stars, and each gap in those had more and more, too, and then—

"Don't look." The words grated painfully beside me, such a wretched sound that at first I didn't recognize Rook as the speaker. I surfaced as though dragged up from drowning, and groped blindly in the direction of his voice until he took my hand. I lowered my gaze from the terrible, infinite sky. But I could not obey him. I could not look away from what I saw next.

A road stretched before us and behind us. The fair folk cavorted along it in a line, pale forms flickering like sepulchral flames, a procession of ghosts. The forest rose on either side of the path, but it wasn't the same forest that existed in the world we had been in before. The trees were as big around as houses. Roots rose from the ground at such a height I wouldn't have been able to climb them if I'd tried. The fair folks' white luminosity cast flitting shadows across the bark.

While I stumbled forward, years raced around me. Mushrooms erupted from the soil, withered, and tumbled over. More grew in their place. Leaves swarmed onto the branches and fell, new buds already twitching and swelling in their place. Moss raced across the ground like sea-foam, surging and retracting in different shades of green. A fawn picked its way shyly from the undergrowth, only to undergo a strange spasm and then fall dead to the ground, a stag with a gray-furred muzzle and full set of antlers. By the time I passed it, its skeleton was half sunk into the ground, absorbed by layers of decaying leaves that rippled as they consumed it, like devouring maggots.

How many years had passed already? Twenty? Thirty? Fear overtook me. I rounded upon my hand in Rook's, expecting to find my skin wrinkled and spotted with age. But it was the same. Wasn't it? The light was so odd—I couldn't trust anything I saw . . .

"Think of it," Rook forced out, "as an illusion. When we leave the path, only seconds will have passed. You will not be changed. Not in any physical way."

His hand shone with eerie light. I almost thought I saw the outline of my own showing through it, and the ring seemed to cast a shadow through his finger. I dragged my gaze upward—

"No," he rasped.

—to his face. His countenance was ghastly, contorted with agony. Translucent shadows ringed his eyes and darkened his sunken cheeks. It wasn't until I realized that I could faintly make out his sharp teeth through his closed mouth that it occurred to me the light came from within, burning from his very bones. He barely resembled himself. He looked like a revenant that had just crawled from the soil, clinging to life only through desperate hunger.

"Is my ring killing you?" I asked.

Ever so slightly, he shook his head. Even that small motion cost him. Not dying, perhaps, but in unspeakable pain. "I would not have you see me this way."

"I'm still not afraid of you," I whispered, and finally closed my eyes.

"What a peculiar mortal you've found." Hemlock's voice buffeted me as an icy, howling wind. "A pity. I do like them better when they're frightened. They're so pink, and so small. It suits them better."

I couldn't say how long the journey lasted. Even without my vision, I got a sense of what was happening around me. Branches creaked and rustled as though the trees were alive. Roots squirmed through the soil beneath my feet. The mushrooms, ferns, moss, and buds flourished and died with a damp squishing sound, like someone stirring a bowl of congealed pudding. The cruel laughter of a fair one occasionally rose above the cacophony, but as time drew on the forest grew louder and louder until I feared my eardrums would burst. I became aware of stranger noises then: a low, shuddering groan emanating from deep within the earth itself. A crystalline ringing I knew must be the stars.

I almost lost sense of who I was—I became a blind animal stumbling along senselessly, cowed by the ageless, implacable enormity of the universe pressing down on me.

Until suddenly, it all stopped.

Only Hemlock's hands beneath my armpits kept me upright. My eyelids fluttered, golden light flickering through my lashes. A dull roar buffeted me. It was the sound of hundreds or perhaps even thousands of voices speaking at once, but compared to the symphony of time passing it was quiet and faraway, muffled by wads of cotton. I couldn't bring myself to care about whatever was happening. The earth spun quickly enough that by the stars' reckoning, I was already dead. It didn't matter if I survived today, or tomorrow, or the next month. My life was more trivial than that of a single leaf in a forest. A golden afternoon, I remembered, and smiled, with no thought to how I must appear.

My head lolled. Through a crack in my eyelids, I registered that we stood on a platform raised a story or so above the ground. Knotted roots coiled around my feet, blackened by an ancient fire or lightning strike and glistening with beads of hardened sap. The roots descended, forming an uneven spiral stair, to a shining, crowded hall that awaited us below, suffused in what appeared to be bright evening sunlight, but couldn't possibly be that, since it was night. Rook had said seconds, and I believed him. A struggling thought came to me: the light was reflected by mirrors. Great mirrors stood behind the balconies crowded with fair folk, which surrounded us in tiers like a huge theater, or a courthouse . . . no, not mirrors—sheets of water cascading down, perfectly smooth, reflecting the room into gilded, gleaming infinity.

I tried to focus on the stooped figure beside me. He was saying something, but I couldn't comprehend its meaning. Clinging to the memory of us so long ago, I pushed a scattering of words past my lips. "That's why you . . . inadvisable."

"Yes. You remember! Come back, Isobel. Come back to me."

"Oh, Rook, just leave her alone. It doesn't matter if she's gone mad or not—and if she has, she's better off staying that way. I'm the one who has to hold on to her, after all."

"Isobel," he said again, and pressed his lips to mine.

It was a rushed kiss, his chapped mouth bumping hard and chaste against my own, but it felt like inhaling a breath of fresh air after hours of suffocating underground. I blinked rapidly, the blur around me shifting into focus. Nausea burned a trail up my throat, and every sparkling jewel and pillar and fairy light threw off a dizzying halo, but I remembered I had things

to live for after all. If I was going to die, I would do so remembering how much I cared about Rook, and Emma, and March and May, whose fleeting lives mattered terribly, the truths of the fairy paths be damned.

All the fair folk in the audience hall gaped at us. Most clung to the rails, craning their heads as though they'd been watching a familiar play only for an actor to burst in unscripted from the rear doors. Having witnessed Foxglove's disgust at his earlier display, and having served as an intimate witness to the depths of Rook's shame, I knew that kissing me in front of the entire summer court was one of the most courageous things he'd ever done.

"I find it awfully trying, you know, that you never take my good advice," said Hemlock somewhere above and behind me. I wasn't listening. I was gazing at Rook as he gazed back, bent double by the fair folk restraining him. I almost laughed when it occurred to me that we were at the same level, and I was nearly standing up straight.

He was panting with his teeth bared, and his breath stirred the loose locks of hair hanging in front of his face. "I made you a promise the last time we were in the summerlands. I still mean to see it through."

"Are you saying that you have a plan?" I inquired, not feeling very well at all, which explained why I found this rather funny also. "And if so, is it arrogant, ill advised, and likely to result in both our deaths anyway?"

"Yes," he replied, and gave me a quick half-smile in between catching his breath. "I'm afraid there isn't time just now for you to come up with a better one. Otherwise, I would wait."

"Go on, then. I know how much you love showing off."

His expression sobered. "Impossibly, it seems I love you quite a bit more," he said. He hesitated, gathering his strength. Then he made a sudden, sharp jerking motion, and his glamour came flooding back. Before I understood what he had done he'd thrown off his detainers, drawn himself up to his full height, and shouted in a voice that echoed across every corner of the hall, "I challenge the Alder King! I challenge him for sovereignty over the four courts!"

His severed finger, still wearing my ring, lay curled among the riven oak's roots.

Twenty

THE FAIR FOLK surrounding us stepped back. My knees buckled, but Rook caught me by the elbow before I fell and threaded his arm through mine. I wondered why no one was attempting to stop him, until I saw his face. I hadn't seen him like this since the night he confronted me about his portrait. He blazed, fiercely incandescent, somehow less human than ever even with his glamour returned, projecting that if anyone came near us, he would strike them down on the spot. One advantage of their horrible fairy customs, I supposed: strength was everything, and with the iron gone Rook was the most powerful fair one in sight. More than that—he didn't have anything to lose. Even Hemlock looked wary.

"Your hand," I said.

"It will bleed quite a lot, I imagine," he replied in a satisfied tone. "Can you walk? I need you close."

Right, the plan. The plan in which Rook tore off his own finger and, apparently, challenged the Alder King to a duel to the death. What could possibly go wrong?

I squeezed my eyes shut, searching inside myself, evaluating my reserves. "I think so. Not for long."

"Then let us go."

Together we descended, my dress leaving a trail of petals on the uneven steps. When we reached the bottom, I looked back once. The riven oak from which we had emerged grew suspended on a balcony, its dark roots entangled around the platform and its branches halfway grown into the wall. I saw no door, no archway, no other entry anywhere. The Alder King's seat of power could only be reached through the fairy paths.

We strode forward arm in arm. The straight avenue stretching down the center of the room was lined by tall pillars of the same sparkling, translucent stone as the walls and balconies. The stagnant heaviness to the air and the absence of any hint of sky alerted me to the possibility that despite the brightness, we were underground. As we passed the first pillar I saw a bark pattern on its surface and realized they were not stalagmites or carvings, but rather petrified trees preserved so long beneath the earth they had turned to crystal. I took a deep breath and leaned on Rook, conscious of the chamber's unfathomable age, and the claustrophobic weight that crushed down on it from above.

The hall's end was lost in a haze of dazzling light, impossible to look at directly. The Alder King could be seated, watching us approach. Or perhaps he was yet to arrive. I did not know.

Sound carried far here. It reminded me of a cathedral between choral movements, when everyone sat down, whispered, shifted, and flipped through the pages of their hymnals, filling the vaulted ceiling with a noise like hundreds of birds rustling their wings. Rook's hard soled footfalls echoed. I could even hear the enchanted petals dropping from my dress, whispering silkily against the reflective floor. Individual words and phrases jumped out of the blur of voices, sometimes indistinctly, sometimes as clearly as though they'd been shouted in my ear.

"Rook," a baritone said, and it took me a panicked moment to grasp that it was a spectator speaking to his companion up on a balcony, not addressing Rook firsthand. "Did you—" someone else murmured, followed by the sharp, carrying sibilance of "*kiss*." "Isobel!" a girl's voice yelped, and my heart kicked against my ribs like a spooked horse.

"Pay them no mind," Rook said, gazing straight ahead. "Pretend it is just you and I, walking alone. They are but the wind."

With the way my vision blurred in and out, I almost could. "I never knew the wind had such an appetite for gossip."

"You mortals, with your limited perceptions." Though he didn't turn his head, I felt his regard shift. A small smile touched one corner of his mouth. "Watch me."

Showing off even now, I thought. But I couldn't deny that a spark of excitement galvanized my veins and caught my breath in anticipation of whatever he was about to do. Cavalierly, still smiling, he raised his wounded hand and unclenched the fist he'd made of his remaining fingers. Drip, drip, drip. His blood spattered a trail across the floor. Someone gasped. Another cried out fearfully. Shoes stomped and shuffled as fair folk jostled against the railing for a better view. One woman seized the long curls of another and yanked her backward to clear a spot. In the brief gap I spied a silvery-blond head ducking past, its color a stark contrast to the rich chestnuts and auburns of the summer court. *Gadfly?* No, it couldn't be . . .

The nearest pillar exploded in a cascade of sparkling crystal shards. Then the next, and the next, and the next, all the way into the distance. Living branches unfolded from their shattered husks, aflame with scarlet leaves. Roots bulged from the floor, splitting the stones in violent upheaval, sending cracks zigzagging in every direction that struck the corners and raced jaggedly up the walls. Screams rang out as chunks of masonry sheared away from one of the balconies and came toppling down in an avalanche of sundered rock, drowning out the tinkling of falling crystal. Residue filled the air, glittering like diamonds.

I stumbled over the broken floor, but Rook steadied me, helping me over a root that still grew, writhing and distending as it inched wormlike across the ground, spilling forth hairs. He did not favor his injured hand. He couldn't afford to.

Unyieldingly, unstoppably, his autumn trees pressed against the ceiling and spread. Their foliage muted the hall's blinding light into the jeweled tones of stained glass. Now, for the first time, I saw what awaited us.

The Alder King. He sat slumped forward on a throne elevated at the level of the highest platforms, vines entangling him against the wall like a heart ensnared in a web of arteries. His face, his beard, his robes, the throne, and even the vines were all the same pale, powdery gray, lifeless as marble, as though he had become part of the room itself. His sleeping countenance gripped me with a terror I couldn't explain. Somehow I knew he wasn't as lifeless as he looked. I felt his slow awareness turning toward us, as surely as a lighthouse beam circling in the dark. And oh, I didn't want to see him wake up.

Rook squeezed my arm, and his next step hesitated a split second before his boot struck the floor. He'd felt it too. Unlike me, he couldn't show his fear—his weakness. Glancing at his face, I found his eyes fixed on the Alder King with haughty, slightly disdainful anticipation, as though he were merely someone the prince planned to beat at shuttlecocks. But his confidence was fake. Just minutes ago I'd seen him slumped broken and pleading against the Green Well. By now I had witnessed him holding the pieces of himself together enough times to recognize the sight instantly.

I wished that just once I could tell him I loved him and it wouldn't be a curse upon us both.

The hall had gone silent. Fair folk stared upward like children at the autumn leaves falling. The rubble was already softened by a blanket of foliage, as though it had collapsed long ago. In the newfound quiet, yellow ivy twined over the balconies and spiraled up tree trunks, and my dress fluttered against my legs in a clear night wind. Rook's branches snaked closer and closer to the Alder King's motionless form, blooming red.

One of the king's fingers twitched.

Dust trickled from his antler crown, a thin stream at first, then a cascade as he raised his head. We were close enough now to see the powdery texture of it clinging to his beard. He blinked, revealing filmed-over, colorless eyes that wandered like an old man's.

"Why do you wake me?" he said in a dry whisper. Though spoken low, his querulous words swept down the hall and scattered in every corner like a gust of dead leaves. Heat followed, and the smell of rot. Sweat broke out on my palms. "I have been dreaming . . . dreaming of ripe grapes, and a sunset reflected on the water . . . I wish only . . ." Puzzled, he glanced around at the vines that had grown over him, imprisoning him against his throne.

"I am here to challenge you, Alder King." Rook's words rang out, echoing. "Your endless summer has fallen to corruption. All can see it. Masterless fairy beasts roam the forest, and your own lands decay while you slumber. And tonight," he added in a yet louder voice, angling his body toward the balconies with his injured hand still upraised, moss spiraling down his sleeve, "a mortal has destroyed the Green Well."

Shouts followed his pronouncement. "No!" "So it is true!" "The Green Well!" "How will we make the mortals love us now?" Squabbles broke out on the balconies. A few fair folk sank to their knees, clutching the railing in exaggerated attitudes of devastation. They all went silent at a gesture from the Alder King that sent a curtain of dust arcing through the air.

"No. What you say is . . . impossible. The Green Well is eternal."

Somehow, I found my voice. "Fair folk cannot lie," I reminded the king, torn between my fear and a sudden curious pity for him. "The well is gone."

His eyes narrowed. More dust crumbled from the webwork of wrinkles surrounding them, revealing patches of papery flesh. He looked down at me. The heat simmered. Every bit of skin touching my dress itched foully, and phantom grasshoppers buzzed as pressure mounted in my skull. That was all I was to him, regardless of what I had done: an insect crawling at the foot of his throne. He meant to kill me with the sheer force of his attention. And he would have, if Rook's ensorcellment hadn't stopped him.

The moment he realized I was immune to his magic and why, alarm and uncertainty sparked deep in his clouded eyes. "Her will remains her own."

Rook showed his teeth in a smile that wasn't a smile, looking so utterly mad I forgot to breathe. "Yes. Now come down and fight me, if you can."

An indrawn breath. Then the throne room erupted.

Screaming ravens rushed inward from every direction, clotting the air so thickly they smothered the hall in midnight darkness. Their flight was a deafening thunder, drowning out the Alder King's roar of protest, swallowing whole the fair folk's surprised cries. A stinging assault battered my face. I coughed on feather fragments swirling about like chaff, only the warmth of Rook's arm reassuring me he was still there. Between the beating wings I caught piecemeal glimpses of the chaos around me. A woman on one of the balconies clawed at her head as a raven thrashed, caught in her elaborate hat. Another tumbled off, pecked at by dozens at once. Fair folk flooded the stairs, attempting to escape the onslaught to no avail, fights breaking out between them as they trod on one another's shoes and gowns. A fair-haired girl— *Lark?*—grinned while she kicked a man in the shin, and then turned toward me, seeking approval.

Fairy blood flowed. The fragrance of summer phlox overwhelmed me with its sickly sweetness, and I struggled to keep my balance as the world spun in a feathered maelstrom.

A towering shape reared from the darkness. Its antlers cut a swath through the ravens, scattering broken bodies to the floor. Rook spun to protect me from the thane's hooves. At the same moment, a pair of cold hands seized my arms and yanked me away from him, pulling me flush against the nearest tree.

"Stop thrashing about," Lark said into my ear. "Some of us are here to help you."

I grabbed Lark's wrist hard. "Rook doesn't have a sword!"

"A sword?" She grinned. "Why would he need one?"

As it turned out, he didn't. Rook ducked and whirled beneath the thane like a dancer, plunging his left hand upward into its chest. It froze and trembled all over. Autumn ivy burst from first its nose, then its mouth, and then its eyes, and rapidly spread over its body until it resembled a giant topiary. He wrenched his hand free, already crushing the ancient brown skull in his hand as he tossed it away. With a swirl of his coat, he neatly sidestepped the cascade of bark tumbling down. He gave Lark and me an assessing look. The ravens now surged around the three of us in a circle, an opaque black wall studded with glinting eyes, as though we stood at the center of a storm. Rook had his back turned when a second thane crashed through.

I cried out to him, but he'd already sensed it. In one smooth motion he dropped to his knees and slammed his palm to the ground, meeting the whirlwind of feathers already rising to engulf him. The thane's antlers whistled through empty air, missing the large, purple-eyed raven soaring away. Rook vanished into the cyclone, one bird indistinguishable among many. Then he burst free near the ceiling, angling down, crooked legs extended, arrowing toward the thane like a falcon descending upon prey. Once more he disappeared. I strained for any sign of where he might have gone this time, and didn't have to wait long. The thane listed first one way and then the other, its stumbling hooves crushing the rotten fragments of its companion, and then fell with an earth-shaking crash, disintegrating in a cascade of vegetation that tumbled far across the floor.

Rook strode free of the remains in human form, dusting off his sleeves.

"Did he really cut his finger off?" Lark's voice held a note of grisly delight. "He did, didn't he! I haven't heard of anyone doing that before. It's permanent, you see—his glamour won't hide it—and the power won't last long."

I swallowed. "Is he . . . can he fight the Alder King?"

A horn blast shook the ground and vibrated up through my shoes. Time stopped. Or at least that was how it appeared at first, but then Rook stepped back, and I slowly raised one of my tingling hands just to make sure I could. The ravens encircling us hung suspended in midair, frozen midflight, unblinking. Not a feather stirred. The horn sounded again. And the ravens fractured like brittle glass and sheeted down, an obsidian cataract crashing at our feet.

The Alder King stood at the top of his platform. The vines had slithered off him; they were still crawling away across the back of the throne. He took one step down. A second. Each impact knocked dust from his body, and as he descended he shed the weight of centuries, as though a mantle of years slipped from his shoulders. An emerald robe revealed itself by inches, trimmed with dark, antique gold. His thick gray-shot beard was braided in places like an ancient warrior-king's, fastened by golden clasps, and a signet ring glittered on his finger. Heavy brows concealed his eyes, revealing only the stern nose and merciless slash of a mouth I recalled from the engraving in the summerlands. Where was the flaw in his glamour? He had none.

All around us the other fair folk ceased fighting in midmotion, assuming the various strange attitudes of actors in a pantomime. I was dimly surprised by how many appeared to have been fighting not only the ravens, but also one another. Whether some were on our side, or whether the violence over trodden-on shoes had merely proven infectious, I could not guess. They crouched frozen, their claws at one another's throats as the flowering vines and moss created by their own spilled blood grew over them.

Rook did not move. His back was straight and his face unreadable. My heart in my throat, I chanced a look at Lark, not liking the way the world blurred out of focus when I turned— this was not the time to start swooning like a storybook maiden. She stood frozen as well, staring at the Alder King with wide, glassy eyes as though hypnotized.

The king took another step down, looming in the corner of my vision, and that was when I figured it out. His size. His size was his flaw. He towered above the other fair folk, inhuman in his dimensions, a head taller than even Rook.

Finally Lark answered my question. "No," she gritted out, the barely audible word squeezed from her lungs by sheer force of effort, passing between her still lips as an exhalation of air. "No one can."

"I recall now why I sat down on my throne and did not rise again for an age." The Alder King's voice rolled over the chamber like thunder boiling over the horizon. The air grew heavy, crackling with latent power until the hair on my arms prickled and stood on end. "I grew tired of your squabbling. Your small lives wearied me. Wine . . . embroidery . . . trifles . . . why? You would claw your neighbor's eyes out for a mouthful of dust. Yet dust is all around you. The whole world is made of dust, and always returns to it. There is nothing else."

I must have mistaken the fear I'd glimpsed in his eyes. This being did not know fear. He felt nothing at all, I thought, laboring to raise my chin. Black spots swarmed before me like gnats.

"And now the Good Law is broken, and you have failed to mete out just punishment. For what reason does this one . . . and that one . . . yet live? It is no matter what the mortal has done. I do not desire," he said, "to see either of their faces."

He had almost reached the bottom of the stairs. I swallowed the bitter taste of ozone and fumbled for my bond with Rook, and into that shared silence I *screamed* at him.

He staggered as though a rug had been pulled out from beneath his boots. Then he shook his head and, to my dismay, gave the Alder King a crooked smile. The smile was too savage to be called charming. "What a fortuitous coincidence," Rook declared. "I confess neither of us wanted to see your face, either. In light of these circumstances, I think it best we take our leave." He folded his arm over his chest and bowed. "Good day."

The Alder King's compulsory return bow cut off his darkening expression.

"Quickly, to me," Rook said, turning and holding out his uninjured hand. A wave of leaves crashed against him as Lark lifted me, hoisted me onto a stamping horse's back, and pulled my arms around his neck. We took off in a bone-jolting lurch. Powerful muscles bunched beneath my cheek. Faces flashed past, gaping in surprise, shrinking away from the stone chips thrown up by his striking hooves. They stung my own legs, icy pinpricks of pressure without pain. I wondered if I bled.

We clattered up the stairs, Rook's shoulders heaving as he conquered the too-small steps. The mirrorlike curtain of water grew closer and closer, reflecting his charge in rippling silver, and my own too-pale countenance as I clung astride. He was going to jump through it. I braced myself as best I could.

"*This* was your plan? Oh, Rook," I mumbled half-conscious into his warm, rough mane. What he was doing was the last thing anyone would expect. "You're running away."

Twenty-one

OUR FLIGHT from the summer court passed in a blur. Only the shock of water streaming from my hair and dripping down my back kept me sensible enough to cling to Rook's mane. My thoughts lapsed in and out of a stupor, my mind struggling to stay afloat.

At some point early on, Hemlock's cold voice chased us down a dim hollow lined by half-dead pines. I quailed at their leaning shapes, whose stripped lower branches bent inward over the stream bed like they meant to pluck me from Rook's withers.

"Oh, do come back!" she called. "We could have tried to take him together, you and I. We could still try. He's after you, you know. Just think what a battle it would be!"

The horn sounded then, hollow and commanding in the night. Hounds bayed in the distance. The sharp spice of pine resin rose from the needles crushed beneath Rook's hooves, and his unrelenting pace didn't falter.

"Please!" Hemlock cried. "I failed him. He's set them on me. Please—please—please—"

Her screams swirled down with me into the dark.

The next time I regained full consciousness it was to Emma standing in the doorway of our house, holding a skillet in a white-knuckled grip, about to swing it at Rook's head.

"I don't care who you are or why you're here!" she shouted. "You put her down *right now* and *leave*."

"Madam, I—"

"Do you want to know how many times I've shoved a man's intestines back into his body? Fair one or not, I'm sure I can manage it the other way around."

I tried to speak, but my throat was so dry it closed up. All I managed was a sort of gagging sound.

"Isobel!" Rook and Emma both exclaimed at once.

I coughed, saliva flooding my mouth at the surge of nausea that followed. "It's all right. Don't hit him. He's"—another gut-wrenching cough—"he's helping me."

Grim and tight-lipped, Emma lowered the skillet. "Bring her inside and put her on the settee. And then explain yourself, please, beginning with why you were just a horse."

The walls tilted crazily as Rook carried me through the kitchen and the hall to the parlor, the air redolent with linseed oil, the shapes of the props familiar even in the dark. Home. I was home. An ache swelled bigger and bigger in my chest. I hadn't expected to be here again—I'd thought I'd die without ever coming back. When he laid me down on the settee, the hot tears spilled over. I had a great deal of other, more important things to say, but my miserable relief hijacked my brain, and all that came out was "Emma" in a strangled wail.

She pushed Rook aside, and he had the good sense to retreat to the foot of the settee and hover there like a scolded toddler. Her arm slid between my back and the settee's cushions, pulling me against her. I clung weakly, sobbing into her shoulder.

"Oh, Bell, where are your *clothes*? Why are you wearing a dress that's shedding petals all over the place? Are you hurt anywhere? Did they hurt you?"

"I'm all right," I bawled against her nightgown, not because it was true, but because I wanted it to be.

Eventually I subsided into wracking gulps and hiccups, and she laid me back down. I was grateful I couldn't see the enormous wet spot I'd left on her shoulder in the dark. "I'm going to fetch some water and a lantern. You," she added, pinning Rook with her gaze, "behave yourself."

"Er, yes, madam," he said.

The moment Emma left the room he was before me like a shot, gathering my wet fingers into his hands. He hissed in pain and pulled his left hand back, fumbling around for a handkerchief to cover up his slip. I touched his cheek, and he stilled, the gleam of his eyes intent on my face in the shadows. I marveled at how hot his skin felt, which meant I must be very cold indeed.

"Isobel," he asked, "are you well? Truly?"

I considered the question. Though I lay motionless, every muscle in my body jumped with overexertion. My heartbeat rocked me slightly, the shell of my ear scraping a rhythmic *shuff, shuff, shuff* against the cushions, as though I had burned up to a husk as light and frail as paper.

"I don't know. Are you?" I whispered.

He started to nod and stopped, unable to complete the motion. How silly of us to ask that question of each other, knowing neither of us would ever be well again. Yet I had the strangest feeling, wrapped up in this cocoon of darkness and exhaustion, resting on the almost-uncomfortable stiff brocade of my settee, that nothing that had happened to us was real. The autumnlands, the Barrow Lord, the spring court, the Alder King—all of it impossible, vivid as a fever dream, contrary to the solid reality of home.

"You promised to bring me back," I said.

"If only I had done so sooner. I—"

Still cupping his cheek, I brushed my thumb over his lips, and he fell silent.

"Don't blame yourself," I said. "We made that choice together. But we can't stay. The Alder King is on his way, isn't he? Emma and the twins are in danger. If anything were to happen to them . . . we must leave as soon as we can."

"Isobel!" The lantern Emma held at the doorway illuminated her shock, both at my words and at the position in which she found us. "You are not leaving this house again, no matter what. Do you hear me?"

She rounded on Rook. His winded and disheveled appearance in the lantern light gave her pause. She narrowed her eyes. She suspected the same thing I would have until recently, that the only reason a fair one would present himself like this was to deceive us. Certainly, it would never occur to her that he was conserving every scrap of magic he could.

"Explain," she said, voice hard. "In detail."

To my surprise he rose, squared his shoulders, and did. He

glossed over certain parts, for which I silently thanked him, but left out nothing of importance. My dreamlike trance faded as he went on. With every word, the memories returned with sharp-edged clarity, tearing holes in the insubstantial veil separating me from the night's horrors. Emma's face went whiter and whiter, until eventually she sat down with an expression like stone.

Humiliation prickled my skin in waves of hot and cold, warring with a tight knot of defiance in my chest. The thought of seeing judgment—or worse, disappointment—on her face when she next looked at me made me want to curl in on myself and never face the world again. I had no way to prove that the love Rook and I felt for each other was real and that we deserved every desperate, foolhardy inch of it, and I was already tired, so tired, of bearing its weight as a failure. A crime.

The minutes I waited for Emma's reaction were the longest of my life. She listened without interrupting. When Rook neared the end her gaze drifted down to his left hand, and a line appeared between her eyebrows. She had never seen an injured fair one before. He shifted at her scrutiny, the only sign of nervousness he'd shown since beginning the story. Despite being a prince among fair folk, in that moment he looked awfully young, not so very unlike a human suitor meeting a girl's family for the first time.

But usually, a suitor didn't deliver news of his and his sweetheart's impending demise.

"And that was why I arrived as a horse," he finished, "and why we must leave soon."

Emma turned to me. I braced myself, believing I was prepared for the worst, but I wasn't. I couldn't bear her pinched, ashen devastation. No judgment, no disappointment, and the fact that she didn't blame me for any of this was the hardest thing of all.

"What of the enchantment on the house?" she asked.

"He's the Alder King, Emma," I said. "I'm sorry. I'm so sorry."

She looked at Rook.

He bowed his head. "I fear Isobel is right. Nothing will stand in the Alder King's way."

For a few seconds, none of us spoke. Emma rubbed the heels of her hands up and down her thighs as though easing a muscle cramp. Her expression betrayed little, but that tense, repetitive gesture was one of aimless despair, and I felt it too—a sick acceleration, a quickening slide, like someone had just tipped me over the crest of a hill in a wagon. There was no turning back. There was only the fall, and the inevitable crash at the bottom.

"Rook, thank you for bringing her home," she said finally. "Isobel, I want you to know that I'm proud of you. Don't leave yet, please. Is there anywhere you can go from here?"

Rook and I exchanged a glance. "We can make for the World Beyond," he said, careful in his phrasing. It was a kindness to Emma, and nothing else. We'd never get that far.

A furtive shuffling came from the stairwell. Then two pairs of bare feet slapped down the steps.

Oh, god. The twins must have heard everything. They'd probably been eavesdropping since Rook and I came in. My stomach clenched at the sight of their wide eyes as they crept around the corner. March hesitated in the doorway, wringing her long linen nightshirt against her legs. May had a squarish object tucked under her arm. They both looked petrified to see me lying on the settee half dead in an enchanted ball gown.

May recovered first. Scowling, she stomped over to Rook and thrust the thing she was carrying up at him. Next she cleared her throat, commanding the room's undivided attention.

"A creepy stranger gave us that while we were playing outside." (*"What?"* Emma exclaimed, shooting to her feet.) "He told us to hide it and not open it, since it's a present for you and Isobel. We tried anyway," she added, narrowing her eyes, "but the lid's stuck."

It was a slender box about the length of a man's forearm, like a box one might store hat ribbons in, but I was well aware that it wasn't a hat ribbon box, even disregarding the way Rook held it as though it might explode at any moment. My insides gave an uneasy flip.

May glanced at me, feigning indifference. Then she gathered up her courage and declared, "I hate you."

"May—"

Her hands balled into fists. "Don't say you're sorry, because it won't change my mind!"

I knew she didn't mean it. She was confused and betrayed and frightened, and being angry at me was her only way of seizing control of the situation. But that didn't stop my heart from sinking to the floor as she whipped around and stomped into the kitchen. March shot me a skittish look and scampered after her sister. Emma gave us a long, fraught stare—its meaning clear, *stay*—before she hurried after the twins.

Through it all Rook wore an expression of aloof perplexity, as a cat might watching its favorite furniture get moved about without its permission.

His bewilderment was the last straw. I didn't have the energy to translate our humanity for him. Grief smashed through my final defenses like a battering ram. I gave a strangled sob, so tired I couldn't tell if my scratchy, aching eyes owed themselves more to exhaustion or tears.

Rook sank onto the end of the settee. He hesitated, then peeled his coat off and laid it over me. It was warm and smelled of him. Overwhelmed by his gentleness, I began weeping again in earnest. He drew back in alarm, clearly thinking he'd made things worse.

"Er," he said. He patted the nearest part of me he could reach, which was my foot. "I apologize for . . . that. If you would stop crying now," he added, a trifle desperately, with a note of princely command.

It was no use. Just then, a random thought renewed my anguish. "Oh, I destroyed your raven pin!" I choked out. "I'm so sorry."

"Well, I think I've found that I don't need it anymore."

Because he loved me. I covered my face with my hands.

"Isobel, I appear to be . . . shall I leave the room?"

"No, it isn't you." Muffled by my fingers, my voice was smudged pitifully with tears. "I'm just, I'm being really human right now, all right? Give me ten seconds."

I sucked in a deep, shaking breath and counted to ten. When I reached it, I had stopped crying. Mostly. After a shuddering exhale, I rubbed my face on my sleeve, which turned out to be a bad idea; the lace scraped my swollen eyelids like sandpaper. Reaching out, I enlisted Rook's help in wedging myself up into the corner of the settee, because I wasn't sure I could sit upright on my own, and determinedly pretended I didn't have a bright red face and a snotty nose.

Good enough. "There. Now, let's open the box."

His fingers tightened around the box's edges. Its varnish gleamed in the lantern light. A gift, May had said. My best guess was that it was some sort of cruel joke, a prank played on the two of us for breaking the Good Law. But that didn't make much sense, did it? One didn't play pranks on people who were supposed to be dead. No one had expected us to survive the night, much less return . . . return to my house. Unless . . .

Gadfly.

A chill rippled up my legs, over my arms, and into my scalp. There was something going on here I didn't know about. Something, I suddenly felt certain, that like most things I didn't know about, I wasn't going to like at all. The room shrank away, its familiar odds and ends blending into an ominous clutter.

Rook passed his hand over the locked latch. I forced myself not to look away from the stump of his little finger. He had already used his glamour to make it appear healed, and for the sake of his pride I would not dispute him in the matter. The wound must have hurt terribly, but aside from that single noise he'd made earlier, he revealed nothing.

He snapped his fingers, and the lid sprang open. Inside, upon a pillow of black velvet, lay a newly forged dagger. Its point glinted, needle-sharp.

I asked, even though I didn't need to, "Is it iron?"

"Yes," he said.

Whether it was due to the ensorcellment, or simply that we had grown familiar with each other, I knew we had the exact same thought simultaneously. Gadfly, standing over us at the Green Well, describing the terms of our violation and the limited means by which we might escape punishment. The way

Rook had pleaded with him to end his life, and thus spare mine. He played games with us even now.

Without another word, Rook passed the box over. I wouldn't take it, so he set it down on the cushion beside me. Our eyes locked. A silent argument raged between us. When he drew a breath to break the stalemate, I emphatically shook my head.

"No," I said. "Stop it."

He leapt up from his seat and knelt on the floor in front of me. He took the dagger from the box and turned it against himself. It shook so badly in his grasp he'd drop it before long, and I took cold comfort in the assurance that he couldn't use it without help. But when his glamour flowed away I wasn't prepared for the sight of his true self. His skin held a terrible pallor; his overlarge, queer-looking eyes were shadowed by exhaustion and pain. Sweat had left streaks in the dirt on his face.

"Listen to me," he croaked. "Both of us need not die tonight. Isobel, you cannot break the Good Law alone. If the fair folk sense I am no more—"

I seized the dagger from him. Having no idea what to do with it afterward, I lifted the cushion I was lying on and shoved it underneath, then threw my weight back on top. "Stop being melodramatic! I am not going to *kill you* in my *parlor*!"

He stared at me in disbelief. "Did you just sit on it?"

"Yes," I said mutinously.

"But there is no other way."

I must have gotten quite a ferocious look on my face, because he leaned back a little. "Have you considered what it would be like for me to go on with my life after murdering you? Imagine if it were the other way around!"

He paused, and looked ill.

"Exactly!"

"No—yes—you are right. I should not have asked it of you." His eyes flicked toward the hallway. Emma. A vise squeezed the air out of my lungs. If Rook asked Emma, she would certainly slay him to spare me, just as she would have killed the fairy beast to save her sister, if only she had had the strength. She wouldn't let another family member die because of the fair folk.

My pulse roared in my ears. I no longer felt the settee's cushions or the tears drying on my face. In the stories, maidens drank poison and jumped from high towers upon hearing of their princes' deaths. But I wasn't one of them. I still wanted to live, and in fact I had lived seventeen perfectly functional years before I'd ever met Rook. I had a family who loved me and needed me. I couldn't ask Emma and the twins to suffer through the pain of my loss. If this was the only option . . . if this was what we had to do . . . but I couldn't countenance it; I ached to think of him gone, a vast empty ache I couldn't face head-on for fear of drowning in it.

His fingers stroked a strand of hair behind my ear. "It would not be like a mortal dying," he said. "You have seen it. I will leave no body behind. There will be a tree, perhaps. A bigger one than that absurd little oak outside your kitchen."

I couldn't stand it. I choked on a laugh. "Show-off."

"Yes." He gave me half a smile. "Always."

I twisted and dragged the dagger back out from under the cushions. I closed my eyes, squeezing the blade so tightly I almost drew blood. I pictured a version of myself, perhaps a year or two from now, walking up the hill to my house. Still grieving, but getting better every day. In my mind March and May ran out of the kitchen door to wrap themselves around my legs—no, around my waist, for surely they'd grown taller. A majestic tree dropped leaves that painted one side of the roof scarlet year-round, demonstrating an arrogant disregard for the state of our gutters. Clouds scudded across a blue sky. Heat simmered. Grasshoppers buzzed in a ceaseless, mind-numbing chorus.

I recoiled from the image. No. I couldn't accept that world, a world where we had lost and the Alder King had won, a world where nothing ever changed, and the evidence of it surrounded me every day.

My palm stung. I blinked and the dagger came into focus, silvery against my red dress, light shivering over its surface like water. For the first time I truly understood what I had been given, and what it could do. Or rather, what it *would* do. Because with this understanding, I made a decision.

The dagger would kill a fair one.

Just not the fair one Gadfly had in mind.

Twenty-two

BRING ME vermilion. And indigo, please. May, I know you aren't talking to me right now, but you can still carry things, can't you? Emma, would you mind finding something I can use to prop up my arm while I work? Rook, that's not a paint palette, that's a serving tray. Oh—never mind, bring it here. I suppose it'll do."

My parlor had transformed into a whirlwind of activity. I'd toppled over the second I tried to stand, so I was enthroned on the settee, propped up by half a dozen pillows, as everyone waited on me hand and foot, which would have been nice if they hadn't all been tasks I'd rather have been doing myself. To their credit, no one tried arguing me out of my unhinged-sounding scheme. Emma and Rook had taken one look at the glint in my eyes, glanced at each other in sudden communion, and started fetching brushes.

I'd never done work like this before. I didn't have time to draft it, for one. Morning light already stole across the room, setting my linseed oil jar aglow and casting a pink rectangle on the wallpaper. I'd decided not to look over my shoulder, because once I started I wouldn't be able to stop, but Emma kept peeking out the window, and it wasn't long before she gasped and dropped a pillow.

"What did you see?" I asked.

"Nothing." She hurried over to stick the pillow under my elbow. "My nerves just got the better of me." A blatant lie— Emma could mix deadly chemicals with someone playing the cymbals next to her head.

May stood on her toes and looked. "There's something running around in the field," she announced in a would-be-casual voice. She turned around with an exaggerated shrug to show she wasn't afraid, even though I could see her shaking from across the room. "I bet it's the Alder King and he's here to kill you and eat you because you're *stupid*."

Emma reared up, clutching another pillow. "May, you will not speak to your sister like that!"

"Well, it's true!"

"The Alder King has not yet arrived," Rook reassured me. "It's only a hound, and it won't be able to enter your home, nor will any of the other beasts and fair folk who follow."

I schooled my breathing, forcing myself to relax. The brush had left bloodless dents in my clenched fingers. "Why?" I asked in a low voice I hoped my family couldn't hear. "The enchantment doesn't prevent anyone from coming inside."

His eyes flashed. "Because I will not let them." He gave the window another cursory glance and then whirled toward the hallway.

"Rook," I said, drawing him up short. "Thank you. Be careful."

I wasn't just thanking him for what he was about to do. I was thanking him for trusting me—for believing in me. It hadn't been easy for him to set the dagger aside.

He gave a stiff nod before he left. The kitchen door bounced shut out of sight behind him. Forcing aside my gnawing fears, I focused on my canvas, losing myself in the glistening paint gliding over its textured surface, the quiet scrape of the brush's dry bristles when I reached the end of a stroke. The background blended from dark burnt umber in the corners to luminous gold at the center, where it would outline the subject in a corona of light. Everything depended on this portrait. It needed to be the best work I'd ever done, completed in a single morning, in my least-polished method—wet on wet—since I didn't have time to let any of it dry. My eyes burned with the effort of staying open, and my brush felt like it weighed twenty pounds. But stroke by stroke, the painting came to life.

Soon I had sunk too deeply into my work to notice anything going on around me. The world consisted only of my Craft. Like an old sailor's map of the earth, nothing existed beyond my canvas's flat borders. Until a great snapping crash came from outside, rattling the glasses on the table beside my easel, and jerking me headlong back into the light, sound, and clamor of real life.

I turned my head in a blinking stupor to find Emma and the twins plastered against the windows. Emma was at the southern window across the room; I hadn't noticed March and May clambering onto the settee, bracketing me between them.

"He tore it in half!" May exclaimed gleefully.

March bounced up and down on her knees.

I spared a look over my shoulder. A tangle of giant, squirming thorn vines surrounded our house, each one taller and thicker than the oak tree, plunging our yard into deep shade. As I watched, one of the vines seized a white shape—a hound— and flung it back into the wheat field, so far into the distance I couldn't tell where it landed. The wreckage of some much larger fairy beast strewn across our grassless chicken run explained the earthquake. I hunted for Rook among the chaos. The last time he'd created thorns of a similar size, he had been grievously injured by the Barrow Lord. How badly had he wounded himself to accomplish *this* reckless feat? I couldn't find him anywhere. And I not only suspected, but knew for certain that he was motivated by a persuasive death wish. A shudder rippled over my shoulders and arms, abating to a fine tremble that seized my entire body. My skin felt tight and white noise rang in my head, crowding out all other thoughts.

March bleated exuberantly as another hound went soaring across the field. The twins' reaction, at least, assured me that if we escaped today intact, I'd have no trouble getting them to like Rook.

Shouldn't we keep them from watching this? I asked Emma with a rather crazed glance.

Emma shot back an equally crazed look that said, *Oh, believe me, I've tried.*

A creaking, groaning noise came from outside. I returned my attention to the window. The thorn vines were freezing in place from the base upward, their heavily spiked tendrils zigzagging into sharp angles as they stiffened, forming a dense, impenetrable-looking thicket. Vertigo swooped through my stomach. I abandoned my efforts at searching the yard and focused inward instead, concentrating on the ensorcellment bond between us. Surely if something had happened to Rook, I would have felt his reaction. The vines weren't dead, just motionless. Whatever was going on out there, he'd done it on purpose—hadn't he?

The kitchen door banged open and boots thudded through the hallway, Rook's long stride unmistakable. I briefly pressed my eyes closed, riding out the relieved dizziness that washed over me. But I didn't have a chance to indulge in the sensation.

"He's coming," Rook said as soon as he entered the room. "We have little time."

His chest heaved like a bellows, and his hair was so rumpled he looked as though he'd been standing in the middle of a storm. One of his sleeves was rolled up, with a dishrag from our kitchen messily bound around his forearm. I tried not to consider the implications of this—he'd never needed to bind his wounds before. Maybe he just didn't want to make a mess with his blood indoors.

Grimly, Emma and I met each other's eyes across the parlor.

"Can you take the twins to the cellar?" I asked.

This might be the last time we ever saw each other alive. The knowledge made holding her gaze like staring into the sun. She had sworn to raise me and keep me safe, but now faced losing me to the same force that had already shattered our lives once. And suddenly I knew with terrible clarity that if she lost me, she didn't know if she'd have the strength to pick herself back up again. In that moment there were two Emmas transposed over each other—the Emma who had raised me, and the Emma she kept hidden from me, an Emma I'd barely even met before. An Emma I might never have the chance to get to know as I grew older.

The spell broke.

"You heard your sister," Emma said briskly, though she sounded very tired. She came over and picked March up. May slid off the settee, subdued. Both twins watched me uncertainly. I couldn't start crying again. Not now.

"I love you all and I'll be done by lunchtime," I declared in my best Isobel's-a-busy-perfectionist voice. When May opened her mouth I interrupted, "May, I know you don't hate me." If I gave her the chance to say it herself, I wouldn't be able to maintain my composure. "Now hurry up."

Before they went, Emma pressed a kiss to the top of my head. I set my jaw and tilted my face toward the ceiling, and waited until I heard their feet thumping down the stairs to let the tears fall. Sniffing industriously, I swiped the wetness away on my wrists, stabbed my paintbrush into a whorl of vermilion and lead tin yellow, and got back to work. It was just finishing touches now. A handful of flaws glared at me from the canvas—a patch of shadow that needed more purple light reflected on it, a slab of the crown that could use more highlights for dimension—but I didn't have time to fix them all. The most important part, I told myself, was done.

Fabric swished as Rook moved to stand beside me. As he absorbed what I had wrought, a profound stillness settled over him. That stillness told me everything I needed to know. A pause, and then I set my brush down. Confidence swelled within me as surely and calmly as the rising tide, filling in every cavernous doubt.

My Craft was true.

A horn sounded, rattling the windows in their frames, low-pitched and sonorous with disdain. Sunlight speared through the parlor as crystal shattered outside—the thorns had fallen to the Alder King. Buoyed by a giddy certainty as intoxicating as wine, I looked up at Rook and smiled.

He tore his gaze from the portrait, startled. At some point his glamour had fled from him. His hair hung in a wild snarl around the disquieting planes of his face. He scrutinized me with inhuman eyes, cruel eyes that weren't made to show kindness or tenderness or love, but they still spoke clearly to the fact that I was behaving oddly, even for a mortal, and especially for me.

"You've run out of magic," I said softly, touching his wrist. Amber-colored blood had soaked through the makeshift bandage.

He flinched, and his expression shuttered. He raised his hand and looked at it front and back, taking in the long, spidery, oddly jointed fingers as if the sight disturbed him as much as it would a mortal.

"The ensorcellment draws upon my strength," he said. "I cannot protect you from him any longer."

"You won't need to," I replied.

A tremor shook the floor. Though I sensed no further movement, the whole house groaned as though lifted several inches from its foundations by brute force. When it settled with a resounding thud, all the boards shook and plaster dust trickled down from the ceiling. Rook glanced around, seeing something I could not. I didn't need to ask. The enchantment on my home was broken. The Alder King had come here for only one reason, after all—to kill us both. And he wasn't wasting any time.

I pushed aside the pillows and stood. My knees gave way for the third time in twenty-four hours, and Rook caught me again, holding me up as though I weighed nothing. I reached for the portrait.

"Isobel," he said. My hand paused. "I am not very good at—declarations," he went on, after a hesitation. And then he hesitated some more, looking down at me, absorbing the sight, and seeming to forget whatever it was he had on his mind.

"I know," I assured him fondly. "I seem to remember you insulting my short legs the first time, among other things."

He drew up a bit. "In my defense, they *are* very short, and I cannot tell a lie."

"So what you're trying to say is that you love me, short legs and all?"

"Yes. And—no. Isobel, I love you wholly. I love you eternally. I love you so dearly it frightens me. I fear I could not live without you. I could see your face every morning upon waking for ten thousand years and still look forward to the next as though it were the first."

"I think we disparaged you too much," I breathed. "That was a fine declaration indeed."

I seized his collar and pulled him down for a kiss, ghoulish countenance and all, ignoring his muffled sound of protest, which did not remain on his lips for long. His teeth were sharp, but he kissed me with such tenderness and care it didn't matter. A flower blossomed inside me, a soft, rare bloom aching for light and wind and touch. In another world, it might have been our last kiss. In this one, I wouldn't allow it.

We broke apart as a shadow crossed the window. Reluctantly Rook released me, and I tottered forward on legs as weak as a newborn fawn's. I took up the portrait like a shield and turned around.

Something was happening to my door. Dark, glistening spots spread across it like an ink spill soaking through a page, or a candle flame blackening a piece of paper from beneath. It wasn't until the sweet stench of decay hit me, and white mold fuzzed over the surface, that I realized the door was rotting. It sagged on its hinges, wood warping. The boards peeled away in strips, disintegrating into spongy lumps as they fell. The brass doorknob clattered to the floor and rolled into a corner. And the Alder King ducked inside, bending at the waist and turning his broad shoulders sideways to fit through the now-empty doorway. The light eclipsed him from behind, transforming him into a black silhouette too bright to see. Heat rolled across the room.

I had had many fair folk in my parlor, yet never one like him. As he straightened, the sun of a different age kindled fire in his beard and glowed on his emerald surcoat, striking him at an angle and intensity for which the room's windows were not responsible. He was from a time that was not our time, and the weight of it enveloped him like a cloak. Conscious that I was so small standing in front of him I might as well have been a child, I took a step forward. He didn't look at me. It was as though he didn't even see me. Beneath the heavy brows his eyes searched through an eternity of years, seeking the present, looking for an hour and a day less significant to him than a single mote of dust suspended in the air among uncountable thousands.

My confidence faltered. My plan had one flaw—it wouldn't work unless he looked down. So I cleared my throat to speak.

"We worshipped you once, didn't we, Your Majesty? I saw the statues in the forest. They were carved by human hands."

He tilted his head as though listening to a distant thread of birdsong.

"I have never heard a tale or read a book in which it was not summer in Whimsy," I continued. "Before you punish us, will you tell me how long you have ruled?"

His voice creaked like living wood. "I have ruled an age. I was king before mortals made the word. First I was admired. Then I was feared. Now, I am forgotten. Strange. I do not recall whether I sleep or wake, or what the difference is between them." His gaze descended, sharpening with comprehension, and my muscles locked as I resisted the urge to flee like a hare from a plummeting hawk. "One day, I came to punish a mortal girl named Isobel and a prince named Rook for breaking the Good Law."

"Yes," I replied, my throat dry as bone. "That day is today, Your Majesty. But first I have made you a gift, just as mortals did before me."

I raised the portrait. His gaze fell to it, and lingered. My heart quailed. He studied my work without recognition, as if it meant nothing to him—I might as well have held up a portrait of Rook or Gadfly, or even a blank canvas. But then he let out a long, slow breath, like the final rattle of a dying man, that filled my parlor as a draft. The otherworldly sunlight gilding his shoulders faded behind clouds, leaving his features shadowed. Once more he became the old man in the throne room. Dust still clung to his features. Revealed by shade, a cobweb hung between two prongs of his antler crown. "What is this?" he asked in a low, hoarse voice.

"It is you, Your Majesty."

He looked at himself. He saw his own face as it wasn't, and

yet was: a ruler who had sat on the throne for countless millennia, but who had felt every loss great and small, endured every burden of his interminable lifetime. A being who had loved once, and was perhaps even loved in return. His mouth trembled. A tear tracked a gleaming trail through the dust on his cheek.

"You said that you dreamed, Your Majesty. You said you wished for something. What is it?" I adjusted my grip on the back of the canvas. Metal, warmed by my body, shifted against my palm.

His face contorted. "How dare you . . . how dare you show this to me?" His words rose in volume until he howled in a broken voice like a storm tearing through trees. The walls shook, and branches whipped against the house outside. "I do not dream. I care nothing for trifles, this dust you call Craft." He raised his hand, preparing to strike me down. Yet still he couldn't take his eyes from his portrait.

Now. I threw myself forward. The Alder King did not see the threat in a mortal girl flinging herself against him, armed with only a canvas and wet paint. What he did not see was his undoing. With the full force of my weight behind it, the iron dagger slid through the painting, between his ribs, and pierced his heart.

I leapt back into Rook's waiting arms as the Alder King dropped to his knees. The portrait tore and fell away—the best work of my life lying in a pile of twisted canvas frame, tattered fabric, and smeared paint on the floor. My pulse pounded like a hammer striking an anvil as I imagined him pulling the dagger from his chest and rising unharmed. But he only put his hand to the yellow paint on his surcoat, as though it surprised him more than his own blood. His glamour began flaking away, and

I made a strangled sound at what it revealed.

The Alder King's height remained, but he was gaunt and emaciated as a corpse, his moth-eaten robes swaddling his withered frame like the raiments of a once-great man eaten away by sickness. His eyes were sunk into deep hollows, and his colorless skin had a soft, frayed quality like rotten cheesecloth. The antler crown turned black with tarnish, hideously spiked where pieces of it had broken off over time, its rim grown into the flesh of his forehead. A nauseating stench rolled from him. When he toppled over, a carrion beetle scurried from his ear and vanished into his beard.

His lips moved. "I am afraid," he whispered, in a tone of dawning wonder. "I feel—"

His eyes drooped shut. Moss foamed up from the rug to engulf him. *He'll ruin the floor,* I thought, strangely practical. *We ought to move the body.* But as soon as the idea occurred to me Rook threw us both aside, shielding me with his back and arms. The world heaved. A barrel-thick root bulged from the floorboards beneath me, splintering the wood like an axe. Flowers surged across the rug and the easel and the settee, over me and Rook, crashing like a wave against the far wall. Glass shattered. Branches scraped the ceiling. Nails creaked, giving way beneath the strain, and then the house shook with a wrenching crash, and loose shingles pelted down all around us. Light sheared through the devastation, blindingly bright.

That seemed to be the end of it. Rook lay atop me a moment longer before he looked over his shoulder, bits of plaster dropping from his hair, and rolled off. He helped me to my feet amid the ruin of my parlor. It was more forest than parlor now: a colossal alder tree had grown in the center of it, breaking through half the roof and felling the southern wall. Dappled light shimmered on an undergrowth of moss and ferns and flowers that gave no hint of the furniture beneath aside from oddly shaped bulges here and there. We had won, but for the moment I felt utterly numb. It was strange standing right in the middle of my parlor, looking out across the wheat field beyond the sagging remnants of Rook's thorn barricade. In the distance, figures fled back into the forest—moving faster than any human, some of them on all fours.

A gust of wind blasted us. Rook shifted, a shingle scraping beneath his boot. Then he stumbled and fell. Panic clutched me. I had a vision of a wooden splinter impaling his back while he protected me with his body. I dropped to the ground beside him, seizing his arm, wondering if he could survive a grievous wound without magic.

He looked more stunned than hurt, however, and as I ran my hands over him, searching for any sign of injury, his glamour flooded back over him. He caught my hand in his. "Look," he said, but it was the expression on his face that made me turn around.

Wind swept across the field, bending the wheat in shimmering waves. As it spread outward, the colors changed. The leaves on the trees turned golden and scarlet and fiery orange. Soon the transformation set the whole forest ablaze. Stretching far into the distance, the only green that remained belonged to the grass verges bordering the fields and a handful of lone, tall pines poking through the canopy. I laughed out loud imagining how confounded the people of Whimsy must be—Mrs. Firth scrambling out of her shop, appalled; Phineas considering the painting hung beside the door. A single red leaf drifted down from the kitchen oak.

"It's so quiet," I marveled. The breeze ruffled my dress, its sweet, longed-for coolness raising gooseflesh on my arms. Birds sang sweetly in the trees. From the edges of the forest, crickets chirped a liquid melody. But the grasshoppers had all gone silent.

A lone figure distinguished itself from the wreckage in the yard, fastidiously picking through the thorns strewn across the ground. His blond hair shone silvery in the sun, and he had changed his clothes since I had seen him last—he wore an eggshell-blue waistcoat and an immaculate, freshly tied cravat.

My gut clenched. Buried somewhere in my parlor, I still had an iron dagger.

Gadfly called out to us in a mild, pleasant voice. "And so the rule of summer is ended, and autumn has come to Whimsy. I do regret that spring is so far away, but that's simply how the world works, and I trust that one day the seasons will turn again. Good afternoon, Rook. Isobel." He halted several yards away and bowed.

Frowning, Rook returned the courtesy. I was bound by no such obligation, and glared.

"What a happy welcome," Gadfly said. "I merely wanted to congratulate you both on a job well done." His gaze shifted to me alone, and he smiled, a warm, courteous smile that wrinkled his eyes while revealing nothing. "You made all the right choices. How splendid. How singular. The moment you slew the Alder King, you destroyed every mandate he has ever made. You and Rook are free to live as you please, unburdened by the Good Law. The fairy courts will never be the same."

Somehow I found my voice. "But you—you wanted . . ."

What *had* he wanted? Abruptly, everything fell into place.

Before I'd made my first bargain with him all those years ago, perhaps even before I'd been born, he'd already begun scheming. Placing my home under a powerful enchantment to gain my trust and ensure that no harm came to me before he set his plan into motion. Arranging Rook's portrait. Bringing us to the Green Well. Planting the iron dagger, which was never meant for Rook after all, but for the Alder King all along. And worse—knowing exactly what to say that would make him my bitter enemy, and set me crashing through the woods, away from my predestined path toward the impossible course of destroying the Alder King. Astonishment and fury washed over me in equal measure. My voice hardened, choked with emotion. "I don't appreciate being used as a pawn in your game, sir."

He looked at me a long moment in silence. "Ah, but you were not a pawn. All along, you have been the queen."

I took a breath. His inflection was laden with some hidden meaning I didn't have the patience to decipher. "And you are treacherous, and I'll never forget the pain we endured by your design, no matter what came of it in the end."

"Spoken, if I may say so, like a true monarch." He smiled again. But a shadow passed over his countenance, and this time, his eyes didn't crinkle. His portrait room sprang to my mind unbidden. All those patient centuries of collecting portraits—not out of desire for them, but because he was waiting for me, for my Craft, a spider at the center of a vast web he'd spun for hundreds of years in solitude.

"I do believe that is for the best," he went on, watching me intently. "Trusting one of my kind is quite enough foolishness for a lifetime. Mortals are always better off not forgetting what we are, and that we only ever serve ourselves."

"Gadfly," Rook said, in a tone that suggested the spring prince was overstaying his welcome.

"Just one last thing, if I may." Gadfly brushed some invisible dust off his sleeve and raised his eyebrows at Rook. "You are aware, I trust, that you are not yet named king? That there is a certain something you must—"

"Yes, I know!" Rook interrupted crossly.

I shot him a curious glance and discovered that he was nervously avoiding my eyes. He looked relieved when tentative footsteps crunched within the house, liberating him of the burden of explaining this "certain something" to me, and for the moment I was happy to forget all about it.

"Emma!" I called. "We're safe! We're in the . . . parlor."

"I can see that," Emma said calmly, picking her way into the room with the twins clutching both her hands. "There are holes in the walls. March, whatever you just picked up, don't eat it."

"Too late," said May.

Emma shook her head. She scanned the parlor, and then the yard, and saw Gadfly, whereupon her eyes narrowed appraisingly. "Now who's going to clean up this mess?"

"Oh, dear," said Gadfly. "I'm afraid I must be off."

Epilogue

I WRAPPED the bandage neatly around Rook's injured hand, pleased to see that this time, he didn't hide a wince. Two weeks later, his finger was nearly healed. We sat at my kitchen table beneath the wavering amethyst glow of his fairy light, still shining brightly after the two dozen enchantments he'd dispensed that day as payment to the workmen rebuilding our parlor. It didn't escape me that he had not yet mentioned returning to the forest, or said anything about taking up the role of king, so the moment he started fidgeting restlessly in his seat, I had a reasonable idea of what he was working up to.

"Once," he said, "I mentioned to you how succession works among my kind. How one prince is replaced by another. Or at least, how it used to work—the law can be different now."

"Yes, and it's awful," I said with feeling. "Killing one another like . . . oh."

Rook hadn't been prepared for me to start figuring it out myself. He paled and continued quickly, "So, technically, as *you* are the one who defeated the Alder King, you're now—well—the queen of the fairy courts. And I . . ."

I took pity on him. He was turning rather green. "Rook, I would be delighted to marry you and make you king. But first, I have one demand. It is of the utmost importance."

I couldn't tell whether he looked more relieved, or more frightened. "What is it, my dear?"

"I'd like another declaration, please."

"Isobel." He swept down to his knees and kissed my hand, gazing up at me in devotion. "I love you more than the stars in the sky. I love you more than Lark loves dresses."

I startled myself with my own yelping laugh.

"I love you more than Gadfly loves looking at himself in a mirror," he went on.

"Surely not that!"

Our laughter carried across the darkened yard, past the chicken house full of sleeping hens, the red-leafed oak, and the autumn wheat whispering in the field, half cropped for harvest. The wild wind swept our voices all the way to the forest, where crickets sang a new song to the crescent moon. Somewhere, fair folk were having a feast. Others swirled in the midst of a ball. Others still traced the edges of a piece of bark, gazing at their portraits in quiet contemplation. A thin mortal woman packed her books, assisted by a girl with sharp teeth and a well-dressed man with silver-blond hair. Yet no matter what they were doing, everyone in the forest waited with an indrawn breath, waiting for the taste of autumn, the smell of change, the first news of a king and queen unlike any the world had known before.

And we wouldn't live happily ever after, because I don't believe in such nonsense, but we both had a long, bold adventure ahead of us, and a great deal to look forward to at last.

Acknowledgments

I wouldn't have had the courage to pursue publication if my family hadn't believed in me. Thanks, Mom and Dad, for your unwavering encouragement and support. You had confidence in me when so much of the world doubted the validity of my dreams—including myself—and I couldn't have done it without you. By the way, I love you most times infinity.

Sara Megibow, my agent, is a superhero. I can't imagine what this journey would have been like without her, in large part because it wouldn't exist. Gratitude alone is inadequate—Sara, you deserve an eight-thousand-dollar ring made of a dozen tiny Fabergé eggs, and also a private island. I'm working on it.

My editor, Karen Wojtyla, is not only a joy to work with, but understands my writing on a level that constantly surprises and delights me. Karen, it's a privilege to work with you, even if you did have me take all the pockets out of Isobel's Firth &

Maester's dresses (you were absolutely right, as usual). Thank you for believing in this book.

I'd also like to thank everyone at Simon & Schuster, including Annie Nybo, Bridget Madsen, Sonia Chaghatzbanian, Elizabeth Blake-Linn, and Barbara Perris, for all your help and hard work.

Thank you to my brother, Jon Rogerson, and also Kate Frasca, for making sure I have a place to stay, feeding me, and buying me the comfiest sweatpants.

I wouldn't be who I am without my friends Rachel Boughton and Jessica Stoops. You have my eternal gratitude for never being more than a message away, for knowing me like no one else does, and for putting up with some truly questionable writing over the years. I don't deserve you. Write your books.

Kristi Rudie, thank you for dragging me out of the house for TV marathons. It helped more than you can ever know.

Thank you to the Swanky Seventeens, a community who provided invaluable support during the journey to publication, and connected me with my friends Katherine Arden and Heather Fawcett. You two are an endless source of inspiration and encouragement. Here's to many more really, really long e-mail chains.

Nicole Stamper, Liz Fiacco, Jessica Kernan, Jamie Brinkman, Katy Kania, Desiree Wilson—thank you for being my partners in crime.

Jessica Cluess, for your advice, even as I fangirled deliriously.

Allison, for calling this book "moist." You understand.

Finally, a huge thank-you to Charlie Bowater, who did an absolutely incredible job bringing the cover to life.